High Intensity

FREYA BARKER

HIGH INTENSITY

Copyright © 2024 Freya Barker

All rights reserved.

9781988733951

Cover Design: Freya Barker
Editing: Karen Hrdlicka
Proofing: Joanne Thompson
Cover Image: Golden Czermak — FuriousFotog
Cover Model: Andrew Flanagan

FREYA BARKER
Just ordinary people with extraordinary stories

Dog trainer and handler, Jillian Lederman, is moving with her pack to Libby, Montana, a place where she has made friends and hopes to find a fresh start. It's time. For years, she's just been keeping her wounds fresh by staying in Missoula—where there were regular reminders of all she's lost—while the rest of the world has continued to move forward.

Perhaps the new house, the beautiful mountains, and a certain pair of clear, blue eyes hold the promise of new beginnings.

Since changing careers years ago, former FBI agent Lucas Wolff has found a much better work-life balance as a member of High Mountain Trackers. Still able to serve his community, he has also been carving out a comfortable existence for himself and is not looking to make any changes to it anytime soon. Not even for a particular bold and ballsy redhead he's been trying to avoid.

That turns out to be an impossible feat when a plane crash during a blizzard sets both of them on the trail of a young girl, all alone in the mountains. But it soon becomes evident they are not the only ones looking, and staying safe means sticking close together.

One

JILLIAN

"You guys be good, okay?"

I get whines and whimpers from Hunter and Murphy, who are crowding around my legs as I try to get out. Emo is being her aloof self, curled up on the carpet in front of the fireplace, pretending not to care whether I come or go, but I know the moment I walk out the door, she'll be up on the chair by the window to watch me leave.

I already put Peanut and Nugget in the back of the SUV. They have their noses pressed against the glass, tongues lolling, excited to be the ones to come with me this time. More often than not it's one of the others, needed for their specialized noses. Today, however, it's Peanut's sweet disposition, and Nugget's cuddly nature that are important. Where we're going no one will care Peanut is partially blind or Nugget has deformed hind legs.

This will be our first visit to Wellspring Senior Living, an assisted-living facility in Kalispell. I got this gig through my friend, Sloane, who is also the one who suggested I move up here from Missoula in the first place.

It was less than five months ago; I was called out to Libby with Emo to search for human remains in the mountains. I still have occasional nightmares about the boneyard my dog sniffed out; a dumping ground for what turned out to be a pair of serial killers.

That's when I met Sloane, who was a detective for the Lincoln Sheriff's Department, and my local contact. She and I connected right away and stayed in touch after I returned home, forging the kind of friendship I've been lacking in recent years. All my old friends have slowly disappeared over time, and I haven't exactly done much to hang on to them. They'd all been part of a life I no longer fit into.

Connecting with the dogs had been the first tentative step on a new path. The friendship with Sloane had been the next one. If not for her, I wouldn't have been able to gather up the courage to pull up stakes in Missoula and seek out a fresh start here.

When I was up here to celebrate Thanksgiving with Sloane, her fiancé, Dan, and their families, the subject of relocation came up. It was over a cup of tea on her front porch early the morning after. She asked why I'd seemed preoccupied during dinner, and I mentioned toying with the idea of a fresh start, even though I didn't give her the background. She didn't ask why—which is one of the reasons I like her so much—and simply suggested moving closer to her. She pointed out there would likely be plenty of work for me and the dogs here in the mountains, since I already had connections with law enforcement in the region and left a good impression.

The idea had been churning through my head the entire drive back home that afternoon, and by the time I got to

Missoula, I'd mostly had my mind made up. The next day I called the realtor, who helped me buy my property on the outskirts of Missoula five years prior, and set the wheels in motion.

Two months later, and here I am; just settled into the dogs' and my new digs, off Terrace View Road, halfway between the town of Libby and Sloane and Dan's place. The single-story, rustic ranch house came with a couple of acres of property backing onto the banks of Big Cherry Creek. The place even had an outdoor run and kennels since the previous owner had hunting dogs.

As I drive away, I glance back at the house and catch sight of Emo's shadow in the large front window. Then I notice the gutter hanging down from the corner and the missing downspout, and realize the term "rustic" may be giving the place more credit than it deserves.

The bones of the house are good, and the previous owner had made a good start on renovations but ran out of money and enthusiasm, which is why I was able to pick it up for a relative steal and on very short notice. And the property itself is amazing, with beautiful views from the back deck, which had been put in new in the past two years.

Most of the windows have been replaced, but the roof definitely needs work, as does some of the stonework on the big river-rock chimney. The siding is actual wooden boards that were stained a gray-blue color. I don't hate it, but it's looking a little weathered.

Inside isn't too bad; the only thing left to do are the extra bedrooms and main bathroom. The kitchen cabinets and concrete counter look fairly new, and so do the floors; nice, light, extra-wide hardwood boards. The focus in the living space is the large stone fireplace, which—along with the view—is what sold me on the house.

The day before yesterday, when the movers arrived, I had them place the big pieces of furniture, but leave the boxes in one of the extra bedrooms for me to tackle bit by bit.

Which is what I'll get back to later today when I get home.

There is snow on the ground, but the roads are clear and it's a beautiful day for a drive. Despite the cold outside air, I have the window behind me open a crack so Peanut can stick her large nose outside. She easily gets carsick otherwise. Mostly Great Dane, she is large enough to stick her head over the back seat and I can hear her sniffing at the fresh air.

Nugget is probably already asleep in the large dog bed I have in the back of the SUV. These two are my therapy dogs. They love affection and they love people, which is a bit of a miracle, given where they came from. As unmatched a pair as they are, these two are best friends.

I pull my knit beanie farther down over my ears against the cold chill. Then I turn up the radio and sing along full-blast to Duran Duran's "Hungry Like the Wolf" as I make my way to Kalispell. I can't hold a tune to save my life, but luckily my dogs don't care.

"You must be Ms. Lederman," the sweater-vest-wearing administrator waiting for me at reception greets me. "David Gentry, we spoke on the phone."

I shake his offered hand. "Please, it's Jillian. Nice to meet you."

"Of course. Jillian, would you follow me? We already have quite a gathering in the community hall. Sadly, our facility isn't equipped to handle live-in animals, so a lot of our residents had to give up a pet. They miss them."

"I can only imagine," I reply. "I don't know what I would do without my guys."

Ten minutes later, Nugget charms his way from lap to lap, doing the rounds as he's bound to do. Peanut is a tad more discerning with her affections and has picked out her favorite person in the room; a frail-looking, elderly woman in a wheelchair. Peanut is sitting down beside the chair, her head resting on the lap of the woman, who absentmindedly scratches Peanut behind the ears.

Both woman and dog have their eyes closed, a look of satisfaction on their faces.

I catch David's eye, who seems pretty pleased as well. It's amazing how simple and effortless it really is to bring a little joy to people's lives.

It brings me joy as well, and provides me with some balance for the rewarding, but often heart-breaking search and recovery work I do.

~

Wolff

"Did you find everything okay?"

I pile the items I picked up on the counter.

"I think so." I quickly check the list on my phone. "Yeah, that's it."

And thank God for that.

Even just being in the proximity of a shopping mall gives me fucking hives, so after wandering the aisles of the women's clothing department in Target for the past half hour, I'm sweating like a pig. Good thing I only need to do this once, maybe twice, a year.

I wait for the woman to ring me up and pull out my credit card. Then I watch her pack up my purchases, and with a curt nod for her, grab the bags, and walk as fast as I can out to the parking lot.

My phone vibrates in my pocket as I'm getting into my truck.

"Yep."

"Ama says you're in Kalispell?" Dan asks.

Ama is both housekeeper and office manager at High Meadow. She's also the most well-informed person at the ranch; she seems to know everything about everyone. So, I'm not surprised she was able to tell Dan my whereabouts, even though she didn't get that information from me.

"Yep."

"Good. I have a favor to ask."

"What do you need?"

"Any chance you could swing by Home Depot on your way back? I just started a new project and need a few things."

I chuckle. "A new project? Aren't you still doing work on your house?"

Dan and Sloane moved into the new log home Dan built just before Thanksgiving, a little over two months ago. I thought he was still finishing up the inside.

"I am, but something else came up that has priority."

"Oh?"

"Yeah…" I hear him chuckle. "Don't tell Sloane, but I'm building a stable out back. I'm buying Aspen a pony for her birthday in April."

Aspen is Sloane's baby daughter. Dan is not the biological father, but you'd never know from the way he dotes on the kid. The fact he's buying her a pony shouldn't surprise me. Still, I stifle a bark of laughter.

"You realize she's just turning one, right?"

"So? She's already starting to pull herself up, and have

you seen her crawl? She can cross the room in three seconds flat. Mark my words; she'll be able to walk by her birthday, and getting her in the saddle is the next step."

"If you say so. Happy to lend a hand on the new project, but in the meantime, shoot me a text with your wish list and I'll swing by Home Depot on my way back."

"Will do. I appreciate it."

I'm still grinning when I take off my hat and walk into the lobby at Wellspring fifteen minutes later. I wave at Marcela, the receptionist, in passing. I'm halfway down the hall to my mother's unit, when her voice calls me back.

"Lucas! Your mother isn't there."

Anyone calling me by that name is associated with my mother in one way or another. The rest of the world knows me by my last name.

I backtrack my steps and stop in front of her desk.

"She's not? We were supposed to have lunch."

The pretty woman smiles at me as she shakes her head.

"Guess she got a better offer, she's in the community hall. But..." she adds with an over-the-top flirty hair flip. "I'm free for lunch."

"I'll be sure to keep that in mind," I tell her with a wink.

Marcela is a happily married woman with a couple of cute kids, and the flirting is all in good fun. She'd never step out, and I'd never step in.

I head down a different hallway, leading to the communal areas. When I walk into the main hall, I spot my mother's wheelchair right away. Hard to miss since she's half obscured by a dog the size of a small horse cuddled up to her.

"She made a new friend."

I turn around to find David Gentry, the home's administrator, standing behind me.

"I see that. Since when do you allow pets in here?"

"Certified therapy animals are allowed," he clarifies. "Board approved and all. Your mother was instrumental in getting that approval."

I vaguely recollect her telling me about a resident petition she was having everyone sign last month, feeling a little bad I was only listening with half an ear at the time. Despite her small stature, and her failing health, my mother is still a force to be reckoned with.

I turn my head to look at her and catch her eye.

"Lucas! Come meet Peanut."

Who the hell would call an oversized animal like that Peanut?

The dog lifts its head off my mother's lap when I walk over. That's when I notice it's missing an eye. The animal looks scary enough and I'm sure could snap my mother in half with those jaws, but it seems friendly, its tail thumping the linoleum floor as I approach. Bending down, I kiss my mother's papery cheek.

"Peanut?"

Mom beams up at me. "Isn't she precious?"

Precious is not exactly the term I would've come up with for the less than attractive dog, but she's definitely sweet, leaning her weight against my leg and staring up at me with one adoring eye as I rub her head.

"Good girl," I mumble at her.

The next moment the hair on my neck stands on end when I hear someone walk up behind me, and say, "It's almost time to go, Peanut."

I don't need to turn around to know who the owner of that voice is, but I don't have a choice when my mom speaks up.

"Oh, Jillian, I'd like you to meet my son, Lucas."

I meet those pretty green eyes, now sparkling with amusement. Of course a dog named Peanut would belong to this woman. She named her cadaver dog, Emo, after all.

Hell, I knew she recently moved to the area—Sloane mentioned it more than once—but I wasn't expecting to run into her at my mother's assisted-living home. That's a little too close for comfort.

"So you *do* have a first name; Lucas, huh?"

"You already know each other?" Mom looks back and forth between us.

"We do. How are you doing, Jillian?"

She adjusts the small furball she's holding in her arms. "Good, thanks."

I turn to my mother to explain, "Jillian and I met working on a search last summer."

Despite my immediate attempt to identify our connection as a professional one only, I see Mom's mind already at work behind the gleam in her eyes.

Great.

"Is that so? Well, what a happy coincidence this is then," she says in a chipper voice and with a satisfied smirk on her face.

My mother has never passed up on an opportunity to try and hook me up with any seemingly available female we've come across. She has never given up hope to get me tied down and settled, despite the fact I've told her often enough I'm not looking for anything permanent. Certainly not with someone my mother hooked me up with.

"It certainly is a coincidence," Jillian agrees with a kind smile for my mother. "Unfortunately, I have to run. My time is up here and I have to get these guys home and fed, but I'll be back in two weeks."

Mom leans forward to give that ugly mutt a hug, before

Jillian heads out with both dogs. Then she nudges my hip with her elbow.

"She seems like a nice girl. Maybe you should walk her out."

"*Mom,*" I warn her.

The tiny redhead with the big smile is already enough of a temptation without my mother's interference.

Two

JILLIAN

"He's such a pretty boy."

Sloane scrunches up her face.

"He may be handsome, but he's a big menace," she corrects me.

I bend down and comply when her dog, River, flops on his back, big paws in the air, for a belly rub.

Big is an understatement for this almost eight-month-old, oversized puppy. River was a rescue I picked up from a kill-shelter near Helena when I was out there with Hunter and Murphy, helping on a search. I couldn't leave him behind.

When Sloane called me a week later, asking me to help her find a dog for her fiancé, it felt predestined.

"What is he doing?" I ask her.

She called this morning, asking if I could take River for the day. She didn't want to leave him with Aspen at High Meadow, because she said he'd been acting up. I told her of course, and that if I got called out, I'd keep him in the kennel out back with my guys.

"Eating my underwear." She makes a gagging sound that makes me snicker. "He's attached to me like Velcro and shadows me everywhere. When I leave the house without him, his howls follow me down the driveway, and then when I get back, I find half-eaten panties he steals from the laundry hamper."

"Is this a new thing?"

I straighten up and walk over to my coffee maker to get a pot started.

"Yeah," she says, taking a seat on one of the stools at the island. "Started last month, sometime before Christmas. Oh, none for me," she adds when I start loading grinds into the filter. "I've been off coffee. It gives me heartburn."

I drop the scoop back in my coffee tin and turn to face her, folding my arms in front of me.

"Have you considered the possibility you could be pregnant?"

First her face freezes. Then, slowly, her mouth drops open, even as she starts shaking her head.

"No. No, no, no."

I tilt my head and watch her go through the motions as she processes my suggestion. Pregnancy would fit with River's behavior as well. Some dogs can react strongly to any changes in physical condition, including pregnancy. I'm starting to wonder if River might have done well as a support dog.

"Oh my God," Sloane mutters, her hand coming up to cover her mouth. "I've barely had a period since Aspen was born. I thought maybe I was still getting regular." She turns wide eyes on me. "I'm gonna have two kids in diapers."

I grin. "Why don't you do a pregnancy test first? Make sure before you panic."

"Dan's gonna flip his shit."

"Highly doubtful," I assure her. "I don't know him that well, but I've seen him with Aspen."

"It's too soon," she laments, tears welling in her eyes.

I'm guessing that might be hormones, since drama and tears aren't necessarily Sloane's MO. River, concerned about his "mother's" mood, sidles up beside her and drops his head on her lap, which only seems to encourage the waterworks.

"I'm making us a pot of tea instead of coffee, while you get a grip," I announce resolutely, turning to reach for the roll of paper towels, which I deposit in front of her. Then I grab the kettle. "I'll reiterate; do a test and make sure first. And if you are pregnant, you'll be just fine. It's not like you don't know the drill, except this time you're far better equipped."

I realize I'm sounding rather harsh, perhaps even a bit insensitive. I'm not, but the subject matter will always be a bit of a struggle, I guess. Plugging in the kettle, I round the island and throw my arm around Sloane in a side hug.

"Look, there's a reason babies take nine months to get here; to give the parents time to get their shit together. You'll be fine," I repeat, giving her a final squeeze.

"Ugh, the timing just sucks. My shift starts in half an hour, and Dan is dropping off Aspen at the ranch and then taking off on a call. I have no idea how long he'll be gone."

"It'll give you time to pick up a test and know for sure before you tell him. One step at a time, my friend. Now," I firmly change the subject. "Did you have breakfast? Can I toast you a bagel or something?"

Twenty minutes later, I watch Sloane drive off for her

shift, River whimpering by my side. I nudge him back inside and close the door.

"You stay out of my laundry hamper, mister."

River throws me a glance before he boldly jumps onto my couch and makes himself a place between Peanut and Hunter, who shoots him a half-hearted growl before going back to sleep. With the dogs settled in, I head to the bedroom to tackle another box. I feel the need to keep my hands busy, mainly so my mind doesn't wander off to places I'm not in the mood to revisit right now.

Hard to do, and as soon as I start stacking my linens in the hallway closet, my thoughts drift back to when I first discovered I was pregnant. It was a lifetime ago. The memories come with a stab of pain, right in the middle of my chest, like a sharp jab to my sternum. Even after all these years, it steals my breath for a second.

Then I shake my head; this isn't about me, this is about Sloane, and I'm happy for my friend, even if she doesn't yet realize how lucky she is.

This morning's visit went in a slightly different direction than I had thought. I'd hoped to be able to pick her brain over coffee, but the topic of conversation came out of the blue, and we ended up having tea.

I never got a chance to ask her about Lucas Wolff.

Bumping into him at Wellspring had been a surprise. I don't know what shocked me more, the fact Wolff actually had a mother—the man gives off loud *alone-in-the-world* vibes—or that this funny, tiny, firecracker of a woman could've given birth to such a reserved and seemingly humorless man.

I'd hope to find out from Sloane if he was this aloof and borderline asocial with everyone, or if that is something he reserves just for me. I have to admit, it's intriguing—he's intriguing—and it makes me want to rattle his cage, get under that impassive front he seems to put up around me.

But there are a few cracks, I've seen one or two, most recently yesterday at the Wellspring facility.

~

Wolff

Fuck, it's cold this morning.

It's in part the brisk wind bringing in a system from Alberta, which is supposed to hit sometime tonight. They're expecting upward of ten inches of snow in the region, which is why we're out early this morning, making sure we're ready for the storm to hit.

Usually, before the first snow of the season hits, we bring the horses in closer to the ranch. There isn't enough stable space for the entire herd, but the pastures immediately surrounding the ranch have field shelters where the animals tend to huddle during inclement weather. Those shelters also have warmed water troughs, and we make sure they're always stocked with fresh hay.

This morning we're out here dropping extra bales of hay. Also, to make any repairs to shelters with damage, like loose boards that could injure one of the animals.

"Grab the toolbox too," I yell out to JD, who is already by the truck, getting a couple of new boards.

I'm tossing hay in the opposite corner, from where one of the horses kicked through the wall to get them out of our way. This is a smaller band of seven colts; generally speaking, a rowdy bunch. All between two and three, and learning to assert themselves. It's not uncommon for us to find one or more horses with injuries when they decide to mete out their dominance.

One of the splintered boards has some bloody hair stuck to it, which leads me to check out the horses' legs for damage.

"It was Ares," I inform JD when he walks in.

I point out the flap of skin hanging down the feisty buckskin's left rear leg, from a few inches above the hock to halfway down to his fetlock. It's an ugly gouge and an open invitation to infection.

"Stupid bastard," JD mumbles.

Then he turns and drops the toolbox and lumber by the damaged back wall, while I pull out my phone and dial the office.

"Hey, it's Wolff," I identify myself when Jonas answers. "We're gonna need Doc Richards out in the northeast paddock. One of the colts, Ares, kicked through a wall and ripped his leg open good. He's gonna need some stitches."

"How long is it gonna take you to patch up the wall?"

"JD's with me. It's just two boards, so fifteen minutes, tops."

"Okay, I was going to put a call in to Doc Richards anyway, Bo says two of the mares are snotty and coughing. He put them in the birthing stalls to separate them from the rest."

Coughing can be a sign of EIV, horse influenza, which is highly contagious. Even though the herd is regularly vaccinated, like any other virus, EIV has many variant strains with new ones developing all the time.

"Rather than have Doc come out there, one of you can walk Ares back to the ranch. He should probably be inside until he's healed anyway."

"Sure thing."

JD has already ripped off the remainder of the broken boards and is pulling out any exposed nails when I join him.

"Jonas wants Ares at the barn," I share as I fit a new board over the opening in the wall. "Couple of the stabled horses may have the flu so he was calling Doc Richards anyway. Ares is gonna be a handful though."

"I'll bring him in," JD offers. "Unless you wanna?"

I shake my head. "You're better at handling the difficult ones."

It's true. I do all right with the horses, but I know my limitations. Dan and JD really have a knack with them—particularly the ornery ones—they grew up around these animals. My contact with horses was limited to summer camps at the dude ranch my parents sent me to as a rebellious teenager. I did catch the equestrian bug, fell in love with the majestic animals, and rode every chance I had.

Which wasn't very often until I met the High Mountain Trackers team. I liked working in law enforcement—catching the bad guys—and I worked hard to become a federal agent. Unfortunately, that job comes with a lot of paperwork and red tape and even the occasional corrupt agent. So, when Jonas Harvey offered me a place on his team, I didn't hesitate.

How often do you get the opportunity to live out a childhood dream and get paid handsomely for it?

"I'll take the truck and hit the next shelter. We've gotta keep moving before the snow hits," I add.

"Okay."

He sounds and acts indifferent, but I don't believe for a second he is. Like his father, JD Watike isn't exactly a talker and tends to be quietly observant, which is what makes him and James exceptional trackers. But I'm no slouch either, and observing was my bread and butter working as a federal agent, which is why it hasn't gone unnoticed that JD likes to hang around the stable when Doc Richards pays the ranch a visit.

I have to admit, when I first met the new vet, I was pleasantly surprised. We talked a few times and I thought she was nice, smart, and definitely attractive, but I don't like playing so close to home. It reeks of messy entanglements.

Of course, since meeting Jillian Lederman just a few months after that, I barely even notice Doc Richards anymore.

You could've knocked me down with a feather when she showed up at my mom's residence yesterday. So much for steering clear of the petite woman now my mother's radar is pinging. Mom knows me too well. She's always had the ability to see right through me, which is why I was never able to get away with anything growing up.

That, and I lie for shit.

Jillian has my full attention, and I'm not happy about it. She doesn't even have to try to worm her way into my awareness, she's simply there. Has been from the start, which is what set off all kinds of red flags for me.

Don't get me wrong; I like women. I like spending time with them, sharing a meal, having a conversation, and some of them I like taking to bed. Hell, I'm not even averse to a longer arrangement—I've had a few of those—but nothing serious or binding or restrictive.

The bottom line is, I like my bachelor life, and I don't want to let it go.

Jillian freaks me out because she's the kind of woman I could see giving up my independence for. Hell, we haven't even had a proper conversation, and yet I can't stop thinking about her.

I'm fucking obsessed.

When I make it back to the ranch hours later, the snow has started coming down and combined with the heavy winds, visibility is reduced to near nothing. I hope Dan, Fletch, and Sully were able to find some shelter from the elements. They went out to find a couple who left to go snowshoeing near the Nordic ski trails but never returned home last night.

I pull up to the barn, shove my hat down on my head as I get out of the truck, and dart for the doors. Inside, I notice right away the overhead lights are off.

"Power's out," JD announces, stepping out of one of the stalls.

I can just see Ares move restlessly behind him.

"I see that. How's he doing?"

"Being a pain in the ass, but otherwise fine. Stitched up, and she put him on antibiotics."

"Good. What's the deal with the other two horses?"

"Probably EIV. She took swabs and wants them isolated."

"Hope that'll be enough to contain it."

Sadly, even horses without symptoms could be carriers, so it's hard to keep it from spreading.

The overhead lights flicker briefly before coming on.

"Generators," JD clarifies. "Jonas went to start them up. Main transformer along the thirty-seven east of town got knocked out. All of Libby is down. It's a fucking mess."

No shit. Power outages are not uncommon during storms out here—hence the generators at the ranch to keep the barn and the main house up and running—but having the entire grid go down is rare. Not everyone has the luxury of a generator.

"Any word on the team?" I ask.

"They found them. A snow slide swept them off the

trail and the woman messed up her leg in the tumble. The boys got back before it got bad out there and hightailed it home when the power went off."

Probably checking on their families in person. With the whole grid down, it likely impacts power to the cell towers as well.

From there my thoughts jump to Jillian, alone in her new house and probably without any way to connect to the outside world. I wonder how she's staying warm.

My feet are already moving when I call out to JD over my shoulder.

"I've gotta go check on something."

Three

Jillian

Dammit.

All I can find are these two measly tea light candles and they don't do much for either light or heat. No oil lanterns or at the very least a damn flashlight in sight. I'm woefully unprepared for this power outage.

The wind is howling outside and I can feel the temperature dropping in here. I've been so focused on getting my house together and the boxes unpacked, I haven't even thought about building a fire. Of course, I hadn't considered I might need a fire to heat the house, to me they're mostly for ambiance.

The dogs are huddled on the couch. My four plus River, who looks to be the only one sleeping fitfully. The others follow me around the house with their eyes, restless and maybe a little spooked by the storm. I haven't heard anything from Sloane, but I assume she's got her hands full just dealing with the storm, let alone the power outage.

When I tried to check the forecast, I noticed I had zero reception, so she won't be able to contact me either.

It also means I won't be able to reach out to anyone, so I'll have to do my own problem-solving.

Starting with heat.

There's no firewood in here, and the supply the previous owner left stored in the garage is limited. Still, it's better than nothing. Walking over to the window, I peer outside, barely able to see the detached building.

Well...I'm going to have to go out there eventually, unless I want to freeze to death. And who knows? Perhaps I can find something useful, like a goddamned flashlight.

Emo and Peanut start whining and jump off the couch when they see me getting dressed to go outside.

"No, we're not going out now, guys. You've gotta wait here."

Peanut immediately jumps back on the couch with a grunt, but Emo throws me a recriminating look, letting me know she's not happy. It can't be helped. I pull my knit beanie down over my ears, tie a scarf around my neck, and shove my feet in my snow boots. Then I carefully slip out the door.

Jesus, that wind is cold. My boots sink down in the fast-accumulating snow the moment I step off the porch. Shoving my hands in my pockets, I trudge in the direction of the garage. I have to squint my eyes to find my way and brace my shoulders against the near gale-force gusts.

It's a bit eerie out here, without the lights from the house or the street, just a pale reflection off the blanket of snow. My lot is fairly treed, so I can't really see the neighbors' houses, but I assume if the streetlights are out, their houses will be without power as well.

I quickly realize I should've brought my phone so I

could've at least used the flashlight on it, because when I step inside the garage, it's very dark. I'm forced to hold my arms out in front of me to prevent running into things as I go in search of the firewood.

A stubbed toe and a couple of cobwebs in my face later, I find the woodpile and quickly load up with as many logs as my arms will hold. If I'd have thought this through, I would have grabbed an empty box or a bucket from the laundry room for easier transportation, but it is what it is.

As I exit the garage, I try not to think about the possible critters I might be carrying. I'm generally okay with bugs— I'd better be, I spend enough time outdoors—but that doesn't mean I enjoy them in my house, or worse, on my body.

Despite not being able to see much and having my arms full, I make it back to the porch, where I dump my load. I figure since I'm out here anyway, I might as well haul as much wood as I can to the porch. It'll be dry out here and I'll have easy access. Who knows how long this storm or this outage is going to last?

Inside one of the dogs starts barking. They can probably hear me out here, so I quickly poke my head in the door.

"It's just me, guys. I'll be right back."

My eyes are getting used to the dark and this time is easier loading up with wood. I'm on my way back, carrying more logs up to the porch, when a deep voice behind me has me jump out of my skin.

"What are you doing out here?"

I hang on to my load as a shield when I swing around. The brim of his hat is tipped down, obscuring his face, but I have no problem recognizing Wolff.

"Me? I live here. What are you doing here?"

Instead of answering me, he brushes past and sets the

big box he's carrying on my porch. Inside the dogs start barking again as I swing my head around to look down the driveway. I don't see any vehicle and have no idea how he got here, but I doubt he walked. I intend to ask him when I'm suddenly relieved of the load of logs in my arms.

"Fireplace? Wood stove?" he asks brusquely.

"Fireplace."

The brim of his hat lifts, and I get a glimpse of his piercing blue eyes fixed on mine.

"It works?"

I open my mouth to confirm, but then realize I don't really know for sure. It's not like I've had a chance to check.

My face is frozen and my teeth are chattering when I respond with, "Since I'm hauling firewood from the garage, I sure hope so. Otherwise, we'll freeze."

"You're freezing now. Grab that box and go inside. I've got this."

"What's in it?" I want to know, but he's already heading for the garage.

"Jillian, get inside and calm down your dogs," he tosses dismissively over his shoulder.

Oh-kay.

Rude, to put it mildly. The man avoids talking to me at all costs and now shows up out of the blue, ordering me around on my own turf? Never mind my freezing hands and chattering teeth.

Pissed, I bend down to pick up the box and just about throw out my back, which doesn't do much for my mood. I have to set it down to open the door and end up shoving it into the hallway with my foot.

"Hey, guys! Quiet!"

The only two dogs still curled up on the couch are River

and Murphy, the other three rush up to greet me, Nugget in the lead.

"Well, hello, and I love you too," I mumble at the enthusiastic greeting. You'd think I'd been gone for a day and not fifteen minutes at most.

I give each of them attention before I get to my feet and catch sight of Wolff's box. Which reminds me, I still don't know how or why he's here. Part of me wants to peek inside, but I have other priorities; it's getting really cold in here and I need to get a fire going. I look around for my phone, which I spot on the kitchen island in the faint light of the two tea lights. I'm going to need that flashlight to make sure the inside of the chimney is clear.

Peanut crowds me when I get to my knees in front of the chimney, and I have to nudge her aside before I can stick my head in. Aiming the light on my phone up, I can see the flue is closed. Not thinking too clearly, I reach for the lever and have to yank a few times before it gives with a squeal.

The next thing I know, my face is covered in soot.

Wolff

Thank God I was still wearing my heavy winter gear, otherwise I'd be a popsicle by now.

Damn truck slid in the ditch turning onto Jillian's street. There were some high drifts along the road, distorting the landscape and making it hard to see whether you're on the road or next to it. I had to leave it there and hoofed it the rest of the way, carrying the box of supplies I thought she might need.

I'm annoyed, because I know I'm going to have to wait until after this damn storm passes before I can get someone to come and pull my truck back on the road. So, it looks like I'll be stuck here until that happens, and I'm not too sure how that is going to go over.

Still, I don't regret coming because it's obvious the woman was not exactly prepared for emergencies. She'll be lucky if she can last the storm on this meager wood supply.

Instead of adding the last logs to the pile on the porch, I open the door and carry them inside. I'm greeted by six dogs, two of them growling. I don't recognize the Lab, but I know the other one, Emo, although she apparently doesn't remember me, and of course I know River, and the two therapy dogs I met yesterday.

"Guys! Friend," I hear Jillian call out.

In the faint light of a couple of candles, I can make out the large stone mantel. It's not until I ditch my boots by the door and navigate my way through six dogs and round the couch, I see Jillian sitting on the ground in front of the fireplace. Her head and shoulders are covered in grime and her eyes are like angry, glittering jewels in a blacked canvass, daring me to comment.

I never back down from a dare.

"You didn't have to climb up the chimney."

She throws me a dirty look before clambering to her feet.

"All I did was open the flue," she shares a bit defensively.

"Looks like you forgot to duck."

I move past her and start stacking the logs next to the fireplace. Then I crouch down and give the dogs a little attention.

When I turn around, she is standing by the coffee table, glaring at me as she wipes her face with her scarf.

We're caught in a bit of a stare-down when she finally relents, asking, "What is it you're doing here, Wolff?"

"Figured you may not have had a chance to prepare for bad storms or power outages. Came to drop off a few things you might be able to use."

When I point at the box just inside the door, she heads over, picks it up, and carries it to the kitchen island. While she starts digging through the contents, I turn my attention to the fireplace and a few minutes later have a small, compact fire going.

As I get to my feet, I see the dogs have taken control of the couch. Jillian seems to have found the LED lanterns, as well as the MREs, and the single butane burner I dug out of my camping gear. The lanterns are on, she already has a pot on the burner, and she's currently using the empty box to load with the content of her freezer.

"Luckily, I'm on city water, so I'm boiling some for tea since there isn't much else in the house I can offer," she announces when I approach. "It's the least I can do after being an ass, when you were just being a good neighbor," she surprises me by adding.

I get a brief flash of her eyes.

"You weren't an ass," is all I can think to say. "I probably was. Nothing to do with you, but I had to leave my truck in a ditch after driving it off the road at the end of your street, which annoyed me."

What mostly annoyed me was trudging through the deep snow in a blizzard for what turned out to be a fair distance from the main road.

"Oh shit. Yeah, I can see why it would," she commiserates. "Maybe I can help pull you out?"

Her hands pause and her attention is on me.

"I'm afraid no one will be pulling me out anytime soon. Not until this storm passes and they clear the highway."

Her face betrays a reaction I can't quite place, but she nods as if she's taking the realization I'll be stuck here for a while in stride. Then she closes the box and picks it up.

"Could you open the back door for me?"

I do as she asks and watch her set it down at the far corner of the deck, pushing it down in the snow.

"I don't want it to go to waste, and its more likely to stay frozen out there than in here," she explains when she steps back inside.

"True, although not all wildlife hibernates through the winter."

She pulls the beanie from her head and static makes her red hair stand on end. She runs an impatient hand through it.

"If that's the case, at least it'll get enjoyed by someone," she returns pragmatically.

Guess that's a valid point.

She kicks off her boots and leaves them by the back door, then sheds her coat, hanging it over the back of a kitchen chair.

"It's already warming up in here," she observes, as she starts bustling around the kitchen, grabbing mugs and a box of tea from a cupboard.

I unzip my parka and slide a hip on one of the kitchen stools. Then I quietly watch Jillian pull the pan off the burner, pour hot water in the mugs, and slide one of them toward me.

"Want sugar or milk?"

I throw her a look she seems to think is funny, because she bursts out laughing.

"So noted," she mocks me, before changing the subject. "Well, thanks to you, I'll be able to warm up the white chicken chili I made last night, I would've hated to throw that out. There's enough for both of us, but sadly, I don't think I can do a decent cheese and garlic toast as I had planned without an oven, so I'm going to have to offer you a rain check on that."

Although I've never heard of white chicken chili—and am admittedly a bit apprehensive at the sound of it—I guess I'm invited to dinner. I'm not going to object.

"Do you have tinfoil?" I ask her.

She looks confused, but opens a drawer and pulls out a roll. "I do."

"I left the edges of the fireplace free. As long as your garlic toast is wrapped in tinfoil, we should be able to toast it in there."

One side of her mouth pulls up as she grins at me.

"Well, aren't you clever?"

~

Two hours later I'm at the sink, taking care of the dishes I offered to wash, since Jillian was responsible for what turned out to be an awesome meal. The woman sure knows how to cook.

She's letting the dogs out back, and I can see her hanging over the deck railing, keeping an eye on them. It looks like maybe the winds are dying down a little. Even though the snow is still heavy, visibility appears to be a bit better.

If this trend continues, the plows may be able to go out tonight, and I can get Sully or Dan to come haul my truck from the ditch. I would've jumped at that a couple of hours ago, but I'm not in any particular hurry to get out of here now.

Surprisingly, conversation over dinner was easy once it got going, and that was thanks to Jillian. She started telling me about each of her animals and how she discovered she had a knack for dog training. Then she asked me how I got into tracking, and I found myself telling her about my disillusionment with the FBI and my switch to the High Mountain Trackers team.

We ended up swapping favorite rescue stories, and I was amazed to find how easy it was to talk to her. It seems the more I get to know her, the bigger a threat to my uncomplicated bachelorhood she's becoming.

Yeah, coming here was a mistake, but one I seem to be enjoying the hell out of.

Four

All it takes is a large wet tongue on my face to snap me out of my momentary disorientation.

Peanut's large head hovers over me when I blink my eyes open, and it all floods back to me. I'm stranded at Jillian's place and ended up crashing on her couch.

The first thing I notice is how bright it is, clearly morning, and it looks like the storm has cleared. But when I flip back the blanket Jillian gave me last night, the intense cold hits me. One glance at the fireplace shows me the two logs I recall tossing on sometime during the night, in an attempt to keep the small fire going, have completely burned up.

My bladder is about to burst, but it'll have to wait until I get that fire going again. I swing my legs down and plant my feet on the floor.

Fuck, that's cold.

My ass has barely left the couch when Peanut curls up in the warm spot I just vacated. She's cold too. Last night all six dogs disappeared into the bedroom with Jillian, and I remember suppressing a fleeting moment of jealousy that they would get to snuggle up with her.

Luckily the wood is nice and dry, so it takes hardly any effort to get the fire going again. Then I take care of business in the bathroom. Despite trying to be as quiet as I can, the activity seems to rouse a few more dogs that slip through the partially opened door to Jillian's bedroom.

It's her dog Murphy, the Lab mix, who makes a beeline for the back door. Yeah, they likely need to pee as well.

"Hold on, buddy," I mumble, quickly grabbing my boots and my parka.

I'm assuming—since she went out to keep an eye on them last night—her backyard may not be fenced in. At least not completely.

The sun greets me when I have to force open the back door against the drift that formed during the night. The snow is thick. It's hard to tell because the wind was blowing it around, but I'm guessing we got a good foot.

Murphy squeezes past me in his rush to get outside, and judging from the clicking of nails on the wood floors behind me, the rest of the pack needs relief as well. I wade through the snow to the railing to keep an eye out.

The view is phenomenal from here.

It doesn't really show at the front of the house, but it's built on a slope, so the back looks to be higher than the front. The yard slopes down into the tree line, which is pretty barren looking now, but I imagine will fill out nicely in the spring. Because of the lack of foliage, you can see the creek that runs behind the property. Of course, there's no missing the mountains beyond and they are as stunning in the summer as they are now, covered in a white blanket.

We're not out here long. The dogs quickly return to the

deck once they've done their business, eager to get back in. I stomp the snow from my boots and toe them off as soon as I step inside.

"Morning."

I look up to find Jillian curled up on the couch in front of the fire, wrapped in the blanket I left there. The dogs are already climbing up there with her.

"Hey."

"Thanks for the fire. It was cold in bed with all my doggie heaters gone."

I have to bite my tongue to keep from offering to wrap my body around her to keep her warm.

"I tried to keep it going overnight, but unfortunately fell asleep on the job," I tell her instead.

I shrug off my parka, toss it over a stool and grab the pot she used last night for water, fill it at the tap, and pop it on the butane burner.

"Coffee or tea?"

She points at the copper pot on the counter next to the stove. "Coffee, please. And there's a reusable filter in the coffee maker, or I can go dig up my French press, which is somewhere in the leftover boxes I haven't gotten around to unpacking yet."

"Don't bother," I tell her, pulling the effectively defunct coffee maker toward me. "I'll use this."

I like that she doesn't jump up and take over, but seems perfectly comfortable snuggled in with her dogs as she watches me putter around the kitchen.

"Have you tried your cell phone yet?" she asks at some point.

"I haven't," I admit.

I'm not ready to examine too deeply why it is I didn't do that first thing when I woke up. Or why I left my phone in my coat pocket instead of keeping it close all night in the first place. In fact, I should've thought to bring a two-way radio from the ranch office, but didn't.

No longer able to feign ignorance, I reach for my coat and dig out my cell. I notice it's already after eight.

"Looks like it's still down," I inform Jillian.

"I'm sure with the storm cleared out, they'll have things up and running again soon enough," she volunteers, looking pretty comfortable and not at all put out by our current predicament.

It shouldn't surprise me she seems unflappable, the work she does requires being adaptable to all circumstances. Although I hate to admit it, I'm pretty sure my impulsive attempt to somehow rescue her was entirely unnecessary. She was already well on her way to rescuing herself by the time I got here.

I watch her untangle herself from the pile of dogs and notice the long johns and fuzzy socks she's wearing, as she bends over to throw another log on the fire.

The woman has a great ass in jeans, but it's fucking spectacular in thermal underwear. She catches me looking, so I pivot around and busy myself scooping ground coffee in the filter. *Damn.*

"I'm thinking the plows are already out. After coffee, I'll probably head back to my truck, but first I'll shovel your driveway...you do have a shovel, don't you?" I catch myself.

"I do." Her voice is closer than before. "I'm pretty sure it blew off my porch sometime during the storm though, but I'll dig for it after, and I promise I can manage my own driveway. You've been helpful enough."

I hold my breath when I feel her place a hand in the middle of my back. I'm almost afraid to turn around, until I hear her question, "But first, how do you feel about oatmeal?"

"Oatmeal?"

My voice comes out hoarse and I clear my throat.

"Yes," she confirms, her hand falling away when I turn to face her. She's wearing that lopsided grin. "It seems most people either love or hate it. What camp are you in?"

"It's a good solid breakfast. I like it all right."

She nods. "Good. I'll make us a quick pot before you head out."

We move around each other surprisingly smoothly in the relatively small space, as I work on the coffee, and Jillian does something with bananas and cinnamon that makes the oatmeal smell fantastic. I pour us coffee, while she ladles the oatmeal in bowls, and we sit down at the small kitchen table.

"This is good," I share after scarfing down half of my bowl.

It earns me one of her grins. "Good. It's the way I used to cook it for—" She appears to catch herself. Her face blanks as she lowers her eyes, nervously tucking a strand of her messy hair behind her ear.

I open my mouth to ask her what's wrong, when my phone vibrates in my pocket.

"It's Jonas," I tell her when I check the screen.

Clearly service is back up and as I answer, I watch Jillian dart down the hallway to her bedroom. I assume to grab her own phone.

"Morning."

Not one for pleasantries, Jonas gets right to the point. "Where are you?"

"Went to check on someone and got stuck here."

"Well, get yourself unstuck, we've gotta mobilize the team."

"I promise I'm fine. I'll drop by with River as soon as I can get out of my street."

Cell service is obviously back up, and electricity came back on maybe half an hour ago, not long after Wolff left. I'd just gotten out of the shower when Sloane called me back. I'd left her a message earlier.

"I'd swing by, but Aspen is running a fever, and Dan had to go in to work early. Apparently, some plane went missing and the team's being called out for a search."

"I heard," I share without thinking.

After Wolff got off the phone, he told me the team had been called out to search for a smaller airplane that had gone missing in the mountains during the storm last night.

It's been on my mind since he left. I can't help but think, if that plane went down with the storm raging out there, the likelihood there are any survivors is virtually nonexistent. It makes me sad, how one moment we're here, and the next all we are is memories.

"You did?" Sloane interrupts my wandering thoughts. "Who'd you talk to?"

Oh dear, here we go. I'm not about to make up some story, since I can't lie for shit, but I'm afraid my friend's imagination is going to run amok at the truth.

"Wolff. He was here when Jonas called him."

"Wolff?" There's a brief pause, and then at a slight increase in pitch, "At your house?"

"It's not what you—"

"Oh my God, I knew it! I could tell there was something going on at Thanksgiving. Wolff looked like someone gut punched him when he caught sight of you. When did this happen? Boy, he did not waste any time, did he?" she rambles excitedly. "I can't believe you didn't tell me."

"That's because there's nothing to tell. Nothing's happened. His truck got stuck in a ditch when he was dropping off some survival stuff for me, so he rode out the storm here. That's it. You're creating fantasies, my friend."

"Well, shoot me for trying to find something happy to think about."

My antennae perk up.

"Did something happen since you dropped off the dog yesterday?" I probe. "Did you buy a test? Talk to Dan?"

She scoffs, "I never had a chance. I barely made it home last night, and then Aspen was sick and Dan had been waiting for me so he could head over to the ranch on the snowmobile to help out with the animals. He was there all night. I didn't even talk to him until he called me this morning to let me know the team was being called out. I was so annoyed, I ended up doing the pregnancy test I picked up on my way in to work yesterday. I intended to do it with Dan there, but since he wasn't and I didn't feel like waiting..."

It's like she suddenly runs out of energy, or maybe she's simply done venting, but she doesn't finish her sentence.

So, I gently prompt her, "And?"

"You were right." She sniffles softly. "And now I don't know when Dan will be back...and Aspen is sick...and I don't have my dog...and I'm just a mess."

"You'll be fine," I try to appease her.

"I'm a mess," she reiterates with emphasis. "It's like I have no control over anything. Not even myself."

In the background I can hear her daughter start wailing, which only makes Sloane sniffle harder.

"Oh God, I can't do this."

"Sure you can," I tell her firmly. "Take a deep breath, go look after your daughter, and I'll be there as soon as I can."

As soon as I can still ended up taking a couple of hours.

It's after noon by the time I pull up to Dan and Sloane's brand-new log home. It was a pleasant surprise to find their driveway plowed. After spending the past two hours breaking my back shoveling my own, I'm seriously considering hiring a service to take care of snow removal in the future.

I considered bringing my guys for a visit as well, but thought better of it. They may have just added to the chaos. Instead, I let them have a good run in the back before I left, and they're generally quite content at home.

Beside me, River starts whining when he recognizes where we are.

"Hang on, buddy," I tell him when he tries to climb over me to get out when I open the door. "I'll come grab you from the other side."

The moment River's paws hit the ground, he takes off for the house, where Sloane is already waiting in the door holding Aspen. As soon as I reach them, I pluck the baby from her arms and shoo Sloane inside before closing the door.

The poor little one is like a stove, so warm, and rather lethargic. I manage to shrug out of my coat by shifting her from arm to arm, and kick off my boots in the entrance before following Sloane into the living room.

"Has she had any fluids today?" I ask, noticing a bottle and a child's cup with a straw on the coffee table.

"Probably not enough. I've tried. We've been up all night," Sloane shares, looking—and sounding—exhausted.

"What about you?" I press on as I lay Aspen down on her back on the couch.

"I...I can't remember. I had tea at some point."

She moves closer as I unzip Aspen's sleeper and inspect her, running my fingers lightly over her chest and belly.

"What are you doing?" her mother wants to know.

"She seems to have a bit of a rash on her torso," I report as I gently flip her over and check her back. No rash there.

Next, I palpate her throat with my fingertips and find her glands substantially enlarged.

"I'm gonna need your help for a sec," I tell Sloane. "If you can lay her on her back on your lap so your knees support her shoulders. I want her head to fall back a bit so I can have a look in her throat."

Sloane sits down and does as I asked. Then I gently press on Aspen's chin. She's not happy with me and makes it known. Her crying actually helps me have a quick look in her mouth using the flashlight on my phone. Her little throat looks raw, and I notice some white dots.

"Oh, you poor baby. Auntie Jillian thinks you have strep throat," I coo at her. I lift her off Sloane's lap and cradle her against my shoulder. "You may want to give your doctor a call, she probably needs to be seen."

"I already tried calling this morning. The message says he's out of the office until next Monday and for anything urgent to go to the emergency room. I wanted to take her but was afraid I was overreacting. Do you really think she has strep? I don't know where she would've picked that up."

I pat her knee. "Sure looks like it. Come on, let's bundle

this little nugget up, and I'll take you. My SUV is already warmed up."

Ten minutes later we're on our way into Libby. I was able to move the car seat from Sloane's Jeep to my Toyota, so Aspen is safely strapped in and it looks like she may be nodding off.

"Looked like you knew what you were doing back there," Sloane observes. "Do you have medical training or something?"

I guess it was inevitable the day would come I'd have to share more about my past than perhaps I'm ready for. It has nothing to do with trust, it has to do with not wanting to open up wounds that always stay raw right under the surface.

"I do. I'm a registered nurse."

Five

JILLIAN

I dislike hospitals.

Kind of ironic, given I worked in one for at least a decade. Still, they represent a bit of a trigger for me now. Not just the hospital itself, but the smells, the sounds, the sense of pain and fear and anxiety is almost tangible within these walls. So strange how I am able to handle visiting when I have my animals with me, but without them I become overwhelmed.

Sloane and Aspen were taken into a treatment room, while I stayed behind in the waiting room. I told her I'd wait here, but that was over half an hour ago and I'm finding it progressively difficult to breathe.

I shoot Sloane a text and don't go too far. Just outside, in the small park at the edge of the parking lot behind the hospital, I find a bench. It's still pretty chilly out and I have to brush a hefty layer of snow off before I can sit, but the sun is out and it's very peaceful. No one is here.

It's a good spot to just sit here with my feelings, which inevitably triggers the tears. I allow myself a few minutes of grace before I pull it together again. This is how I deal with grief, letting it out in controllable measures, otherwise I'm afraid, even after all these years, it will sweep me away.

I haven't shared my past with anyone here, mainly to give myself a break. It's not that any of it is a secret—anyone doing a little background search will be able to find every sordid detail—but I wanted a chance to establish myself in this new place as just a woman, not a woman with a cargo hold full of baggage.

I lived like that for the eight years I remained in Missoula, where every day I risked being confronted with a reminder that would hit like a punch to the gut. It could come out of nowhere, finding me vulnerable and unguarded.

The last time that happened, I was going about my business, grabbing a few groceries on my way home. I was testing some avocados for ripeness when I caught sight of them. They didn't see me at first, and I was frozen on the spot. By the time I forced myself to move, Chris noticed me and his expression went from surprise to one of guilt in an instant. It took me a second to figure out why, and the next moment I was walking out of the store, my cart left in the middle of the produce department.

That experience triggered my decision to move here to Libby. To a clean start. But I suspect it won't be long before my history will start coming to light. It's that Sloane was distracted by her baby's condition, otherwise I'm sure she would've probed my admission I am an RN. More importantly, why I'm no longer working as one.

I don't know if I'm ready to talk, but I'm not going to lie about it.

"Here you are."

I turn around to find Sloane walking up and immediately get to my feet.

"I needed some fresh air. How is she? Where is she?"

"She's dehydrated, and because of her age they want to treat her here. The doctor agreed with you on the strep throat, but he swabbed her to make sure. They put us in a room, and she's asleep now." She restlessly glances back at the hospital. "I don't have any idea how long we'll be here, and I didn't want you waiting around forever."

I hook my arm through hers and steer her back to the entrance.

"If they'll allow me in the room with you, I'll stick around for a bit."

The fact she doesn't immediately tell me that's not necessary assures me I'm making the right call.

"Have you had a chance to get in touch with Dan yet?"

"He's on a search, I don't want to bother him."

"Fair enough." I suggest carefully, "But maybe it wouldn't be a bad idea to contact your uncle, or someone at the ranch to let them know what's going on."

She immediately shakes her head. "There's no need to worry anyone."

I squeeze her arm. "Unless someone drops by your house—maybe to see if you need help after the storm—and finds your Jeep in the driveway but no sign of you or Aspen. They'd worry unnecessarily."

One of the reasons Sloane and I get along so well is because we're very similar. Both of us are fiercely protective of our independence. Sometimes at our own detriment.

"You're pushy," she mumbles as we make our way into the hospital.

"You're stubborn," I fire back.

We stop at the nurses' station, where we're told Aspen is still sleeping, and yes, I'm allowed to join Sloane in the room. She appears tiny in the big crib, which looks more like a dog kennel on wheels. It doesn't seem to bother her, she looks quite peacefully asleep with her hands relaxed by her face, and her mouth soft and slightly open.

She's so precious.

When I turn around, Sloane is on her phone, typing a message. Good.

"I let Ama know," she volunteers when she catches me looking.

I've only met Ama briefly, but it was clear off the bat the woman is a force. I can see why Sloane would pick her to pass the information to.

"Good call."

"Why don't you sit down?"

Sloane takes the chair beside the crib and points me to the recliner in the corner of the room. I have a feeling there's a reason she wants me comfortable. The moment my ass hits the seat I'm proven right.

"So...a nurse? How come I didn't know this?"

I shrug. "I don't know, it's never really come up. I haven't worked as a nurse in eight years."

"Why not? What made you change careers?"

A little honesty goes a long way. At least I hope it does.

"I specialized in palliative care; it starts to wear on you after a while."

A sympathetic expression slides over her face.

"I can only imagine. That has to be a tough job."

"It is. Although, it's gratifying at the same time. Supporting terminal patients and their families through those final steps feels like a privilege too."

"Right. Still..." she nudges gently, probably sensing this isn't the easiest subject for me.

"Still..." I pick up on her prompt, "It's hard dealing with someone else's loss when you're grieving yourself."

"You lost someone," she confirms.

I swallow the lump in my throat and blow out a sharp breath.

"I did, but I don't know if I'm ready to talk about it."

She tosses me a sad little smile. "Then don't. Why don't you tell me how you ended up working with the dogs?"

I'm grateful she steers the conversation in a different direction, and for the next half hour or so, I tell her about volunteering at the animal shelter because I had to stay busy but couldn't handle people. I share how I ended up with Peanut and Nugget, who were deemed unadoptable, but ended up being exceptionally wonderful support dogs to me, and as it turns out, to others as well.

Sloane doesn't pry, but seems genuinely interested when I tell her about my growing passion to give these animals, rejected by the people who were supposed to care for them, a new purpose in life. It's my favorite topic and I'm so deep into it, at first, I don't notice the door opening, but Sloane does.

"What are you doing here?"

Dan stalks into the room glaring at her, all broody and hot under the collar.

"What am I doing here? Where would you have me be when our daughter is lying in a hospital bed?"

Yikes. I sense a come-to-Jesus discussion in the air, and they certainly don't need me for that. But when I ease my way to the door, I find it blocked.

By Lucas Wolff.

Wolff

"Out."

I'm surprised when she plants a hand in the middle of my chest and forcefully backs me out of the room.

"Whoa, hold on."

"Let's give them some space," she mutters, not letting up.

I cast one last glance into the room before Jillian pulls the door shut. Then I follow her down the hall to a waiting area.

"How's the baby?" I ask when I take a seat next to her, running my hand through hair that's getting too long again. I could braid it.

"Suspected strep throat, and she's dehydrated. They want to at least make sure she can keep liquids down." She shifts in her seat, turning toward me. "I thought you guys were out on a call. In fact, so did Sloane, which is why she didn't wanna bug Dan."

Guess that makes sense. We were, in fact, out on the missing airplane call most of the day, but because of the cold temperatures, Jonas doesn't want us out there after sundown.

It's a complicated search, because all we have are the coordinates where the private jet last pinged on the radar before it disappeared. That doesn't necessarily mean that's where the plane went down. All day, helicopters have been flying over Elephant Peak while we set up a base of operations along a forest development road near the Howard Lake Campground. With any visible irregularities they reported, Sully would dispatch our state-of-the-art Matrice drone to get a closer look. Based on his findings, we'd go in with the horses, but so far today we haven't had much luck.

If that plane went down and on the off-chance someone survived the impact, it is doubtful they'd last the night.

None of us had been happy going home for the night, but there is little we can do in the dark, except risk the safety of our horses.

"We were out, but were losing light. We'll be heading back out there first thing tomorrow. Dan happened to be in my truck with me when Ama called him so we came straight here. He's in a bit of a state, but he loves that little girl," I add in defense of my teammate.

She grins. "I know. And Sloane is still not used to sharing responsibilities when she's been used to carrying those by herself," she points out, defending her friend.

"Fair enough," I concede, nodding.

"So, no sign of the plane?" She diverts conversation to the search.

"Not yet. Either it veered completely off its set course or the snow is obscuring any signs of a possible crash site."

She leans forward with her forearms on her knees, twisting her head to look at me.

"How many people on board?" she asks somberly.

She knows as well as I do, even if someone survived the crash, it's unlikely they would've survived the elements for long.

"Three crew and four passengers," I share. "The plane belongs to Vallard Logistics and members of the Vallard family were on board."

We were told it was the family matriarch plus her oldest son and his family who were on the plane. The son is acting CEO for what apparently is a large, worldwide transportation company. We're talking big money, which is probably why Ewing said we'd not only have multiple state and federal agencies involved in this search, but the press wouldn't be far behind.

"Oh no. A family? Kids?"

"I heard one kid. An eleven-year-old girl, both her parents and her grandmother."

Jillian turns to face away, softly shaking her head.

Yeah, I feel the same way. Any time kids are involved—hurt, or possibly dead—it hits hard.

I'm sure I am not the only one still experiencing an occasional nightmare after we discovered the body-dumping ground of a couple of perverts who snatched young girls off the street last summer. We were able to rescue only one girl who survived hell and will never know a carefree life again.

Jillian had been the one to actually find what was left of the bodies of the other missing girls with the help of her cadaver dog, Emo.

"Do you think my guys and I could be of help?" she suddenly asks.

I glance over. "Right now it would be a wild-goose chase. Maybe once we have a more defined area, but it'll be tough going on foot."

She straightens her back. "I have snowshoes."

"I'll mention it to Jonas," I offer.

She nods and her eyes drift off to some place unseen. We sit lost in our own thoughts for a bit, but I'm the one to break the silence when I remember a promise I made this morning.

"By the way, sorry I didn't end up doing your driveway as promised. Were you able to find your shovel?"

"I did, and as I told you this morning I would, I managed fine doing it myself."

The clearing of a throat has me turn my attention to the door where Dan is standing, his eyes narrowed on me. I'm guessing he caught some of that exchange and has some thoughts on the subject, but to his credit, he keeps them to himself.

"I'm gonna stay here with Sloane," he announces. "You guys should go home."

"Then how are you gonna get back?" I ask him.

"I'll figure it out."

"Why don't you take my truck," I offer, fishing the keys from my pocket and tossing them at him. "I'll catch a ride with Jillian."

Dan's head snaps around to check on Jillian, who is looking at me, a smirk tugging at her pretty mouth.

"Sure, I'll give you a ride, cowboy."

Six

WOLFF

Almost thirty-six hours since that plane disappeared off the radar.

The mood turns more somber with every passing hour. Chances any of the seven occupants have survived not only the crash, but the frigid temperatures are virtually nonexistent.

It doesn't help we've basically been sitting on our asses, waiting for even the slightest of indications of where to start looking. Glancing around me, I can tell I'm not the only one it's getting to.

JD, who drove out here with me this morning, has whittled that hunk of wood he's been working on to not much more than a sliver, and Dan is pacing like a caged tiger. After apparently spending a good chunk of the night in the hospital with Aspen before she was released, Jonas told Dan he didn't want to see him until he'd had at least eight hours of sleep.

Sully and Jackson, Jonas's stepson, are the only two on our team actively doing something. Sully operates the Matrice, our drone, and he and Jackson are scrutinizing the video feed coming in. Jackson has a sniper's eye and can detect irregularities at great distances.

I get up to stretch my legs and walk out of the shelter we set up. It's a clear day with stark blue skies, but at this time of year that generally means brisk temperatures. It's supposed to get a little warmer, but I'm not sure that'll do much for those poor people out there.

I walk up to one of the two fire drums we set up out here, and warm my hands on the radiating heat as I take in the surroundings. It's pretty country up here, the crisp white snow covering the dark pines you see most at these elevations. Only the steady hum of the generator outside the shelter disturbs the silence.

Hard to believe this pristine, picturesque landscape hides the ravaged fuselage and victims of a plane crash.

"Anything?"

I watch Sheriff Junior Ewing's approach. He's been here since yesterday, coordinating efforts and calling in resources for the aerial search. I can see the strain on his face. Responsibility weighs heavy, and I'm glad I don't have his job.

"Nothing yet," I share.

He sidles up next to me and shoves his hands toward the heat.

"It's not bad enough I have the National Transportation Safety Board sending in a team and having nothing to show them," he grumbles, "but families of the victims are blowing up my phone, and now I hear from my boys that the press started arriving in town. Everyone is fucking pushing for answers and I have nothing to give them."

For lack of anything constructive to say, I grunt sympa-
thetically.

The rumble of an engine has both of us turn our heads
toward the trail.

"It's Bo," I share when I catch sight of his truck pulling
up to the camp.

He's already pulling a crate from the back of the crew
cab when we join him.

"Delivery from Ama," he clarifies, motioning for me to
grab the massive thermos on the floor behind the driver's
seat.

"Yes. I'm fucking starving," JD mutters when he catches
sight of us entering the shelter.

"Stew, sandwiches, and coffee," Bo announces as he
pulls a large pot from the crate.

It's not often we have the luxury of a home-cooked meal
when we're out on a call, but we happen to be stuck at a
base camp just over half an hour's drive over a bumpy
forestry road from the ranch.

Over the hearty lunch, I listen to Bo filling the sheriff in
on the ramped-up activities in town this morning.

"We even had a KCFW-news van pull into the rescue
this morning." He chuckles. "Lucy had her shotgun out and
about blasted them off the porch."

Bo's wife is a tiny firecracker with a big attitude and runs
Hart's Horse Rescue, just down the road from the ranch.

"What the hell were they doing at the rescue?" Junior
wants to know.

"Never got a chance to ask, but when I got to the ranch
after, Ama mentioned they'd been there earlier, looking for
the latest on the search. Apparently, the crew was pretty
pushy, and were reluctant to leave after Jonas shut them
down." He barks out a laugh. "But they moved when

Thomas stepped outside waving the old double barrel shotgun."

"Guys...I've got something."

I turn my head to catch Jackson pointing at something on the screen. Everyone scrambles to their feet, crowding behind him as he zooms in on what appears to be a couple of snapped tree tops as the drone slowly flies over.

"There's another one," he points out. "Can you stay this course but go in lower?"

Sully adjusts the altitude to where the drone almost skims the tops of the trees. The camera mounted under the drone can pan a hundred and eighty degrees, giving us a wide view of the area.

"Right there," JD pipes up. "Debris on the left of that ridge."

He points to the downslope of a rocky outcropping at the center of the screen. In the drift of snow at the bottom, you can clearly see discolorations and pieces of torn metal.

"How far is that?" Dan asks, even as Jackson pulls up a map on the second screen.

Our location is already marked and he puts in the drone's coordinates.

"Two point seven miles as the crow flies," he informs us.

Normally a distance our horses could easily do in record time, but considering the rough terrain combined with the snow, it'll likely take us some time to get there.

"Have a look..." Jackson indicates a thin line on the map. "This looks like one of the old logging trails. It runs on the north side of that ridge. If we can find it, that might make the going a little easier."

These mountains are riddled with old logging trails, a lot of them unused and grown over. However, they generally provide the smoothest passage through what otherwise is unpredictable landscape. A trail would definitely speed up the process.

On the screen it looks like the drone is hovering low over the location, the camera zoomed in on a larger piece of metal, a partial tail number visible. It matches the first three digits of the missing Cessna 560 Citation. Just visible from under the section of the tail is a hand, palm up with the fingers curled in.

Jesus.

Ewing is already on his radio, calling it through.

"All right, guys," Sully calls for attention. "Get the horses ready. Load up the sled with the medical kit, the second generator, and the floodlights; sundown is only four hours off. But your first order is to look for survivors. Oh, and as you go, make sure to leave clear markings on the trail.

"Jackson, I'm going to need you to take the second sled, load it heavy with logs, then follow them, and tamp down the snow on that trail as best you can. Make a few runs if necessary; we're going to need vehicle access as close to that location as we can get."

Less than half an hour later, we start making our way through the deep snow. It's not only hard work for the horses, but there is a considerable risk they could get injured. One careless step could have devastating results, so despite wanting to rush to the crash site, we force ourselves to go slow.

It takes almost two hours to get to the first evidence of the downed plane—a part of the landing gear sticking out of the snow. Faster than I'd anticipated, but still not fast enough to my liking. At this point it's safer to leave the horses secured and continue on foot to get closer.

We have seven crash victims to find, and, even though

the odds are not good, I'm hoping we can find at least one, but maybe more of them, alive.

With snowshoes strapped to our boots and handfuls of orange marker flags in our packs, we spread out and start moving into the crash site.

"Hello! James Vallard! Captain Alpern!"

My voice is swallowed by the snow and greeted with ominous silence. In my gut I know there is no one left alive. Still, I continue moving, bracing myself for the inevitable as I search.

When I spot a complete seat, upside down, long brown hair from underneath trailing in the snow, I close my eyes and silently pray this isn't the little girl.

"Bo! I've got one," I call out.

In a previous life, Bo was a nurse, before he joined the armed forces as a field medic. His medical training is definitely an asset to the team and comes in handy out here. He lumbers over and pulls off a glove, reaching under the chair.

"Cold," he states simply. "Give me a hand."

Between the two of us we manage to flip the chair upright, the body frozen in place, still strapped in her seat. I wince at the sight of her head, which sits at an unnatural angle to her body, her neck clearly broken. This definitely isn't a child, but an adult woman. From her apparent age, I'm guessing we've found the girl's mother, Theresa Vallard, but it's not on me to make that determination.

"I'll radio it in."

I've just reported the first confirmed mature female casualty to Sully when I hear JD call out.

"Bo!"

While Bo heads his way, I shove an orange flag in the snow next to the body before continuing on my search. I don't encounter anything else until I come upon the portion of the tail we spotted on the drone's feed. I already know there's a body under here, and I can tell from the hand it's another female, but I need confirmation there is an entire body underneath and not just part.

"I could use a hand over here," I call out.

There's no way I can lift this section by myself.

While I wait for Bo, I scan the landscape around me, wondering where the rest of the tail could've gone. In the denser trees to my left, I notice a reflection of metal about twenty feet in. I'm going to check that out next.

"JD found a man," Bo shares when he joins me. "Deceased. What do you have?"

"This is the arm we saw on the screen back at base camp. Looks female."

Bo crouches down and lightly touches the hand. "Young," he mumbles, and my heart sinks.

It must've shown on my face because he immediately clarifies, "Not quite that young."

So, that leaves the twenty-six-year-old flight attendant, her name was Sylvia Hansen.

We each carefully grab at opposite ends of the torn metal and lift it aside. I briefly glance at the body it covered, only long enough to confirm it is not the kid. I'm starting to realize this is not going to get any easier until we've found all the victims.

Sticking another orange flag in the snow next to the young woman, I point at the trees.

"I think there's a bigger piece over there," I tell Bo.

"I'll tag along," he offers, and I hear the soft thud of his snowshoes behind me when I head for the trees.

What we find is a substantial portion of the rear of the fuselage. When I looked at drawings of the various layouts for this model Cessna earlier, I noted in all of them the bathroom is at the rear of the plane. When we round the side, we find a big gaping hole where this section was attached to the rest of the plane. The ceiling is caved in, but a single, empty chair still appears to be bolted to the floor, it's back against what I believe is the wall of the bathroom. The door is open.

"I'm going in," I announce, brushing aside a cluster of dangling wires.

"Be careful," Bo rumbles.

Ducking down, I find my way past the chair, taking a deep breath before I stick my head around the bathroom door.

Empty.

"It's clear."

Twenty minutes later JD and Dan find both pilots in the nose of the plane, which must've broken off on impact. Both are dead. It's one of the sheriff's deputies who ends up recovering the matriarch's body when a few of them show up to join the search.

By nightfall, six bodies have been moved by sled to base camp.

The girl is still missing.

Seven

JILLIAN

I lift my hand at the guy in the truck as he drives off.

I don't think he even glanced in my direction.

Then I look back at the load of firewood he literally dumped at the end of my driveway. I guess it was naïve of me to think I'd be left with a tidy, stacked pile on my porch without putting in some serious elbow grease myself.

The prospect of carrying every log up to the house is a bit daunting, but maybe I can find a bucket or a bin in the garage. I haven't been in there since I stumbled around in the dark during the power outage, but this time at least I'll be able to see something.

Cobwebs are the first thing I notice, and a light shiver runs down my back. Not a big fan of spiders, at least not indoors where I don't expect them. I grab the broom leaning against the wall just inside the door, and with a few well-aimed sweeps clear most of them away.

Other than some drywall sheets leaning against the back

wall, and an old workbench with a few rusted tools under the single window, there isn't much there. No bucket or bin in sight. But when I glance up, I notice a rope hanging down from a plastic sled up in the rafters. Now that could be useful.

It helps to be able to drag the wood to the porch steps, but I'm still sweating buckets when I finally put the last log on the pile. Still, while I have the sled out here, I may as well load it up with the empty boxes I've been collecting on the back deck as I unpacked. I'll load them in the back of the SUV and drop them off at the recycling depot just up the road when I head into town later.

Ten minutes later, I'm on my way to the bathroom to get out of my sweaty clothes and hop in the shower, when the ringing of my phone in the kitchen stops me. The phone number on the screen doesn't quite register until I already have the phone to my ear.

Shit.

"Jill?"

Chris is the only one who calls me that, and I've grown to hate that name. But that might be because of the visceral reaction I have to the sound of his voice. I feel instantly ill.

My instinct is to hang up on him, but a kind of sick curiosity stops me.

"What do you want?" I snap, none too graciously.

"I actually stopped by to talk to you after seeing you at the grocery store, but I discovered you sold your place. I've been worried about you."

"*Now,* you're worried about me?" I remind him.

"Come on, Jill, please..." His tone is patronizing, and anger starts to burn in my gut. Even more so when he adds, "It doesn't have to be like this."

"Oh, I know it doesn't," I fire back with a healthy dose

of sarcasm. "So, I'm asking you again, what is it you want, Chris?"

I can sense his annoyance in the heavy silence, but I can play this game as well—if not better—as he can. Call me petty, but I feel a faint sense of victory when he caves.

"Fine, I was trying to be considerate so you don't get blindsided. Rachel delivered a healthy baby boy last Saturday."

Hot bile surges up and coats the back of my throat. I don't know why I react like this. It's not like this is unexpected after bumping into him and his very pregnant wife at Albertsons, but I didn't need it in my face.

Still, I force myself to say, "Congratulations."

Of course, Chris can't simply leave it at that, and pushes his luck.

"You know, he actually looks just like—"

I immediately cut him off with a warning.

"No. Don't you dare go there, Chris. This conversation is over."

Without waiting for his response, I end the call and immediately block his number. Whatever connection remained between us over the years—maybe shared grief is all it was—is no longer there.

Chris has moved on by recreating what we lost. I guess that's what upsets me; I know there is no way to get back what is gone, and to even try feels somehow like a betrayal to the memories that remain. That doesn't mean I'm stuck in the past; I'm simply moving on in my own way.

I hold it together until I'm in the shower and then I allow the memories to flood me. Images of Macy's dimpled grin. The strawberry-blond braids she favored to a ponytail. The stuffed bunny she dragged everywhere. Her adorable squeaky little voice. Reading her *Llama, Llama, Red Pajama* at bedtime.

Then inevitably come the darker flashes. Macy as an infant, struggling for air when she had pneumonia. Her first bloody scrape after tripping on the sidewalk. The sheer panic when I found the backyard gate wide open. The squeal of tires. Her lone new butterfly hair clip in a spreading pool of her blood.

The tears follow; hot, plentiful, and never quite as healing as I wish they were.

I don't allow myself the indulgence of crying often anymore. There was a time it was all I did, and it absolutely drained all the life out of me. It doesn't bring any relief, only makes my heart feel emptier.

Chris wanted to fill the hole in his with another child and couldn't understand why that felt offensive to me. The void Macy's loss left in my heart will always be there, but I found other ways to give me purpose and nourish my soul. Those differences turned out to be insurmountable and, to be honest, I don't think either of us tried very hard.

When I open the bathroom door, I find Peanut and Nugget right outside.

"I'm fine, guys," I reassure the dogs, giving them scratches before I continue to my dresser.

Maybe I'll take the crew for a nice long walk along the creek. We've had nothing but blue skies since that storm came through, and today the temperature has actually been quite bearable. They could do with the exercise, and frankly, so could I.

I dress warmly, strap on my snowshoes while sitting on the bottom step of my deck, and walk out my backyard. It's one of the things I love about this house, there is nothing between me and Mother Nature, but a chain-link fence and a gate.

My dogs don't run off, they tend to stay in a pack when we're out on a hike. They monitor each other, so I can just enjoy my surroundings. The snow is pristine back here, untouched, and I watch as the dogs walk in front of me, sniffing everything. You'd think the snow would obscure scent, but often times a snowfall will cover and actually preserve a trail, making tracking easier.

When we return, it's close to six and the sun is already down. I'm carrying Nugget, whose little legs couldn't keep up with the rest of us, but my lungs are full of fresh air, my face is flushed from the exercise, and my head feels clear. I lead the pack around the side of the house to the front, so I can dry the dogs with a towel on the porch before letting them inside.

I'm crouching down, trying to wipe as much snow off the animals as I can, when a truck pulls into my driveway. The dogs immediately start barking.

"Quiet," I tell them as I get to my feet.

I recognize Wolff as he gets out.

"Hey," I greet him, wondering what he's doing here.

Wolff

I'm not sure why I'm here.

We were ordered to go home, get some rest after thirty-six hours of searching. The last twenty-four of those we spent trying to track down the final crash victim.

Eleven-year-old Hayley Vallard has been missing for

almost seventy-two hours since the plane dropped off the radar.

Last night, the NTSB investigators took over processing the crash site, and we were able to focus on the search for the girl. Unfortunately, it has been frustratingly fruitless so far, but none of us was willing to give up. So Dan, JD, Jackson, and I kept pushing through the night, hanging on to the unlikely hope we might find her alive.

Then a couple of hours ago, Jonas, Fletch, and James showed up at base camp, calling us back for a briefing. The four of us were sent home for the night, told to rest up while the old guard took over the search.

I was home long enough to have a shower, but felt too restless to even contemplate hitting the sack. So, I hopped in my truck and drove here.

"Hi."

I'm feeling a bit ridiculous now, standing here with nothing better to say.

Jillian tilts her head and studies my face for a few beats before jerking her head toward the door.

"Come in. I picked up some beer yesterday."

I kick off my boots on the porch and carry them inside with me, dropping them on the boot tray next to Jillian's. The dogs give me a good sniff-down as I follow her into the kitchen.

"Sloane mentioned you found the plane," she prompts me as she sets a beer bottle in front of me on the island.

I nod. "We did."

I don't volunteer anything more and watch her fill a kettle with water. Then she grabs a mug down from the cupboard and tosses in a tea bag.

"You're not having a beer?" I observe out loud.

She shrugs. "I prefer tea."

Interesting. I briefly wonder who she had in mind picking up those beers yesterday, when she returns to the subject of the crash.

"That can't have been an easy scene."

I take a reinforcing drink from my bottle before answering her.

"Pretty horrific," I concede.

"Never gets easier, does it?"

Her comment reminds me she's not a stranger to death in all of its grisly forms. Maybe that's why I was drawn here. She's someone I could talk to, she'd get it.

"It doesn't. These people didn't even see it coming. Makes you wonder what the fuck they were doing out in that storm in the first place."

I realize that question has been bugging and angering me since I heard of the crash.

"And now a young girl is still out there somewhere."

"The girl? You haven't found her?"

"She wasn't with the wreckage, and we've been looking for her since last night."

"Do you think she could've survived? I don't know— gotten injured, maybe confused, and wandered off?" she suggests.

"It's possible, but it's hard to believe we wouldn't have found her by now. We covered a decent amount of ground."

She does that head tilt again, like she's sizing me up.

"What?"

Her generous lips stretch in a soft smile.

"You wanna be out there."

"Damn right I do," I admit. "But the boss sent us home to get some rest."

"And instead you're here, having a beer," she points out, as she turns to the water kettle which is boiling.

"It would appear so..."

She pours water in her mug and leaves it to steep, as she opens the fridge and starts pulling out ingredients.

"I assume you haven't eaten yet?"

"No, I haven't."

"You okay with double-decker grilled cheese?"

"Can't say I know what it is, but it sounds pretty good."

Looks amazing too.

I watched her layer four pieces of sourdough bread with a thin spread of pesto, sliced tomatoes, turkey, and fresh mozzarella, stacking two together to make two massive sandwiches. Then she popped those in the toaster oven on the counter.

She's just pulled them out, all browned and oozing.

Damn. I didn't think I was that hungry, but my mouth is watering and my stomach is growling.

We don't talk much while we're eating, Jillian apparently starving as well. I'm surprised to see the petite woman devour her entire sandwich in equal time.

"Thank God for yoga pants," she announces, sitting back as she pats her stomach.

Who knew a woman with a healthy appetite could be all kinds of sexy?

Or maybe it's because it is Jillian.

It's probably a combination of a full stomach, the beer, and a serious lack of sleep catching up with me, but I find myself suddenly yawning big. It doesn't go unnoticed.

"Think you'll be able to sleep now?" Jillian asks as she gets up from the small kitchen table and gathers our plates.

Probably, even though I'm enjoying sitting in her kitchen, watching her putter around.

"Yeah, I should get going," I reluctantly admit, pushing

myself to my feet. "That 6:00 a.m. briefing will be here soon enough."

"Like I said before, if you think I could be in any way helpful, I'm here. The snow does not affect the dogs' sense of smell. In fact, they sometimes track better."

I'd actually been thinking about that. Maybe I should bring it up with Ewing tomorrow morning.

"Yeah, I do. I don't make the calls though, but I'll make the suggestion at the briefing."

She follows me to the door and waits for me to shove my feet in my boots and shrug my coat on. Then I turn to face her.

"Dinner was great. Again." I bark out a laugh. "Jesus, you'd think I only show up to mooch a meal off you."

She flashes me a pair of pretty, wide, green eyes. "Damn, and here I thought you sought me out for my sparkling personality."

Her comment throws me for a second, but then she starts laughing. A free, lighthearted sound I could listen to all night.

"One of these days I'm gonna knock on your door and take you out to dinner."

She seems as stunned at my promise as I am. That came out of the blue.

She nods pensively, then steps in and gets on her toes, pressing a soft kiss to my cheek.

"I think I'd like that."

Eight

"We can't have civilians stomping around the crash site."

Greg Polman, the NTSB lead investigator, is clearly not on board calling in the dog team.

It's not just my hackles that shoot up, but I can sense the guy's callous dismissal garners a similar reaction from the others. But it's Junior Ewing who pipes up first.

"Miss Lederman is as much a civilian as most of the men assembled here. Her dog team has extensive experience working with law enforcement agencies. Last year, she assisted with the investigation into a pair of serial killers, who used these mountains as their dumping ground, and was instrumental in finding the remains of their victims. We've all worked with her and she's a consummate professional."

Jonas decides to add a sobering reminder.

"And let's not forget we're talking about finding an eleven-year-old girl here."

Polman focuses on him.

"Are you suggesting the kid is still alive?"

"No way to tell for sure until we find her," Jonas fires back.

"Plus," Ewing fills in, "You said yourself it looked like someone may have gone through the airplane pantry."

Polman asked earlier whether any of us had opened the cupboards or the small fridge, since they were found empty when they examined the front section of the plane. The fact he even posed the question was an insult in itself, which didn't exactly ingratiate the man to any of us. This whole discussion isn't helping that.

"She could've raided it for supplies," Junior continues. "Plus, these guys reported bumping into some winter sports equipment. Skis, snowboard, snowshoes and the like."

"Yeah, the family was on their way back from a vacation in Whistler, British Columbia," the investigator clarifies. "Surely you're not suggesting the kid might've packed a bag, strapped on a pair of snowshoes, and taken off, are you?"

"It's possible," the sheriff proposes.

It's clear Polman doesn't agree.

"Why the hell would she do that? She stands a better chance of being found by staying with the wreckage."

"Unless she thought she could go for help," I suggest. "She may not have been the only one who initially survived the crash."

"Or she doesn't want to be found," Fletch adds.

He would know, he spent years trying not to be found in the Canadian Rockies.

"We're wasting time on assumptions," Jonas intervenes, "when we should be out there getting answers, and the bottom line is; Jillian Lederman and her dogs could help us find some of those answers."

Polman slaps a hand behind his neck and tilts his head back, looking up at the roof of the temporary shelter, before responding.

"Fine. Call her in, but you are responsible for her."

The moment he leaves the tent, Jonas speaks up.

"One thing though, she should not go out there alone. Out here and under these conditions, she follows the same rule as the rest of us; always at least one other person within sight. Winter is dangerous in the mountains."

"I'll tag along with her," JD offers.

He's glancing at me and I know he's trying to get under my skin, but I still can't keep myself from reacting. Especially after that not so innocent, innocent kiss last night.

"In your fucking dreams," I tell him, before turning to Jonas. "I'll go get her. She'll have a hard time finding us otherwise."

Jonas shares a look with Ewing before nodding at me.

"Go."

I call her on my way down the mountain, as soon as I have reception again, to give her a heads-up. When I pull up to her house a while later, she's already waiting on the porch, with two of her dogs by her side. I note neither of them are Emo, her cadaver dog.

"I'll follow you in my SUV," she announces.

"You're not gonna get up those roads without chains," I point out.

"Shit, I don't have any," she admits. "I thought I could double my chances and bring both Murphy and Hunter, so I can search with one while the other rests."

"Well, why can't you?"

"Because the crate is in the back of my SUV."

"Bolted down?" I ask.

"No."

"In that case, we can throw it in the back of my truck and put it inside the shelter at our base camp. We've got a heater going in there for the equipment, so it's probably more comfortable for the dogs than the back of your SUV."

"That'll work."

She opens the rear passenger door to my truck and whistles between her teeth for the dogs. They respond instantly, jumping down from the porch, running over, and hopping straight into the back seat.

It takes us a few minutes to get the aluminum travel crate from the back of her SUV and secure it in the bed of my truck with some straps. While Jillian goes back to the porch to grab her backpack and snowshoes, I get behind the wheel and start the engine.

"I wasn't expecting to get called out already," she says, buckling herself in. "Guess you weren't messing around this morning."

"My team and the sheriff were on board right away," I share.

"But?" I glance at her, and she flashes me a grin. "I could swear I heard one in there."

Perceptive.

"The lead investigator for the National Transportation Safety Board, who's in charge of the crash site, required a bit of convincing," I admit. "What can I say, he's government, but he saw the light in the end."

"I hope you didn't make an enemy out of him in the process."

"Not me. I didn't have to say a word. Ewing and Jonas did all the convincing."

I catch a glimpse of a smile on her lips. I guess there are worse things than having those two tout your praises.

"Well, I appreciate the votes of confidence, and I hope to God one of my guys can pick up her scent."

I tell her about this morning's briefing, about the possible missing supplies, and the theories we were throwing around.

"I guess it's possible, but she'd have to be an incredibly resourceful and courageous eleven-year-old," Jillian points out. "I really hope she is all those things."

Me too.

On my way here I was mulling over the likelihood the girl could be out there, still alive. You'd think we would've found some trace of her—tracks—but if she started moving while the storm was still going on, the snow and wind could well have obscured them. Especially if she had, say, a pair of snowshoes; the imprints she'd leave behind would be fairly shallow.

So yeah, even though the odds are getting slimmer by the minute, I'd love to find her alive out there.

"I notice you didn't bring Emo?"

I turn my head to catch her looking at me, a shadow in her eyes I can't quite put my finger on.

"Not as long as there is even the remotest chance this child survived," she states firmly before aiming her gaze out the windshield.

Then she adds softly.

"There's still hope."

Jillian

"You wait here, sweet girl."

I nudge Hunter into the crate. She whines softly but curls up in the blankets I keep in there, resting her head on her crossed legs. She's a beagle mix and has a great nose, but she doesn't quite have the same stamina as Murphy and takes a lot longer to recover, which is why I'm taking him first.

Murphy, a black Lab cross, is eager to get going when I walk him out of the large tent.

"Easy, boy," I mumble when he starts pulling on the leash.

Wolff is already standing next to one of the snowmobiles parked outside. He's going to give us a ride to the crash site, which apparently is a bit of a hike away.

"It'll be cozy, but he should fit between us," he suggests, indicating the dog. "I'll strap your gear to the cargo rack."

A few minutes later we head down a narrow trail. Murphy is enjoying the ride with his front paws on Wolff's shoulders, tongue lolling, and his nose stuck in the breeze. There's barely any direct contact between me and Wolff because the dog is wedged between us, but that doesn't stop my heart from beating a little faster.

I like him. I like that he comes across as this somewhat reserved, controlled guy, but shows up on my doorstep last night looking everything but. It's almost as if he seeks me out, despite his reluctance to get close. Call me an idiot, but I find that attractive.

He is attractive. Tall, built like a swimmer with wide shoulders and narrow hips. Not usually a fan of long hair on men, I really like it on Wolff. An almost rebellious contrast to an otherwise pretty buttoned-up guy. Same with the gray-speckled beard; facial hair is not normally my thing but, more than once in the past few days, I've found myself fantasizing how the neatly trimmed bristles would feel on my skin.

And then those steel-blue eyes…

You'd expect them to be cold, yet they're anything but. In fact, I've caught more heat than I would've thought possible in those baby-blues on a few occasions.

It's tempting. *He's* tempting, and I'm not quite sure yet what to do with that.

Any musings on the subject evaporate from my thoughts when Wolff brings the snowmobile to a stop, and I catch sight of the debris field in front of us.

"Don't touch anything."

The order comes from an older man wearing a navy parka with NTSB initials on his chest, who walks up as we are getting off the snowmobile. I know the type: old-school, protective of his turf, suspicious of any outsiders, and maybe even disapproving of women in any professional capacity. In my experience, ignoring the attempts at intimidation and killing with kindness works best to disarm guys like this.

I slip my glove off and hold out my hand.

"You must be the investigator in charge."

"Polman," he confirms curtly, accepting my hand almost as an afterthought.

"My name is Jillian Lederman, and this is Murphy." Before he has a chance to respond, I continue, "We won't disturb anything, we just need to allow Murphy to pick up a scent. I'm sure you would be able to direct us to an item that belonged to the girl, maybe her seat. Something that is most likely to have her scent on it."

He seems a little taken aback, and there's a slightly awkward silence I'm happy to wait out with an expectant smile on my face.

"Right," he gives in. "Would her suitcase be helpful? We started gathering up personal belongings from the site this morning."

He points at an ATV with a small trailer attached.

"That would be perfect, actually."

He starts moving in that direction while I clip on Murphy's lead. The dog's demeanor instantly changes; he knows it's time to work.

"Nicely done," Wolff whispers as we follow the investigator.

I flash him a smile and a wink.

Polman is already flipping back the brown tarp covering the small trailer and pulls out a hard-shell carry-on with country flags printed all over. One side looks almost as if it melted.

"Was there a fire on board?" I wonder out loud.

The investigator's narrowed eyes snap to Wolff behind me.

"Hey, she didn't get that from me."

I point out the deformed edge of the suitcase. "I was just curious about this."

Polman's lips are tight when he answers.

"We have reason to suspect there may have been a small explosion. I would appreciate if you kept this information to yourself. It's an ongoing investigation."

"Of course," I reassure him. "The reason I ask is because the smell of smoke can have a bit of an effect on Murphy's ability to pick up a good scent."

"No, no evidence of a fire," he clarifies.

I reach for the zipper of the suitcase.

"May I?"

He gestures for me to go ahead.

To my surprise there is very little in the suitcase; a few Tshirts, some underwear, a bathing suit, and a pair of pajamas. Considering she was just on a winter vacation, that seems a bit sparse.

"No socks, no sweater, and no toiletries," I point out.

"Astute," Polman observes.

The discovery actually flames my hopes. It would confirm the girl survived and was obviously capable of rational thought if she grabbed things she would need to sustain herself.

"What's the girl's name?"

Wolff is the one to answer, "Hayley. Hayley Vallard."

I grab the pajamas I assume she's slept in, and tuck them in a resealable bag from my backpack. Then I crouch down and hold the bag open for Murphy.

"Ready to get to work, Murphy?"

His tail is wagging as he shoves his nose in. The bag is part of his routine, and every so often I'll take it out of my pack to keep the scent fresh in his nose. I let him sniff his fill before zipping the bag closed and tucking it in my backpack.

The dog sits down beside me, looking up and waiting for my order.

"Good boy. Search, Murphy."

He takes off immediately, zigzagging in front of me. I keep him on the long lead for now, but once he picks up her scent and heads into the tree cover, I'll probably let him off. Give him the freedom to track.

The snow here has been packed down from all the traffic I imagine has gone through in the past few days. No need for snowshoes yet, but that will change if Murphy takes us into the woods.

The dog pulls me away from the ridge and down the slope, into the trees, toward a large section of the plane.

"Careful," I hear the investigator behind me.

But Murphy is already finding his way around the wreckage and darts into the gaping hole, sniffing furiously at the single seat, before ducking inside the open door of a bathroom. I can tell from his reaction he's picking up on the girl's scent; his tail is standing almost straight up and he is hyperalert, almost vibrating.

He scoots back out of the fuselage and almost gets tangled up with Polman, who is right behind me.

"Give them some space," Wolff, who kept a respectful distance, grumbles at the man. "Let them do their work."

Murphy is tracking though, and pulling me in a different direction, so I can't quite make out Polman's response. The dog is no longer zigzagging, but moving in a straight line, right to what appears to be the nose of the plane. There he sniffs around for a moment, before making a beeline for the trees on the far side.

"Hold, Murphy. Wait," I call out quickly, before he pulls me into the deep snow.

He obediently sits down, but he's tense and ready to spring up as soon as I give him any indication. As I'm quickly strapping my snowshoes on, I notice Wolff about twenty feet behind me, doing the same thing.

"You don't have to follow me."

He glances up with a half-smile.

"No team member goes out alone in these conditions. HMT rules."

I open my mouth to tell him I'm not an HMT team member, but I have a feeling that won't make much of a difference. Besides, Murphy is starting to whine, eager to get going.

Instead, I straighten up and pull on my gloves.

"All right, boy. Let's find Hayley."

Nine

The woman is tireless.

I've followed behind Jillian for close to two hours now with only a few short breaks. My inner thigh muscles are starting to burn with the slightly unnatural gait, walking on snowshoes.

I've noticed though, the trail the dog seems to be tracking is all over the place. He's taken us in every direction, at some point even crossing over our own tracks. It seemed to throw him for a moment, the scent leading in two different directions but, somehow, he figured it out.

The girl must've been disoriented in the storm.

But now the dog looks to be a bit confused. Up ahead he came to a sudden halt and is lifting his nose, sniffing the air around him as if he's lost track of the scent.

"Okay, Murphy," I hear Jillian call out to the dog. "Break."

She drops her pack and fishes out a flask of water and the dog's collapsible bowl, as I catch up.

"Did he lose the scent?"

"I think he's running out of steam, but he'll keep pushing until he collapses, unless I stop him," she shares when she catches sight of me.

"How long can he go for?"

"He's good for a couple of hours in decent conditions, but not trudging through a foot of snow. He's gonna need a good rest soon."

I glance around me. "Well, we're actually not that far from base camp. Have you noticed the last half hour we've been going almost parallel to the trail we came up with the snowmobile?"

She nods, brushing some snow off a fallen tree, and sitting down. I take a seat beside her, giving my legs a break. I do better on horseback.

"Remember that rock shelf where we took the last break? Murphy really seemed interested in the shallow crevice underneath. I wonder if she maybe rested there for a while. That ledge would've given her a bit of shelter."

"Could be," I concede. "Maybe she waited for the worst of the storm to be over."

"That would explain why, since leaving that location, the trail has been straight downhill instead of nearly going in circles like it did before." She shakes her head. "The only thing that doesn't make sense is the timing. If she waited out the weather before heading down this way, it most likely wouldn't have been until morning. By that time the search was already in full swing, she was close, she must've noticed the activity. Why didn't she come look for help?"

She's right. It is curious, and ties in with one of the theories Fletch floated earlier this morning.

"Someone suggested the possibility she may not want to be found. Like you said, there has been plenty of activity, and we've covered all of this ground on horseback."

"I guess she could've gotten hurt in the crash and died trying to get to help," Jillian suggests somberly.

"Surely we would've found her."

She shrugs. "She may have holed up in a hiding spot."

I turn my head to look at her.

"What about getting Emo?"

"No," she responds almost angrily. "I'm not ready to give up on her." Abruptly she gets to her feet. "I'm gonna give Murphy a rest and get Hunter out here. Let her have a try."

Clearly, she did not like my suggestion Hayley may not be alive. I decide not to push it. There really is no rush should the girl already be gone.

I pull out the spray can I've been marking our trail with and put an arrow on the log we were sitting on. This way we'll know where we were and when we get turned around. It isn't easy to keep track of where you are in this snow-covered landscape. Everything looks very similar.

It's literally no more than a ten-minute walk to the shelter, where we find Jackson and JD.

"Where is everyone?"

Jackson looks up at me. "The old guard left. Home for a rest, I guess. Except for Dan, he was heading to the ranch with the other horse trailer and said he was gonna stop in at home to see how Sloane and the little one are doing. Then he'll be back."

"Sloane?" Jillian pipes up from where she is crouched down, greeting Hunter. "Is she okay? The baby?"

Jackson shrugs. "As far as I know."

"I thought Aspen had recovered," I direct at Jillian.

"Yeah, she has. I wasn't...I just thought maybe Sloane came down with it too."

She waves her hand dismissively before returning her attention to the dogs. She has Hunter out of the crate and coaxes Murphy in there.

"Your turn for a snooze, boy." She bends down and kisses the top of his head. "You did good." Then she closes the gate.

She goes to leash up the other dog, and we're about to head back out when Dan pulls up. He's got a few hay bales in the back of his truck.

"Your timing is perfect. I brought lunch," he announces when he hops out of the cab.

"Hay?" I observe, hauling one of the bales from the truck bed.

I toss it to the front of the remaining horse trailer. All four horses are tied to the side and covered with blankets. The hay we brought this morning already decimated on the ground in front of them.

"And a tray of burritos and some coffee in the passenger seat," he adds, grabbing the second bale of hay.

"Maybe we should grab a quick lunch first?" I carefully suggest to Jillian, who is waiting. "We've gotta fuel up too."

Also, passing up on Ama's burritos is almost sacrilegious, but I keep that to myself.

"Mmm. God, this is so good," she moans on a mouthful with her eyes closed five minutes later.

The bite I just took gets stuck in my throat as a mental image of Jillian, naked in my bed, pops in my head. I cough to try and dislodge it.

"You okay there, my friend? The heat getting to you?" JD mocks me with a grin as he whacks me between the shoulder blades.

I cough again and mumble, "Asshole," behind my hand.

The interaction escapes Jillian, who turns to Dan.

"How is Aspen, by the way? All better?"

"Yeah, she's good."

"And Sloane? She didn't catch it?"

Dan's face splits in a goofy grin. "Not strep, if that's what you mean."

I glance over at Jillian and catch her smiling as well.

"What was that all about?" I ask when we're strapping on our snowshoes outside ten minutes later.

She can't quite keep herself from grinning again.

"Afraid that's not my news to share."

Ahhh.

Gotcha.

Jillian

The brief moment of joy I felt for Sloane and Dan quickly evaporates as we make our way back to where Murphy lost the little girl's trail.

What was she thinking? I've thought about the possibility she hit her head in the crash and wandered off, but nothing really supports that theory. Every step she's taken has been with purpose, even though I'm not sure of her motivation.

Thinking of myself at age eleven, I'm pretty sure I wouldn't have had the presence of mind—or the courage, to be honest—to have done what it looks like Hayley has. I was a girly girl growing up. My parents took me camping one summer and I absolutely hated it. I was into boy bands, bead bracelets, and Easy-Bake ovens, not communing with nature. Obviously, that changed over the years.

But Macy might've grown up to be an industrious and brave eleven-year-old. Even at five she'd loved going on hiking adventures, identifying bugs, searching for mushrooms, looking for animal tracks. She was fearless in her explorations of the world around her.

My eyes start to burn and I try to shake off the wave of grief. My focus needs to be on finding Hayley, who may still have a full life to live.

"Is she looping back?"

Wolff's voice snaps me back into the here and now.

I glance at Hunter, who looks like she may have finally picked up the scent. Her nose is low to the ground as she determinedly struggles through the snow. Murphy's enthusiasm means I have to keep him on the long leash, but Hunter is much more sedate and will stop on a dime on my command, so I let her loose.

Wolff is right, she appears to be doubling back, heading the other way. For a moment I'm worried she's retracing our earlier steps and I'm about to call her back when I notice her veering off to our right, away from the trail.

I set course after her as Hunter takes us deeper into the woods. She seems to have a strong scent, and is moving with purpose for the next few minutes. Then she abruptly stops and starts pawing at the snow, sniffing furiously at the hole she created.

My heart sinks, and for a moment I can't breathe.

Did she find her?

In the next moment she's moving again, still on the trail, and I blow out a relieved breath. As I pass by where she stopped, I notice something sticking out of the snow. Something bright orange that seems out of place in the woods.

Crouching down, I see it's the corner of a piece of paper and pull it out.

"It's a wrapper."

A Reese's wrapper to be precise.

That explains Hunter's interest; peanut butter is her favorite treat. It also gives me a strange satisfaction to know Hayley had something to eat. I just hope she has more supplies to sustain her for a bit.

Wolff takes it from my hand and tucks it in the pocket of his coat, mumbling something like, "Atta girl."

We hustle to catch up with my dog when Wolff points up ahead, past Hunter. Through the trees I can make out a rock wall.

"I'll bet she went for the rocks in hopes of finding shelter. A dry place to rest," he suggests. "I actually think this may be the same ridge as at the crash site. From the air I remember seeing it runs almost parallel to the trail."

"I can't get over the fact this is an eleven-year-old we're looking for. Not even a teenager, and after a horrific crash and the trauma of having her family wiped out, it blows my mind she can even think of things like supplies and shelter."

"Either she has very good instincts, or she knows a bit about survival in the—"

He doesn't finish his sentence and stops in his tracks, sniffing the air.

"Can you smell that?"

I sniff too but my nose is runny from the cold and I don't smell anything.

"No. What is it?"

He sniffs again. "It's gone now. I could've sworn I smelled smoke."

"Smoke?" I parrot.

"Like I said, it's gone now."

We start moving once more, but I notice every now and then Wolff seems to lift his nose in the air.

I can hear Hunter start whining, when we approach the base of the ridge. She's pacing back and forth, her nose lifted high and every so often she puts a front paw up against a large boulder.

Walking up to her, I put a hand on her back and tilt my head upward.

"What've you got, girl?"

"I smell it again," Wolff says from behind me. "Something burned at some point."

This time I detect it too; the way your clothes smell after sitting by a campfire. "Someone made a fire," I conclude out loud.

"Jillian, come have a look at this."

As I turn to him, Wolff is taking a few steps back and peering up. I move to stand beside him and follow the direction of his gaze. The ridge is steep, but not impassably so, and as I'm looking up, I'm noticing some ledges and crevices that would make good foot or handholds.

"You think she climbed up there?"

He shrugs and looks at me. "Your dog seems to think so."

Yeah. She does. Her focus on something—or someone —overhead is unwavering.

Wolff walks up to Hunter, who is still pacing back and forth and seems to be searching for something—or someone —overhead. Then he leans his butt against the rock and proceeds to take off his snowshoes.

"What are you doing?"

He lifts his head. "I'm gonna have a look."

"And how much climbing experience do you have?" I ask with a hefty dose of sarcasm.

Then I reach in my backpack and pull out my flexible climbing shoes, waving them at him. I have plenty of experience and he knows it from last year's search with Emo.

"Besides," I add, as I pull my left foot out of my boot and fit on the flex shoe. "You'd probably scare her. I know I'd be, if I were a traumatized, eleven-year-old girl, encountering a strange, tall man wearing a scowl in the middle of the wilderness."

I do the same with the other and leave my boots attached to the snowshoes. Already I can feel the cold seeping into my toes.

"I don't scowl."

I pause to shoot him a "yeah-right" look.

"Hunter, you stay, girl." Then I turn to Wolff. "Give me a foot up, will you?"

Not that I need it—I see plenty of footholds to get me up on this big boulder—but I don't want to make him feel useless either. He does as asked, pressing his back against the rock, and folding his hands for me to step on. I'd be lying if I said I didn't enjoy the brief interlude of suspension, where I brace myself on his shoulders and my eyes lock with his.

Then suddenly he hoists me up and the moment is broken as I scramble onto the boulder. From this vantage point I can see what's above me a little better. One of the crevices I noticed earlier looks a little larger than I thought. The shadows seem darker. Deeper.

It's not a difficult route to get up there and I reach for the first handhold as I start making my way toward it.

"Careful," I hear from below.

I'm sure it goes against everything that is Lucas Wolff to stand by and watch me do this.

"Always," I reassure him.

It's an easy climb to get to the narrow ledge. I grab on with my hands and heave myself up.

The first thing I notice is the campfire smell, which is much stronger here. Up close I can see the actual crevice is maybe a foot-and-a-half high and four feet long. However, trying to look into the dark interior, I get the sense it's roomier inside.

A slight shuffling sound from the shadows has me rear my head back, and I almost lose my balance. I should've been more careful; this is just the kind of hiding spot where wildlife likes to shelter for the winter.

Wildlife, or scared little girls.

"Hayley? Is that you?"

No answer, but another little shuffle. As if something is trying to hide deeper in the shadows.

I reach into my pocket and fish out the penlight I always carry on me, flicking it on. When I shine the narrow beam into the crevice, it first reflects on something shiny; the metal buckle of a backpack.

When I pan the light around, it catches on a pair of wide eyes in a dirty face, tucked in the far corner. My heart stills and a sob escapes my lips.

"Hey, sweetheart..."

Ten

Wolff

Since I saw her body disappear into the crevice a few minutes ago, I've been fighting the temptation to go up there after her.

Instead, I'm trying to calm Hunter, who is whining even harder now she can't see Jillian anymore, while I keep my eyes peeled on the ledge above.

I'm not a praying man, but I find myself silently pleading with some unseen force that she found the little girl. Alive.

"Wolff?" Jillian's head pops out over the ledge. "She's here. We're going to need medical here."

Shit.

It's going to be tough for EMTs to find their way up here and, unfortunately, Bo went home to sleep. It would be more efficient if I could carry her down to base camp and meet up with EMTs there.

"Is she injured?"

"I can see some scratches and bruising, but she's weak; probably hypothermic and dehydrated. She's in and out. We need to get her out of here."

"I'm gonna carry her," I make the decision. "Let me radio it in and then I'm coming up."

Her head disappears, as I put a call in to base camp and report the situation to Jackson, who answers. He's going to call EMTs and the sheriff's office to meet us when I carry her down.

My winter boots aren't going to cut it but, since I don't carry climbing shoes in my pack, I'm going barefoot. I leave the boots and tuck my socks inside, so I have something dry to put on my feet. I hope we can do this quickly so I don't get frostbite.

Next, I shrug my pack off my shoulders, pull out the two coils of twenty-foot buckled tie-downs I carry with me, and shove them in my pockets, along with my water flask. Then I climb up on the boulder.

"Good girl, Hunter, you stay. We'll be right back."

I have no idea if the dog gets what I'm saying, but it makes me feel better for leaving her here.

Going up, I'm not quite as nimble or fast as Jillian was climbing to the ledge, but—despite the fact my toes are already frozen and tingling—I make it without losing my footing. I stay flat on my stomach and turn my head to peer into the crevice.

The space is barely large enough for Jillian and the girl, who, I see, has been wrapped up in a mylar blanket. No way I'm going to fit in there as well.

"Jillian, I'm going to give you my parka and I need you to put it on her," I tell her as I sit up to unzip. "It's going to be way too big, but it'll function as padding when we lower her down. Make sure the hood is up to protect her head. I have two straps; we'll fashion a harness with one, and the other I'll use to lower her to you."

I'm going to be fucking cold, but I should be okay once we get moving. Luckily, it's not as bitter cold or windy as it has been recently. I slide my coat toward Jillian and hand her the water flask as well.

"See if you can get her to drink some."

"Careful!" Jillian yells at me ten minutes later.

We were able to get Hayley down safely, but I'm not so sure I'll make it in one piece. My fucking feet are numb and I slipped twice already, trying to climb down.

"I can't believe you were barefoot," she scolds me when I try to put on my socks over my uncooperative feet.

"It seemed like a good idea at the time."

"Well, I hope, for your sake, you didn't do permanent damage," she grumbles.

When I have my feet back in my boots and make sure my snowshoes are attached tightly, I turn to lift Hayley from Jillian's arms. She's been holding her all this time, and shakes out her arms the moment I relieve her of her load.

I peek under the hood and notice the girl's eyes are open, but I don't think it's me she sees. She has dark blond or brown hair like her mother, and her eyes are the color of whiskey, but they're blank. The poor kid is tiny, she weighs next to nothing. It's a damn miracle she was able to last this long.

Carefully shifting her a little higher in my arms, I start moving, retracing our steps to the shelter.

"I can't believe she survived," I tell Jillian in a low voice when she falls in step beside me.

"She's resourceful. Among other things, I found a lighter in her pack, and apparently, she was able to build a small fire up there. The ashes were cool though, so I figure maybe she became too weak to climb down and gather more sticks and bark to burn. I also noticed an empty water bottle, and another one she used to relieve herself in. There was little urine and it was dark."

"That's how you figured she was dehydrated."

"That, and her disoriented and weakened state, although hypothermia would've played a part as well. She was like an icicle when I touched her, and so pale. If I hadn't heard her move moments before, I would've thought we were too late."

We're moving at a brisk pace, the snow easier going since our earlier footprints packed it down a bit. Also, I need to keep moving to generate some heat. You'd think with the girl held so tightly against me, it would be warm sharing body heat, but there isn't much warmth radiating from her.

We only take one short break, mainly to give Hunter a well-deserved drink, but we also try to get Hayley to take some more water. Unfortunately, that is less successful. I don't think she's conscious and most of it dribbles down her chin.

"She needs an IV," Jillian mumbles as I lift the girl up again.

I grunt my agreement as I start moving again, even faster. I'm less worried about Jillian keeping up than I am about the girl slipping away in my arms if we don't get her some help.

There is no more talking as we hurry back to base camp. Despite her small size, my arms are trembling and muscles burning with the effort of carrying her all this time. I feel a surge of relief when I can see the tent shelter through the trees.

The guys must've been keeping an eye out, because Jackson is already pushing the tent flap aside when we approach.

"EMTs?" I ask as I duck past him inside.

They cleared all the electronic equipment from the large folding table and covered it with a horse blanket. I lay her down and, disturbingly, her head lolls to one side.

"ETA five minutes," JD is the one to answer.

"Leave it on," Jillian says, putting a hand on my arm when I start unzipping my coat, which is way too big on the little girl. "Let the medics do it."

On the other side, Hunter hops on the edge of the table with her front paws and shoves her nose inside the hood of the parka, sniffing Hayley's face.

"You did good, girl," Jillian coos at her dog, grabbing her by the collar.

On the table, Hayley softly moans. At the same time, two EMTs walk into the tent.

I blow out a deep breath; she's alive.

Jillian

It was Wolff's suggestion I get in the ambulance with the girl.

My head resisted, despite every instinct pushing me to stay by the girl's side. I used the dogs as an excuse, but Wolff brushed my concern aside by assuring me he could drop them off at home if I'd give him my keys. He then hammered it home when he reminded me she has no one to stand by her, to comfort her when she wakes up, to advocate for her.

Even without knowing everything about me, he knew exactly which button to push.

So, I handed him my keys, asked him to let my dogs out for a pee and make sure they have fresh water, told him where to find their food, and then I hopped in the back of the ambulance.

For someone with a healthy dislike of hospitals, I seem to be spending a lot of time here this week. However, this time I'm determined not to end up in the waiting room.

I jog alongside the stretcher as the EMTs wheel her through the ER. They look at me strangely when I tell a nurse, who asks if I'm related, that I'm her aunt. To their credit, they say nothing, and I'm able to sneak in and stay off the radar while the medical team starts examining her.

I already told the EMTs what I know, and listen as they fill in the physician on her condition and the circumstances that caused it. When the doctor glances my way and asks the young EMT who was in the back of the ambulance who I am, I hold my breath.

"The girl's aunt. She rode in the back of the ambulance," he answers.

I shoot him a grateful smile and make a mental note to thank him properly when I have a chance.

"Ma'am? For now, I'm going to need to ask you to wait outside. There's a small waiting room for family right across the hall. Someone will be in to get some information from you, and I'll come see you when I know more."

Shit. I have a feeling this false claim being related isn't going to hold water for long once they discover I really have no information to give. I assume they'll want to know things like medical history, allergies, insurance, and stuff like that. I know nothing.

As luck would have it, I bump into Sheriff Ewing when I slip out of the room.

"Great job finding her."

I offer a smile at his compliment and put my hand on his arm, leading him across the hallway into the waiting room the doctor indicated. Thankfully, no one is in here.

"So you're not confused later," I tell him as I take a seat. "I lied and told staff I'm her aunt to be allowed to stay close."

He nods, a serious expression on his face. "I see. Well... since the poor kid seems to have lost almost her entire family in that crash, she can probably use an extra relative."

"I'm not sure how useful I'll be. I was told someone will be in to get information, but I have no idea what to tell them."

Ewing sits down beside me. "Don't worry. I stopped at the nurses' station coming in and explained the situation."

That's a relief, I'm not a fan of lying—I'm not particularly good at it—and would've hated to have had to come up with some plausible story.

"You're saying she has some remaining family?" I come back to something he said earlier.

While Wolff and I were on the search, he filled me in on what he knew about Hayley's background. Somehow, I thought her entire family was on that plane, but apparently not.

"Yeah, an uncle. Her father's younger brother. We were finally able to connect with him through the family company. He was in Guatemala on a business trip and is making his way home." He flips his hat back and runs a hand through his hair. "I'll see if I can get word to him; it'll be a relief for him to hear his niece was found alive. The man was devastated."

"I'm sure. Can you imagine what that girl went through these past days?"

"No." He shakes his head and puts his hat on the chair beside him. "I've seen a few things in my day, but that crash site was pretty horrific."

A silence falls over the room, and I rest my head back against the wall, briefly closing my eyes.

The sun was already down by the time we arrived at the hospital, and I hope Wolff got my dogs out for a pee. That's something I don't really have in place yet, a dog sitter. Someone like Kimmie, my next-door neighbor's teenage daughter, who would look after the remaining dogs when I was on a search. She'd stay at my house if I had to go out of town.

I'm going to have to start looking for someone like that around here, but I haven't even had a chance to knock on my neighbors' doors to introduce myself. During the summer their care is a little easier; the pack would be happy outside in the dog kennel where they'd have a small fenced-off run. Of course, someone would have to stop by to ensure they have fresh water and get fed regularly. In the winter, however, they're inside the house, and that would mean trusting someone with the key and alarm code so they can get in.

Normally trust takes time for me. Oddly enough, I didn't think twice about handing Wolff my keys. I'm not sure what to make of that.

Speak of the devil, fifteen minutes later he walks into the waiting room.

"Any news?" he asks, his attention moving from me to Junior and back.

"Still waiting to hear," the sheriff answers first, cocking his thumb at me. "I'm sure they'll come here first, since Jillian here is the nearest family around."

At Wolff's confused look, I confess my minor deception and earn a grin.

"Everything okay with the dogs? You got here fast," I observe.

"They're fine. JD went with me; he's taking them for a run out behind your house. I was going to hit up Best Buds and grab us a quick pizza, but decided to first come to see what was going on."

He's about to take a seat on my other side, when the doc who was looking after Hayley walks in.

"I see you've grown in numbers," she comments, "You're all here for the girl?"

"Hayley Vallard, yes," the sheriff confirms, getting to his feet.

I get up as well.

"I'm Dr. Chahal. The girl's looking better. Her stats have improved. We have an IV established. Fluids going in. Core temperature is coming up," she reports quite businesslike. "Still unresponsive, which may be a way for her to cope after the incredible trauma she survived, but it could also be she's sustained injuries we aren't able to see on the outside. So, we will keep her sedated and run several tests and scans to make sure there is nothing we missed. She'll be monitored closely at all times, but until we've had a chance to do what we need to do, I suggest you try to get some rest, Miss…"

She shoots me a pointed look.

"Call me Jillian," I quickly fill in. "But she's going to be all right?"

The woman smiles what I'm sure is meant as a reassuring smile, but comes across as a tired, perhaps mildly patronizing one.

"For now, I'm going to be reserved and say she's not out of the woods yet, but what I'm seeing is encouraging. Get some rest, Jillian, and make sure to leave a number where you can be reached with the nurse."

Then she turns her attention on Junior Ewing.

"And I'm sorry, Sheriff, but obviously anything you need to know from her is going to have to wait. This probably was a wasted trip for you."

With that she makes her exit, but I have one more question for her.

"Dr. Chahal?" I call out as I dart into the hallway to catch her.

"Yes."

She stops and turns around.

"I have a trained therapy dog I think might have a calming effect on Hayley when she wakes up. I'm more than happy to bring him in if that is something you are open to?"

She looks skeptical, and I prepare to get turned down, but her next question gives me hope.

"The dog is certified?"

"Yes. I can bring his papers," I assure her, trying not to come across as too eager.

She studies me for a moment before giving me a curt nod.

"Sure. Call first, though."

A few minutes later I'm walking out to the parking lot, flanked by Sheriff Ewing and Wolff.

"I take it you don't have a vehicle here?" Junior observes. "I'll be happy to give you a ride home. That is..." he adds, with a quick glance over my shoulder at Wolff.

His voice rumbles behind me.

"I've got her."

Eleven

JILLIAN

"Just lay down, Nugget."

I run my hand down his spine as he stretches out on the white sheets.

My girls are a little upset with me. Poor Peanut looked a little crestfallen when I left her behind, but children tend to respond better to Nugget, whose size is a little less intimidating. I got the stink eye from Emo, who probably feels left out as well, since the other two saw action yesterday, and wanted to make sure I knew it.

Last night when Wolff and I got home with a couple of pizzas, JD had just returned with the dogs. He'd taken them for a long walk, so it's not like they didn't get their exercise. Then today before I left the house, I took them for another good hike.

I called the hospital first thing this morning to see how Hayley did through the night. The nurse I spoke to said she was still sedated but was stable. She didn't want to tell me more on the phone, but said she'd have Dr. Chahal get back to me.

The doctor called fifteen minutes later to let me know Hayley had three broken ribs, a concussion, and deep bruising covering a lot of her body, all of which she felt had been the result of the crash. She also had a few frostbitten fingertips, but other than that—and of course the emotional trauma—no other major injuries.

She also mentioned she was going to start waking Hayley up soon, so if I wanted to be there with the dog, I'd have to make tracks. Which I did.

I haven't seen Dr. Chahal since I got here but the nurse knew to expect me. They'd already stopped the medication that kept her sedated, and only a bag of saline solution is left on her IV pole when I am shown in her room.

I notice right away Hayley's color is so much better than it was yesterday; no more white skin and grayish-blue lips. Someone cared enough to wash the grime off her face and brush out her hair. I never really noticed how long it was yesterday, because the hoodie she'd been wearing under her coat had been covering her head.

She's a pretty girl.

Last night, after Wolff and JD left, I did a little research on my laptop. We'd talked about the crash over pizza, and it got me curious about this family. I figured it couldn't hurt to dig up whatever background I could find. In fact, it might be useful in helping me connect with the girl.

The Vallard family is a pretty big deal, as I've discovered. Their company, Vallard Logistics, is worth a cool seven-point-five-billion dollars. That's not chump change. When I spotted the company logo, the stylistic VL, I realized I'd seen those initials plenty of times on the side of transport trucks.

Vallard Logistics was founded in 1940 by Hiram Vallard,

who would've been Hayley's great-grandfather. He had the good fortune during the WWII years to pick up a number of military contracts. When other men of eligible age were drafted and sent off to war, Hiram —who had lost his left forearm in a farming accident at his uncle's farm—was able to capitalize on an otherwise dark time in history.

He only had one child, Sarah-May Vallard, who was born a year after Vallard Logistics was founded and worked for her father's company since she was just seventeen years old. So, when her father passed away in 1968 from a massive heart attack, Sarah-May—only twenty-seven at the time—took over her father's company.

Hayley's father, James, was born two years after his grandfather died and, like his mother before him, he was groomed from an early age to take over the business. Brother Grant seemed like an afterthought, and arrived nine years later. In 2000, Sarah-May handed over the reins of Vallard Logistics to James but stayed involved in the background.

I also discovered the Vallards were regular benefactors to a variety of charities, which is how I found some pictures online, leading me to the mother's Facebook account. Most of the images Theresa posted were of fundraisers they seemed to attend regularly as a family. There were some of camping trips as well, which it looks like they did fairly frequently. That might explain Hayley's survival skills.

The one thing I took away from the pictures was how much Hayley takes after her mother, who was a beautiful woman. In Theresa's most recent post, she shared several snapshots of their trip to Whistler. There was one image of Hayley with her parents that brought tears to my eyes. They all looked so happy.

"Gram..."

The whisper has me turn my attention to the girl. Her

eyes are still closed but she's becoming restless, moving her legs and rolling her head from side to side. Nugget instantly snuggles his little body against her side. I don't know why he does that, but it seems to calm the girl down.

I reach for the button to alert the nurse, but she already walks in.

"Is someone waking up?"

She turns down the volume coming from the monitor I only now realize was beeping. Then she leans over the bed, a hand on Hayley's shoulder.

"Can you open your eyes, love?"

One eye opens a crack before shutting again.

The nurse takes the girl's hand. "Can you squeeze my fingers?"

When nothing happens, she releases her hand. "That's okay, honey. You take your time."

Then she turns to me. "It's going to be a while for the medication to flush from her system. Let me know if something changes."

As soon as she leaves the room, Nugget scoots up in the bed, nudging the girl's hand with his snout until he's wormed his head underneath her fingers. I sit back and wait.

At some point, my gaze slipped out the window, and I'm staring at the mountains in the distance when I hear the soft thud, thud, of Nugget's tail hitting the bed. When I turn to look, Hayley's eyes are still closed, but her fingers are stroking the dog's head.

"Hey, sweetheart..." I say in a soft voice, when I notice her run her tongue over her chapped lips. "Are you thirsty?"

I grab a cup of water from the bedside table, and bend the straw so I can slip it between her lips.

"Have a sip. It's water."

Her eyes stay firmly shut, but her lips close around the straw as she takes a drink.

"He loves getting his ears scratched," I tell her, looking for something neutral to talk about. "He's the smallest of my dogs and often gets lost in the shuffle, so he loves it when he can get all the attention."

No reaction, but her fingers keep stroking on the dog's soft fur, so I keep babbling.

"My name is Jillian, and his name is Nugget, and as you can see, he loves people. I don't know if you remember but two of my other dogs, Hunter and Murphy, helped me find you yesterday."

At that her fingers still.

"You were really smart, finding that little cave, and you did a good job climbing up those rocks. You were really brave, keeping yourself safe and warm with a fire. It gave us a chance to find you."

I glance over at the door where I see Junior Ewing poking his head in.

"Keep going," he mouths, gesturing for me to continue before his head disappears.

When I turn back to the bed, it looks like Hayley's eyes aren't quite closed all the way.

"Want more water?" I ask her, and at first she seems to ignore me, but I guess thirst wins out when she nods.

I slip the straw between her lips and let her drink a little more before setting the cup back on the nightstand.

When I turn my attention back to the girl, I'm met with two gorgeous, almost copper-colored eyes.

"Hello, there."

It's tough trying to get back into a normal routine after spending most of the week on an intensive search.

I've been restless all day, trying to find my groove doing my regular work.

Today was hauling more hay to the outside herd, making sure their water access isn't frozen over, and no one's gotten hurt.

When I passed by the main house on my way to my cabin earlier, Jonas stopped me, asking if I could take the trailer tomorrow and drive two horses to their new home at a ranch outside Dumas, Washington. It's about a ten-hour roundtrip under good conditions, but Jackson was already roped in and, taking turns driving, we should be able to do it in a day. Although it'll be a long one, I don't mind the drive.

I have no clue why, but as I grab a quick shower at home, I suddenly feel the need to let Jillian know I won't be around tomorrow. The last time I felt compelled to let someone know my whereabouts was before I left for college, when I was still living at home.

Hell, part of the reason I've not been tempted into any kind of serious relationship over the years is that I like not having to justify my every move. Yet, here I am, wanting to tell Jillian.

I grab my phone off the bed where I dropped it.

Hey, are you home?

The answer comes fifteen minutes later when I'm just contemplating whether I want to have breakfast for dinner with the two eggs and half pack of bacon left in my fridge, or head over to the main house to see what I can scrounge up to eat there.

Just walked in the door. What's up?

I take a minute to think about my response. I guess I'd hoped to take her out for dinner, but if she just walked in the door, she may not want to go out again. But maybe I can bring dinner to her.

How do you feel about sushi? Tempura?

A Japanese bar and grill opened a couple of years ago with a pretty wide variety in food choices. I've been there a few times with some of the guys. It even has a twenty-four seven casino. Just a small one, but it's a fun place to kill a few hours.

Pretty good about both, why?

Can't blame her for thinking that, coming from the big city, but in recent years a surprising number of good restaurants have opened in Libby. We have quite the selection now. I can think of a few more I'd like to introduce her to.

I'm calling in my order before I leave, so I won't have to wait for it.

~

"Oh wow. This is really good."

To emphasize, she moans as she licks the tempura crumbs off her fingers and lips.

122

I'm starting to realize the sounds people make in appreciation of good food, and those made in the throes of passion, are not that different. Or maybe that's just Jillian making those noises. As satisfying as sharing good food with her is, it leaves me hungry for other things.

I'm thinking at this point it's almost inevitable, my body is definitely committed, but my mind still throws out faint objections, even as I lean over the table and kiss her shiny lips.

For all intents and purposes, it's an innocent kiss, but that doesn't stop the groan rumbling in my chest at the feel of those lips molding to mine. The temptation is strong to haul her across the table, but I resist.

There's no need to rush. If we are to pursue anything, I want to make sure we're on the same page every step of the way. A quick fling is not a good idea when we live and work and move in the same circles. Not that I believe for one minute a quick fling would be enough for me.

"Wow, again," she mumbles, when I release her mouth and sit back down again. "That was really good too."

She blushes a little when she says that, or maybe the blush is from the kiss, but either way, I like her straightforwardness.

"Agreed."

Then I shove another piece of tuna nigiri in my mouth.

"I was married," she suddenly volunteers out of the blue, lifting her eyes to mine. "I believe in full disclosure. Especially if that kiss is going where I think...hope...it might. We live in a small community, hang out in the same circles. I think transparency is important."

I like her direct approach. No games, no playing coy, just laying the cards on the table.

This conversation is a bit of a departure from the casual

sharing of our days. Jillian just finished telling me how Hayley woke up today but still seems out of it, not really talking. However, having Nugget there for a few hours seemed to calm her down, so Jillian is taking him back to the hospital tomorrow.

Now I have the shape of her mouth branded on my lips, and we're talking relationships.

Surprisingly, I don't feel the urge to bolt out the door.

"I'm good with transparency," I find myself responding.

She nods before continuing, "Chris and I ended things five years ago and our divorce was final the year after. It was a fairly amicable split and I've mostly stayed to myself since."

"I've never been married," I reciprocate. "Never really had a long-term relationship. Mostly due to the unpredictability of my work, which also required me to move around quite a bit. I think you already know I was a federal agent before joining the HMT team. But, if I'm honest, I've kinda liked my autonomy as a bachelor."

"Past tense?" she asks.

The blush on her cheeks is back, but her eyes on mine are unwavering. My mouth quirks with a smile. Jillian is not only being direct; she's making it clear she expects the same from me and won't put up with ambiguous statements.

"I'm not sure it has much to do with the wish to remain a bachelor, but rather with meeting someone who makes you want more than the singular existence you've clung onto for forty-three years."

I reach across the table and take her hand in mine.

"There's a reason I wanted to see you tonight. I mean, not that there has to be a reason, but Jonas is sending Jackson and me out of town to deliver some horses tomorrow, which means we'll be leaving early and coming home late."

"Okay?" She makes it sound more as a question than a statement, and I realize I may need to clarify.

"For someone who's always valued his independence, it seemed interesting I suddenly felt the need to let *you* know where I would be."

Her pretty mouth spreads into a smile.

"You're right, that is pretty interesting."

"That said…" I push myself up from the table. "We need to hit the road at five, and have a long day ahead of us, so I probably should get home and grab some sleep."

"Of course."

She gets up and follows me to the door, where I stop and turn.

When she opened the door for me earlier, I liked she hadn't felt the need to doll up for me. What you see is what you get with this woman, which holds a great deal of appeal to me. The pink slouchy sweater, lounge pants, and fuzzy socks, and even the hair up in a haphazard bun on top of her head look soft and approachable.

I reach out and tuck a hank of hair behind her ear that escaped the bun, before sliding my arms around her waist, tugging her close. I tower over her by, I'm guessing, close to a foot, but she feels perfect in my arms, especially when she places her hands on my chest and tilts her face up.

The invitation is clear, and when I bend my head, her arms come up and hook around my neck, her fingers curling in my hair.

This time when my mouth covers hers, it's not that innocent. I trace the seam of her lips with my tongue, and she doesn't hesitate to grant me access. Her mouth is eager, and I fucking love it.

Oh, hell yeah. That first hit of her taste makes me want to pick her up and carry her to the nearest flat surface. My hands have already found a strip of bare flesh at the small of her back, and I slide my palm under her sweater and up the silky skin of her torso, discovering the absence of a bra.

Sweet Jesus...

I call up every ounce of control to tear my mouth from hers.

"Hold that thought," I whisper, pressing my lips against her forehead, before I regretfully let her go. "We'll pick this up later."

She responds instantly.

"You bet we will."

Twelve

Jillian

I'd been prepared to tell Wolff about Macy last night.

I never got the chance.

I'm the one who brought up full disclosure, but when Wolff responded in kind and said some really meaningful things, I didn't have the heart to bring down the mood.

Then there was the kiss...

The brush of lips over the table was sweet but controlled. But the kiss in the hallway? My lips felt bruised, my skin on fire, and my knees went weak. Wolff always comes across as reserved—someone who has himself firmly in hand—but the man kissing me last night was on the verge of losing control.

It felt fantastic, and I would've loved a chance to push him over that edge, but he ended it before I could try. His promise there would be a follow-up kept me up half the night, fantasizing about what that might be like. Something tells me it'll be phenomenal.

After a restless night's sleep, in the harsh light of morning, I'm thankful things didn't progress any further than they did. I would feel a whole lot better if he knows he's starting something with someone who will always have a hole in her heart. The kind of hole no one can fill.

Not everyone can handle that. Chris couldn't.

It's still pretty early when Nugget and I get to the hospital. I was eager to get going this morning, curious to know how Hayley got through the night. I don't know why, but I feel a sense of responsibility for her. Maybe because she clung onto my hand with both of her icy ones after I found her huddled in that crevice, looking at me like I was her savior.

The girl has no one else in her corner right now, at least not until her uncle gets here.

"Her night was a little restless," the nurse on duty informs me when I inquire about Hayley. "She still hasn't spoken. Nods yes and shakes no, enough to communicate, but that's about it. It doesn't look like she slept too well."

"Poor kid," I commiserate.

But when I start moving down the hall toward her room, the nurse stops me in my tracks.

"I forgot to mention, she's no longer there," she calls after me. "She was moved to a different room at the request of the sheriff's office."

Surprised, I swing around.

"Sheriff's office?"

She nods. "Something about security."

Security? For the girl? That has my mind spinning. Is she in danger? Is that why she was hiding out in that cave? My head is swirling with flotsam of information that is trying to slot itself into a scenario that would require security for an eleven-year-old.

Also, does that mean I won't be allowed to see her?

The disappointment that thought brings with it comes with a few faint alarm bells. I barely know the child and am already feeling way too attached.

Still, I retrace my steps into the lobby and pull out my phone, looking up Junior Ewing's number.

"Shit, I meant to call you," is how he answers his phone. "You're at the hospital, right?" he guesses.

"You would be correct. What happened?"

"Can you hang tight? I'm on my way."

"Sure," I tell him, even more confused now.

Whatever it is, he clearly wants to explain face-to-face. Which doesn't feel very reassuring to me. I take a seat in the lobby so I can keep an eye out for him. Nugget is adaptable and curls up on my lap. He doesn't care much where we are as long as he gets his snuggles in.

Ten minutes later Ewing stalks through the automatic doors, his hat in his hand and his face flushed.

"Sorry, it's already been a crazy morning," he huffs, dropping down in the seat next to me.

"So what's going on with the security?" I prompt him.

Ewing glances around the lobby before responding.

"Precautionary. I got a call from Polman this morning, he's the NTSB lead investigator."

"Yeah, I met him."

Something in my tone makes him smile. "Made an impression on you as well, did he? He must've skipped charm school, but at least the man is thorough. They found some evidence that could indicate the plane crash was not an accident."

"Who would do that?"

The sheriff shrugs. "Your guess is as good as mine. You'd be surprised at the messed-up stuff people do for the stupidest reasons. Anyway, until they can confirm either way, he suggested we put security on the girl. Especially since it looks like her uncle will be stranded in Guatemala for the time being."

"Stranded?"

I sit up straighter. That poor girl, she must feel so alone in the world.

"The Guatemalan government foiled an attempted coup yesterday morning, but there is ongoing unrest and fighting. They shut down all air travel indefinitely. Grant Vallard called me from the U.S. Embassy in Guatemala City where he's been hiding. Apparently, it's a mess down there."

"So now what? What happens to Hayley in the meantime?"

"For now she stays in the hospital, we'll have to take it a day at a time. If Vallard still isn't here by the time she is released, we may have to place her in protective custody. Unless, of course, sabotage is ruled out, in which case it'll likely be foster care."

I don't want either of those things for her. It would mean more strange people.

"Am I still allowed to see her?"

"Normally I'd probably say no, but she's just a kid, and her doc says this guy seems to have a positive effect on her," he says, scratching Nugget's head. "Besides, she already knows you and could probably use a friendly face."

I set Nugget down on the floor and get to my feet.

"In that case, where can I find her?"

He grunts as he gets up too. "I'll take you."

Hayley is staring out the window but her head swings around when we walk in the door. Her eyes immediately search for Nugget at my feet when she recognizes me.

"Hey, sweetheart. I see you've got new digs. Nice view."

I pick Nugget up and deposit him on the bed. Then I walk over to the window, pretending to look outside, but from the corner of my eye I catch Hayley reaching for Nugget. By the time I turn my full attention back to the bed, she has him snuggled against her, his head propped on her belly, and her hand stroking his soft fur.

"I'll let my guys know you're an approved visitor, and I'm trusting you keep her location to yourself."

"Obviously," I return, a bit testy he feels the need to tell me that.

After all, I'm a professional, and it's not like he hasn't worked with me before.

He runs a hand through his hair before fitting his hat back on his head.

"Sorry. Of course that goes without saying. I'm feeling the pressure; Polman was ready to call in the FBI this morning and I pushed to hold off because I didn't want—"

I stop him with a sharp shake of my head when I notice Hayley is observing us intently. I'd almost forgotten she was there.

"Right," Ewing catches on. "I'm going to leave you guys be. I've got things to do. We'll catch up later."

When the door closes behind him, I return my gaze to the window.

"He feels responsible for keeping you safe until your uncle gets here," I tell her with my back turned.

I have a sneaking suspicion this girl may be more aware of what is going on around her than she lets on. In the reflection I catch her looking at me.

She's definitely listening.

～

"Wouldn't take much to take out the tub and put in a shower like I did in mine."

I got an early start this morning and had the horses loaded up by quarter to five before I realized I hadn't seen Jackson yet. When I went to see what was keeping him, he just came walking out the door, pressing a towel against the side of his face.

He'd slipped in the tub and lost his footing, which isn't that hard to do when you only have one foot to begin with. Whacked his elbow good on the way down and hit the side of the tub with his face, splitting the skin over his eyebrow. Hence the towel, which was to staunch the blood.

He's a bit of a broody bastard, even on a good day, but today managed to stay quiet almost the entire drive to Dumas, Washington. I was pretty content to drive in silence, with good tunes on the radio and my mind on Jillian.

It wasn't until we dropped off the horses and stopped for a quick bite just south of Spokane, Jackson brought up the old tub in his cabin. He reluctantly admitted he hadn't been too steady standing in the sloped bottom of the tub and would hold on to the built-in soap dish to keep himself steady. Except, as it turns out, the soap dish was no match when his foot went out from under him.

"You put in a shower?"

I nod. "One of the first things I did is tear out that old tub. Not like I was gonna use it. Jonas was fine with it, he paid for the materials, and the guys helped me with the work. It took a three-day weekend to complete. I can show you what it looks like when we get back."

"Yeah."

He sounds a bit dismissive.

I glance at him from the corner of my eye. His jaw is tight and his knuckles white on the steering wheel, as he stares straight out at the road ahead. I don't pretend to understand what he's been through, either while serving his country or the resulting loss of his leg. I can't imagine it's been easy. But one thing I do know is, when you no longer fit the life you envisioned, you move on to build one that does.

Sometimes it starts with something as simple as a bathroom that suits your needs.

"Dan's gotten pretty good at all the plumbing stuff," I push a little. "I'm sure he'd be happy to lend a hand. Especially since you, along with everyone else, worked on his place."

I add the latter because I suspect asking or accepting help is part of his problem. Doesn't hurt to remind him everyone needs a hand from time to time, and it has nothing to do with the loss of a limb.

"I'll talk to Jonas," he finally concedes after a long silence.

I scoot down in my seat, pull my hat down over my eyes, and sneak a grin. Mission accomplished.

"What are you doing here?"

Despite the dubious greeting, she steps aside to let me in.

As soon as I step over the threshold, I'm instantly swarmed by the dogs. A good distraction while I try to come up with an appropriate answer. When I can't find one, I opt for honesty.

"I've been thinking about you a large part of my day and I wanted to see you."

That smug little half-smile I've seen her flash a time or two makes another appearance.

"I see." She turns and leads the way into the living room, while I scramble to ditch my coat and kick off my boots. "You mentioned you'd be back late, so I kinda figured I wouldn't see you." She abruptly turns around. "Not that I'm complaining, but I might've put something else on."

She's wearing a pair of cutoff flannel men's pajamas and an old slouchy T-shirt. I'm not complaining either; she looks relaxed, cutely rumpled, and extremely approachable. Which is why, instead of telling her so, I show her.

There is no resistance when I walk up and pull her into my arms, and I give myself an inner fist pump when she hooks me behind the neck and lifts up on her toes. That pretty mouth of hers smiles up at me, and I can't resist.

God, I don't think I'll ever get enough of her taste. All five-foot whatever of her is pressed up against me. Soft skin and lithe muscle warm under my hands, as the modest swell of her breasts seems to beg for attention. After spending the better part of my day thinking about the feel and the sight of her, I'm already beyond resisting temptation.

I slide my left hand from the small of her back to her soft belly and up, cupping her perfect handful. Her deep moan vibrates against my tongue, and all I can think about is getting us naked.

So much for my slow seduction plans, with barely a hello, and no conversation of any value before ending up with a hand up her shirt, the other down the back of her shorts, and my tongue down her throat. From zero to high intensity, and my heart is about to beat out of my chest.

Classy, Lucas. Classy.

What snaps me out of my lust-filled haze is the feel of her small hand palming the rock-hard ridge behind my fly. I quickly trap her wrist in my hand before she finds her way into my jeans.

"If I feel your skin on my cock, I'm gonna make a goddamn mess," I pant into her mass of hair, trying to will my body into submission.

I'm not looking for a quick physical release. Not this time, and not with Jillian. If we're taking this step, I want to minimize the risk I fuck it up, and make sure she's taken care of properly.

"Maybe I like things messy," she teases, eliciting a pained moan from me.

Bending through my knees, I gently bite the tender skin where her neck meets her shoulder, while sliding my hand farther down her shorts to slip my fingers between her legs.

"Damn, and I sure like messy on you."

I hear her breath catch as I dip a finger between her folds. It feels like warm, liquid silk.

"Hop up," I instruct her, moving both my hands to her butt.

The moment she jumps, I start moving toward her bedroom, but instead of tossing her on the bed, I slowly lower her to her feet in front of the dresser. Then I turn her around so she faces the large mirror sitting on top.

"Look at you," I mumble against the skin of her neck, my hands already busy sliding her shirt up.

Jillian's face is flushed, her lips slick and swollen, and her eyes smoldering as they follow the path of my touch. My rough hands stand out in contrast against her delicate, pale skin. She voluntarily lifts her arms so I can slide the shirt off her, leaving her with only the flannel cutoffs hanging low off her hips.

Cupping both her breasts, I brush the pads of my thumbs over her pink, distended nipples. In the mirror I watch as she catches her bottom lip between her teeth and tilts her head to offer me her neck. I find her pulse with my lips, opening my mouth to suck on her skin while using one hand to slide down her shorts and cup the neatly trimmed patch of russet hair at the apex of her thighs.

She leans her head back against my shoulder; a strong, independent woman giving herself over to my touch, handing me her trust, and I've never seen anything more beautiful.

Suddenly I'm in a hurry to feel her skin to skin, and with an arm around her waist I gently bend her forward, urging her to brace herself on the dresser. Then I whip off my shirt and unbutton my fly. Her eyes follow my every move.

I retrieve a foil packet from my jeans before shoving them down my hips.

"Commando," she whispers, a soft smile on her lips as she watches me roll on the condom. Then her eyes find mine. "A rebel after all."

She's already lifting her ass when I put a hand on her hip, and with my other hand, I guide myself into her body.

"Oh fuck," she mumbles when I sink inside her, and I immediately freeze.

She's small, I should've been more careful. But when I start to pull out, she reaches back and digs her fingers in the globe of my ass.

"Don't you dare move," she growls, as she does this roll with her hips that sends a charge of pleasure-pain up my spine.

Then she reaches her other arm up and around my neck, chest out and her spine almost unnaturally arched, as she tangles her fingers in my hair. With my mouth latched on to her shoulder, and my eyes fixed on her stunning reflection, I start powering inside her.

Her moans drive me deeper and faster, and as I expected, it doesn't take long for my balls to draw tight against my body.

"Gotta come for me, Jilly," I urge her on as I reach a hand between her legs.

Rolling her clit with my fingertips, I can feel the walls of her pussy flutter before they grab my dick in the most pleasurable vise. I buck a few times, and then my body goes rigid as every synapse fires in concert.

My knees buckle and I curve myself around Jillian's trembling body, her dresser holding us both up.

"Holy smokes," she sighs in a shaky voice.

"Pretty much," I agree hoarsely.

So much for keeping my distance.

Thirteen

JILLIAN

"Her name was Macy."

I'm not sure what drives me to bring up my daughter now.

The sweat is still drying on our bodies, lying in my bed, tangled together in the afterglow of seriously hot and absolutely mind-blowing sex, but I put it out there. Maybe it's the strength of his body cocooning me, shielding me, making me feel nothing could possibly touch me.

Perhaps I needed that feeling of postcoital security to rip open the deepest wound my soul will ever know, to bleed the grief that lives there.

I note he doesn't ask or push me for more information than that. He simply holds me, his grip on me perhaps a little tighter, as if he realizes I may well come apart otherwise. His kind silence gives me a chance to do this at my own pace, and because of that, I give him more than I would anyone who would ask.

"She made the sun rise every day from the moment she was born."

I turn my face into his chest and smile my memory against his skin, even as I feel the first tear slip from my eye.

"She had this halo of red curls, and bright blue eyes that smiled all the time. The happiest child I've ever known. She was small for her age but her personality was big enough to make up for her lack in height. You would've expected her voice to be sweet and high-pitched, but instead she sounded like a jazz crooner, her sound was mellow, almost smoky, but when she turned up the dial, she could produce volume like a foghorn. But then as a reminder she was just a little girl, she had this cute little lisp, and a stubborn inability to say *animal*."

I sniffle as I picture my daughter, clear as day, the shoulder strap of her favorite OshKosh B'gosh bib overalls hanging off her narrow shoulders, a streak of dirt on her cheek, and an infectious grin on her face as she helped me weed our vegetable patch.

My last living memory of her.

"She was five," I continue. "She was helping me in the garden. I'd just gone to turn off the water hose on the side of the garage and was so sure I'd latched the gate."

Wolff makes a guttural sound coming deep from his throat, but to his credit, he doesn't comment.

"I don't think the delivery truck driver ever saw her. A neighbor across the street said he saw Macy dart into the road from between two parked cars, but it was too late to do anything about it."

I may not have seen it back then, but I realize now my daughter's death must've had a major impact on more lives than just mine. Macy's father, of course, but also Jeff across the street, the UPS driver, and my next-door neighbors, who came running outside when they heard me scream. I'm sure that horrific scene left an indelible impression on everyone who was there that day.

"She died six hours later in the hospital. I lost time... after that. I can't even remember her funeral, but I remember exactly how she looked, and what she was wearing that day when she ran into the street."

He hugs me a little tighter and I feel him press a kiss to the top of my head.

"Wait here," he mumbles.

I instantly miss the warmth of his body and the security of his arms when he slips from the bed. I reach down and tug up the covers to make up for the loss, but Wolff is back just moments later with a glass of water and a box of tissues.

I sit up and take some tissues to mop my face. Then I grab the glass he offers and take a sip before setting it on my nightstand. When I lie back down, his arms come around me, tucking my back to his front.

"You'd think after almost eight years it would get easier to talk about it," I muse out loud. "That I'd get over my aversion to hospitals."

"Don't see how it could," he mumbles behind me. "I imagine that kind of loss stays the same, no matter how much time passes."

For a moment I well up again; his words of understanding mean more than empty condolences could.

"True."

"Your daughter would've been thirteen now?" he asks.

I appreciate that after telling him about my daughter, he doesn't shy away from asking about her. People generally avoid the topic, either thinking it would be difficult for me, or simply uncomfortable dealing with grief in general. Ironically, trying to pretend she didn't exist is more painful than remembering she did.

"Almost. Her birthday is in June."

"So twelve. Close to Hayley's age," he observes quite perceptively. "Is that why you're drawn to her?"

I turn around in his arms so I can look him in the eyes.

"I'm sure that's a big part of it. I'd like to think Macy might have developed the same kind of courage and survival instincts. She definitely had the same adventurous spirit," I share, looking into his warm eyes shimmering in the dark. "But also, because I know what it's like to have your entire world ripped away from you, leaving you feeling utterly alone."

"And despite your dislike for hospitals, you show up trying to make sure she doesn't." His smile is soft.

I shrug. "It's a small price to pay."

He hums an acknowledgement before asking, "How was she doing today?"

I haven't had a chance to tell him about today's developments so I fill him in on what Sheriff Ewing told me. Wolff doesn't look surprised when I mention the suspected sabotage of the plane.

"I'd been wondering if maybe the girl was hiding because she saw or heard something," he shares. "Something that scared an eleven-year-old enough to brave the wilderness in a snowstorm."

"She seems to be responding to Nugget, but still not communicating, so I guess that could be trauma *or* fear."

"Or both," he suggests. "Either way, I have a feeling she'll keep mum unless she feels she can completely trust someone. At this time, you're the most consistent person for her, so keep doing what you're doing."

"I told her I'd be back in the morning."

"Good." Wolff presses a kiss against my forehead and rolls on his back, tucking me to his side. "Let's get some sleep."

I put my hand on his chest and hook my leg over one of his. Then I close my eyes and try to remember the last time I went to sleep cuddled up with a naked man in my bed. I know for a fact it's been longer than eight years, since Chris was never a cuddler, and neither am I.

Or so I thought.

~

Wolff

"You're whistling."

I turn my head to find Fletch glaring at me.

"I'm aware," I finally give up on the mini stare-down he challenged me to.

"It's fucking annoying," he grumbles.

"He probably got laid last night," Jackson pipes up as he hands me a two-by-four he just cut to size for the new door opening I'm framing. "His truck didn't show up until this morning. And for the record, I'd be fucking whistling too if I got some action."

"You got laid?" JD walks in, carrying a sheet of green board.

It took us all of three hours to completely gut Jackson's bathroom this morning. Apparently, he didn't waste any time once he'd made up his mind. He was waiting for me when I got back and roped me in as he'd apparently done with Fletch and JD, because they showed up ten minutes later.

I don't have any special skills, but as Jackson pointed out, it was my idea and I live conveniently close. Aside from the fact Fletch has a thing for demolition, he and Jackson have gotten pretty close these last months. Both those guys went through hell and back serving their country, and bear the scars on their bodies and their souls.

JD is the handy one, he also owns a shitload of tools needed, and he did a lot of work on Dan's house. Dan has his own project at home he's working on today, but apparently, he'll be here to tackle the plumbing when we get to it.

I'm ignoring the guys and concentrate on putting in the new door lintel. The basic layout of Jackson's bathroom will stay the same with the sink and toilet in the identical location, but we are building the shower a little deeper than the bathtub was, which meant we had to move the door slightly. The roomier shower will allow for the addition of a corner bench we plan to build in.

The other addition will be a safety bar we're anchoring to double studs. Jackson protested that none of those added features were necessary, but all it took was Fletch telling him not to be an idiot, and that was the end of the discussion.

While I work, my thoughts inevitably slide back to the woman I left warm and cozy in her bed this morning. I'm not usually one to spend the night, but there was no way I could've left her after she bared her soul to me last night. Not that I would've wanted to anyway.

It's so rare reality beats the imagination, but I'll be damned if Jillian didn't blow every one of my fantasies clear out of the water.

"You're fucking whistling again," Fletch complains behind me.

～

It's getting dark out already, and only Jackson and I are left when Dan pokes his head in the door.

"Looks good. When do you figure you'll be ready for me?"

All the new green board is up, and taped, and we've just finished throwing on a sealing primer to dry overnight.

"Tomorrow," Jackson answers him.

My phone vibrates in my pocket. When I see the call is coming from Wellspring Senior Living, I duck past Dan and step outside to answer.

"Wolff."

"Hi, it's Marcela at Wellspring...David Gentry asked me to give you a call. I'm afraid your mother had a bit of a tumble in the dining room at dinner tonight."

My heart seizes in my chest.

"Is she okay?"

"Well, she was talking when EMTs got here. David went with her in the ambulance and I'm sure he will be in touch as soon as he knows something."

"Where did they take her?" I ask, walking back inside.

"Logan Medical Center."

"Thanks."

With that I hang up and poke my head into the bathroom.

"I've gotta go. Family emergency. I'll call."

"Wait!" I hear Dan yell behind me as I stalk from Jackson's cabin to mine.

He follows me into my place where I snatch up my truck keys, grab my wallet and my phone charger off the counter, and snag my coat off the hook.

"What's going on?" he asks.

"Mom fell. She's on her way to Logan by ambulance. Don't know anything more."

"Shit. Anything I can do?"

I shrug into my coat and stuff my wallet and phone charger into the pocket.

"Nah. I'll be in touch when I know more."

"Hope she's okay," he calls after me when I step out and jog to my truck.

Me too, brother. Me too.

The clock on my dashboard says it's a quarter to seven, with a bit of luck I can be in Kalispell by eight. I crank the classic rock station and try to drown out my worries with loud music.

A call comes in forty minutes later when I'm halfway there, and I answer with a press of the button on my steering wheel.

"Yes," I answer curtly, not recognizing the number but hoping it's David with news about Mom.

"Is this Lucas Wolff?"

"It is."

"Mr. Wolff, my name is Dr. Hannon, I'm the on-call orthopedic surgeon at Logan Health Medical Center. Your mother was brought in a while ago as the result of a fall. We were able to determine she suffered a displaced fracture of both bones in her forearm and she needs surgery to set the bones. Unfortunately, your mother is a bit confused at the moment, and I understand you have power of attorney for her?"

Confused? Mom?

"I do," I answer him.

"Good. I'm going to need your verbal consent to operate on her."

"You said she was confused? As far as I know my mother doesn't have dementia," I point out.

"Confusion can be a result of shock, or an undiagnosed

UTI, sometimes dehydration will cause confusion in the elderly. Chances are she'll be fine tomorrow, but at this point I'd prefer to err on the side of caution and get your okay."

"Yes, yes, of course. I'm a little over half an hour away and I'll sign whatever you need."

"Check in at the nurses' desk in the emergency department. They'll have forms for you to fill out."

When he ends the call, I take a moment to process the information, which comes with a bit of relief. I would think a broken arm—even one that requires surgery to fix—is preferable to a fractured hip or skull, but I'll still spend the night in the hospital.

I quickly call Dan to give him an update and ask him to pass on to Jonas I likely won't be there in the morning.

Next, I dial Jillian. Not that we made any firm plans, but I had hoped to drop by her place tonight, and I don't want her to think I'd leave her hanging after spending the night with her.

She answers on the second ring and surprises me.

"How is she?"

"She needs surgery to set the bones in her forearm. How did you know?"

"Dan told Sloane, who called me. I wasn't sure whether maybe you didn't want to be disturbed, so I was waiting, hoping for a call."

"You could never disturb me."

Now I'm surprising myself. For someone whose always valued his privacy, I'm sure quick to give her free access.

"You're on your way to the hospital?"

"Yeah, that's why I called, I'm gonna stick around at the hospital, and am not sure how long that'll be."

"Of course," she acknowledges immediately. "Do you want company?"

Damn, the fact she cares feels good.

"I'll be fine. Besides, I know you're not a fan of hospitals, so I wouldn't ask that of you. Especially after already spending the day in one."

She's quiet for a bit and for a split second I wonder if maybe I hurt her feelings. But then she puts my mind at ease.

"All you have to do is call if you change your mind," she says softly. "I'll be here."

Yeah, feels damn good.

Fourteen

WOLFF

"Mom, you have to leave that in."

I untangle the cannula from the fingers of her free hand, and gently fit it back in her nostrils.

Her blood oxygen had been a little low in recovery so they'd put her on a low-flow feed. Her surgery turned out not to be as straightforward as setting the bones. They had to stabilize her forearm with plates, which meant a longer surgery and more sedative than anticipated. She'd taken her sweet time waking up and has been a bit combative since.

Luckily, the hospital has a café that stayed open until eleven, so I was able to buy something to eat and drink while I waited. As of four this morning, Mom was moved into her own room, and I was able to catch a few winks in the recliner in the corner whenever she dozed.

"It makes my nose hurt," she says, her words still a bit slurry.

The overnight nurse mentioned recovering from the

anesthesia can be more of a challenge in the elderly than it is to come back from the actual surgery. Staff has been very attentive and patient with Mom, but lack of sleep has me running short on patience.

Taking a deep breath, I swallow the sharp words I had on my tongue, and force my tone a little gentler.

"Why don't I go ask the nurse if there is anything they can do about that?" I suggest.

It may not be a bad idea for me to step out for a few minutes, maybe duck outside and get some fresh air. Since it's almost eight o'clock, I can make a few calls to give people updates. I didn't want to do that during the night.

I find a nurse I hadn't seen yet at the nurses' desk and relay Mom's complaint.

"It's probably just dry, but I have something for that. I was about to come and take vitals anyway, so I'll bring it with me."

"Excellent, thank you. I'm just going to pop out for a minute and maybe grab a coffee."

"Of course. I'll keep an eye on her."

I end up popping into the café first, which apparently opened at seven again, and grab a coffee and some kind of muffin I take outside to eat. It looks like a nice day and it's definitely not as cold as it was last week. I spot a bench at the edge of the parking lot and walk over.

"How did surgery go?" Jonas asks when he answers my call.

"Well, she'll be setting off metal detectors at the airport, but other than some added hardware, she should be okay. She's a bit fuzzy though, and keeps pulling on tubes."

"Yeah, I remember Dad was like that after he had that hernia surgery last year. They told me it was the anesthesia, which I guess was true, since he was back to his cantankerous old self a week later."

Right, I'd forgotten about that. The reminder puts me a little more at ease. I'd hate for my mother to lose that sharp mind she rightfully prides herself on.

"I remember that. Anyway, I'm going to stick around at least until the doctor has come by. He's apparently doing his rounds at lunchtime."

"Things are more than covered here. Stay with your mom. I think Dan mentioned he was heading into town later anyway to pick up a couple of things, and offered to drop by the cooler of food Ama is putting together."

"She doesn't have to do that. I can get food here," I protest.

Jonas snorts. "Fuck, have you met Ama?"

He makes a valid point.

"Anyway," he continues. "I'm sure he'll message when he's on his way."

That eliminates the need to give him a call, so the next person I dial is Jillian. I'm half expecting my call to go to her messages, so I'm surprised when she answers.

"Hey, how was your night?"

Her voice is warm and soft, and I wish I could see her face.

"Restless. Mom is okay though."

I quickly fill her in on her condition.

"Postoperative delirium," she interjects. "It's not unusual in the elderly. It can come and go, and usually passes in a couple of days to a week. Too bad she's not in the hospital here, I could pop by with Peanut. I'd bet she'd be able to keep your mom calm and grounded. It wouldn't be the first time."

"How is Hayley?"

"Yesterday was more of the same, and I don't expect today to be any different. She only really reacts to Nugget and for the most part ignores us humans. Yesterday the sheriff tried to question her, but she simply turned her head. She's been staring out the window at that parking lot much of the time."

"I'm sure with time, she'll talk."

"I hope so. I worry if there isn't any progress, my open welcome here will eventually run out, and I still believe Nugget can help. I'm only going for a few hours today though. I need to give my other guys some attention. Emo actually started chewing on my couch, which is something she's never done. I think she's bored."

"Once I'm back, one or a couple of your dogs can hang out with me at the ranch. They'd have a ball."

"I'm sure they would," she confirms with a smile in her voice. "Well, I should probably let you get back to your mom, and I need to get to the hospital. Tell your mother Peanut and I will come visit her soon."

Mom is sitting up in bed when I walk in, her eyes clear and lucid. I immediately notice the cannula is gone from her nose. I'm about to chew her out, but she doesn't give me a chance.

"Don't even start. Last check my stats were perfect so they took the damn thing off. It wasn't me. Now tell me whatever is in that bag is for me...because whatever it was they tried to pass as breakfast was not fit to feed a pig."

I don't bother hiding my grin. It looks like my mother is back.

~

Jillian

• • •

"Excuse me?"

I startle at the voice just as I'm getting Nugget out of the back of my SUV. I turn around and catch a tall, well-dressed, middle-aged man wearing aviator shades, emerging from a black vehicle. The first thing that comes to mind is the FBI has arrived. He definitely looks the part.

"Yes?"

"Jillian Lederman?"

Small prickles crawl up my spine at the thought he may have been waiting for me. He pronounces my name with an accent I can't quite place. It seems a little ominous to have a stranger address me by name. It appears to put me at a disadvantage and I immediately look to level the playing field.

"And you would be?"

The man flashes a disarming smile, the white of his teeth stand out against the darker olive tone of his skin. But when he reaches out one hand and removes his shades with the other, his dark eyes look far from inviting. They look empty.

"Forgive me. The name is Emiliano Rojas," he introduces himself as I give his offered hand a brief press with mine. "I represent Grant Vallard," he continues. "Mr. Vallard has asked me to convey his gratitude to you for finding and looking after his niece while he is making every effort to get here."

"I'm just doing my job," I quickly reply, dismissing him as I start moving toward the hospital entrance. "But tell Mr. Vallard it was my pleasure," I toss over my shoulder.

There is something about the man that doesn't feel right. I can see the girl's uncle maybe wanting to say thanks, but I would expect that to be relayed through the Sheriff's Department who hired me for the job. It just seems odd he would actually send a representative to convey a simple message like that.

I glance back right before stepping through the doors into the hospital lobby, and watch the vehicle pull out of his parking spot. Also pretty damn weird, as if the only purpose he had coming here was to talk to me. And that makes me wonder how this Emiliano Rojas knew he could find me here.

I try to read the license plate of what I believe is a Cadillac, but can only make out the first half before he disappears out of sight. I quickly jot down "H16" in my phone and then continue down the hall and up the stairs. To my surprise, I find Sloane on duty outside Hayley's door.

"Hey, Nugget."

She bends down and greets my dog before acknowledging my presence. My guess is she's ticked I didn't answer any of her several calls or respond to the two messages she left last night. I suppose I wasn't ready to discuss what happened between Wolff and me two nights ago. A development she'd somehow gotten wind of, judging by her messages heavily loaded with innuendo.

"Before you ask, I volunteered for the job since I guessed you'd be here. Apparently, the only way I'm going to get any straight information is to corner you at work."

"I have no idea what you're talking about," I lie through my teeth.

"Don't give me that. Dan says something happened with you and Wolff."

"And he would know?" I know I'm fighting a losing battle, but I can't resist a little sarcasm before I concede defeat.

"Yes," Sloane returns without blinking.

I don't really think Wolff would've told anyone, but it's

possible the fact he'd spent the night at my place hadn't gone unnoticed. Despite the fact women often get the reputation, I've discovered men can be horrible gossips.

"Fine. Something did happen, but I don't want to stand in a hospital hallway and discuss this with you. I promise I will spill all, the first decent chance I have. But before I go in to see Hayley, did a guy by the name of Emiliano Rojas stop by here? He just intercepted me in the parking lot."

She shakes her head, her eyes narrowing on me as her expression turns serious.

"Who is Emiliano Rojas?"

"He claims to represent the girl's uncle."

I tell her about my brief interaction with the guy and closely watch her expression get even more grim. That doesn't give me a good feeling.

"Was he alone?" she asks sharply.

"As far as I know. The car had those dark-tinted windows so I can't say for sure, but I only saw him."

"But you saw him get out?"

I nod and am about to say yes, when I replay the scene in my head and realize something I hadn't clued into before.

"Shit. He got out of the passenger side."

"You're sure?"

I nod. I never saw him get back in, and assumed he was alone.

"I think the vehicle was a Cadillac and I got part of the license plate."

I pull up the quick note I made and relay the partial plate number, which she jots down in the small notebook she has tucked in her breast pocket.

"I'll pass it on to Ewing, he can do a search." Then she waves her pen under my nose. "I'll let you know what I find out, but don't think for one minute I'll be forgetting about your promise to fill me in."

"So noted," I mumble as I pass by her with a wink.

Hayley's back is turned when I walk into the room, and she doesn't move when I pick up Nugget and set him on the bed. I assume she's asleep, so I take a seat in the recliner in the corner of the room and pull out my phone, checking my emails and social media.

In the past few days, sitting in this hospital room with a non-communicating child, my online presence—which was maybe a quick scan once a week before—has increased exponentially. I'm actually finding quite a few groups that interest me. Specifically, about training rescue dogs for different assistive purposes.

One group focuses on support animals for children on the autism spectrum, and I've been reading through some of the posts. I've learned these animals are basically trained to measure the specific needs of a given child, which can be as unique and varied as grains of sand. This makes their training more complicated and time-consuming, which in turn leads to long waiting lists for these dogs.

I'd be interested in picking the brain of someone who trains these dogs for this purpose. I'm curious to know if it would be possible to train rescue animals who already have developed the types of traits required to meet those special needs. I don't even know if it's something I could, or would, want to tackle, but I can at least put the bug in someone else's ear.

If this were possible it would mean the world, not only to those kids, but to the dogs as well.

"What's his name?"

I startle at the sound of her voice, it's soft, a little bit hoarse from lack of use, and deeper than I expected. Her back is still turned but she has lifted her head, peeking at me over her shoulder.

"Nugget," I tell her, forcing myself to stay calm, even though I want to jump up and down. "He's a cross between a Maltese and a poodle."

I watch as her thin fingers brush through the dog's hair before drifting lower to the awkward bend in his underdeveloped back leg.

"Did he get hurt?"

"No," I assure her. "He was born like that. His deformed legs slow him down a little, but not much."

"Oh…"

Seemingly satisfied with my answer, she lies back down and I am once again looking at her back. Part of me wants to prompt her to talk more, maybe ask her a few questions, but I don't want to risk her clamming up again. I have a feeling patience will net better results in the long run.

An hour or so later, when Hayley still hasn't moved despite Nugget occasionally shifting around on the bed, I get up to check on her. She appears to be asleep again and as I return to my seat, the door opens a crack, through which Sloane pokes her head. She glances at the bed before slipping inside the room.

"She asleep?"

"Again. She was awake for a bit and actually spoke."

"She talked to you?" Sloane says a little too loud, slipping into the room.

Behind her one of the nurses pokes her head in.

"She's sleeping," I remind Sloane and inform the nurse.

The woman nods and indicates, "I'll come back in a bit."

"She talked to you?" Sloane repeats on a whisper when the nurse disappears.

"She just asked about the dog and then she went back to sleep. I didn't want to push it."

"Probably best. It's good progress though."

Sloane sits down on the armrest of my chair and I shift to give her some room.

"Reason I came in is Junior Ewing just got back to me," Sloane says in a low voice, leaning in. "The FBI is sending in a team to cover the girl. It's your encounter in the parking lot which prompted that move. They pulled the hospital security feed covering the parking lot and were able to get a good view of the guy. Stefano Puma is his real name, and he's a known associate of the Ovando crime family which, apparently, has been on law enforcement's radar for years. They're responsible for sixty percent of the cocaine production in Bolivia."

"How does a guy like that represent Vallard?"

"As it turns out, he doesn't. Ewing got hold of Vallard, who denied having sent anyone."

I'm so confused. What would a Bolivian crime family want with me?

Apparently, my facial expression betrays my bafflement, because Sloane immediately offers up a possible scenario.

"Vallard Logistics is one of the bigger transporters between the U.S. and South America. For that reason alone, it would hold the interest of a producer of cocaine, if they were looking for alternate ways to move their product."

"Pretend I'm ignorant," I tell Sloane. It's not like I'm well-versed in drug trafficking. "Alternate to what?"

She shrugs. "Cartels. Generally, they control the movement of the drugs and thus reel in the bulk of the profits. If the Ovandos could take control of one of the largest transport companies, they could bypass the cartels."

My mind spins as I try to fit that information in with what happened this past week.

"Are you saying they brought down that plane? What purpose would it serve to kill an entire family?" I mutter under my breath, keeping an eye on the bed.

"I guess they're still figuring that out, but if the objective was to take out the family, they fucked up. Which is why the FBI wants a detail on her..." She indicates Hayley in the bed. "And her uncle is placed under protection in the U.S. Embassy in Guatemala until he can be safely extracted and brought Stateside."

"But why approach me?"

"Who knows? But unfortunately, if they think they may be able to get to Hayley through you, it means you're not exactly safe either."

Well, damn, it feels like someone just walked over my grave.

Ending up on the radar of a Bolivian crime family was not part of my bucket list items.

Fifteen

Sloane pointedly ignores my obvious irritation, which only annoys me more.

I have five dogs—as I've pointed out several times, for Pete's sake—and none of them, not even Nugget, would allow anyone to get too close to me without doing some damage. They may look like placid animals, but I have no doubt each one of them would protect me with their life.

Heck, Emo may be trained as a cadaver dog, but she is a Malinois, a breed also known for their protective nature, which is why they are frequently used as law enforcement canines. They can be fierce.

Aside from that, I have a decent alarm system, I have neighbors, and now that I've been removed from Hayley's approved visitor's list, I doubt they'd even be interested in me. But none of it swayed Sheriff Ewing.

He showed up at the hospital with two FBI agents in tow about an hour ago. After he introduced the two agents, who were on Hayley's guard duty, he informed me for the girl's safety and my own, I no longer would be allowed to see her. Then he mentioned Sloane would follow me home and I'd have a guard assigned to me twenty-four seven, until there was no longer a threat. Since I was doubtful of any threat to me in the first place, I did not take kindly to the invasion of my privacy.

Obviously, it did not stop Sloane from following me home and into my house.

Hayley had woken up shortly before the FBI contingent showed up, so I'd had a chance to prepare her for their arrival. Of course, at the time neither of us had realized I wouldn't be there beyond the FBI's involvement either. I could read the shock on her face when Ewing was asked to escort me out of the room, and part of me wanted to scoop her up in my arms and refuse to leave her side.

Except, I won't take the risk my presence might pose to her, as they apparently think it might.

"Be grateful the feds are letting us take responsibility for your safety," Sloane shares from her perch on my couch. "You might not have been given the option of staying home with your dogs if your safety had been up to them."

"I still don't see how I could be of any interest to them. It's not like I had any information of value to start with, and now I'm no longer allowed to see Hayley, any kind of leverage I might've provided is gone."

"Look," Sloane bites sharply, a serious expression on her face. "I understand it's an inconvenience, but you're just going to have to suck it up for the greater good."

I snap my mouth shut on the knee-jerk objection that wants to escape.

Because she's right; this is a minor inconvenience for me and the last thing I want is to distract law enforcement from doing what they feel they need to make sure Hayley stays safe. Ultimately, that girl's safety is paramount to me as well.

"Point taken," I concede.

Suddenly overwhelmed with sadness I might not see Hayley again, I walk into my kitchen and put on the kettle for a cup of tea. I could use one, and this gives me a moment to get myself under control.

A few seconds later, I can't stop myself from asking, "Will you be able to find out how she's doing?"

"Hayley?" Her expression softens at my nod. "If I can't, my boss can. Or otherwise, we ask your boyfriend to work his old Bureau connections, I'm sure he could still pull some strings."

I roll my eyes at her reference to Wolff as my boyfriend. I have a feeling it won't take her long to get back to the subject of what happened between him and me.

"Speaking about your boyfriend..."

See?

I end up confirming we slept together but that's as much information as I'm willing to share. It doesn't matter to Sloane; she runs with it either way. She gets busy plotting out our future, making suggestions as to where we should live, but when she starts talking about children, I cut her off.

"I'm staring forty in the face; I'm not sure children are on the menu."

"Plenty of women have families a little later in life these days," she argues.

"I'm aware, I just don't think I could go there. Again," I add as an afterthought.

I watch first confusion, then realization, and finally sadness wash over her face.

"The person you lost..." She refers to our earlier conversation when Aspen was in the hospital last week. "A child?"

I pour us both a cup of tea and sink down on the couch beside her before confirming.

"My five-year-old daughter, Macy, was killed in an accident eight years ago."

For some reason it's a little less difficult mentioning her name this time. I'm so grateful when Sloane asks pointed questions about what my daughter was like, and not about what happened to her. I'm able to answer without breaking down. Perhaps the trick was always to focus on who she was and not the tragedy that took her from me.

We talk about Macy and Aspen and Sloane's pregnancy. We share our experiences parenting, and the conversation changes something in our friendship. Deepening it by our discovery of another layer of compatibility.

It's almost five when a knock has Sloane jump up and head for the door. I'm surprised when Wolff stalks in. I thought he'd still be in Kalispell.

"What are you doing here?" I blurt out a bit ungraciously, so I quickly follow it up with, "I thought you'd still be with your mom."

He stalks up and cups my face in his hands and before I can even react, his mouth is on mine.

"Hello to you too," he mumbles, after taking the wind from my sails with that kiss.

When I glance over his shoulder I catch sight of Sloane, shamelessly grinning like an idiot at the display.

~

Wolff

. . .

I got the call from Junior Ewing just as Mom was loaded onto the ambulance.

She was being moved back to Wellspring Senior Living, where she'd made it clear she'd be more comfortable, and staff would be able to keep an eye on her.

I ended up following the ambulance to the home where I told Mom I had to leave. As expected, she shooed me to the door, the promise of a more extensive explanation later was enough for her after I mentioned Jillian might be in danger.

The moment I got back in the truck, I called an old FBI colleague, still working from the Kalispell office, to get the dirt on what was going on. He mentioned the Ovando family name and the hair on my neck stood up.

I don't think there is anyone working for any federal law enforcement agency—present or past—who hasn't heard that name before. A notorious Bolivian crime family, the Ovandos have made waves for years now, shedding blood without hesitation in their bid to put a claim on the pipeline of drugs being pumped onto our streets. They already control the majority of cocaine production in Bolivia, and have been looking for other ways to increase their profit margin.

I have no fucking idea how these guys tie in with the plane crash—although I could think of some plausible scenarios—but to hear one of them accosted Jillian in the hospital parking lot has my blood run cold. I was grateful to hear Junior put a detail on her, but he'd guessed correctly I would be looking out for her safety.

Which is why I rushed back to Libby.

I barely even registered Sloane when the door opened. The only person I had eyes for was Jillian, standing by the kitchen island and looking surprised to see me. A wave of relief propelled me across the room, and my heart didn't slow down until I had her body in my arms and her taste on my lips.

"Well, hello..." Sloane sounds behind me, amusement tinting her voice. "Can't say I've seen that side of you before, Wolff. Not so unflappable after all."

Keeping a firm hold of Jillian, who is trying to wiggle free, I swivel my head to look over my shoulder.

"Are you still here?" I fire back. "Don't you have a family to get home to?"

She raises an eyebrow. "Am I to assume you're taking over?"

"Correct. Check with your boss."

"Fine. I know when I'm not wanted."

"Excuse me," Jillian mutters, putting both her hands against my chest and shoving hard. "I'm not some kind of package to change hands."

"Oh, keep your panties on," Sloane teases as she pulls open the door. "At least long enough for me to get out of here."

Reluctantly I let go of Jillian, who immediately creates some distance.

"It's bad enough I'm being forced to put up with babysitters," she snaps. "But I draw the line at being talked about like I'm not even in the room. What the hell is wrong with you two?"

One now, because Sloane conveniently slipped out the door. Still, I nod, because I see her point. I did walk in here like some caveman, completely disregarding her needs in favor of my own need for reassurance.

"We care, which isn't an excuse, but an explanation," I volunteer, shrugging out of my coat and hanging it over the back of a kitchen chair. "For myself, all I can say is an hour and a half is a long fucking time to be on the road with worry as your only companion."

Her anger seems to deflate as her eyes close and the tension leaves her body.

"I can't believe you left your mom. How is she?"

"She is back at Wellspring, where she will be monitored closely. She actually insisted I come when she heard it involved you."

"Does she…"

"Know I care about you?" I finish for her. "Yes. I was stuck in a hospital room with her for twenty-four hours. My mother is relentless and very skilled at drawing out information I'm not excited to part with."

Her mouth stretches into a grin.

"I knew there was a reason I liked your mother."

"Why? Because she's a master interrogator?"

"No. Because she's smart, determined, and unapologetically goes after what she wants."

I shrug, I have to agree. "She is all of those things."

"I'm glad to hear she's doing better." Jillian opens the fridge and starts rummaging through the contents. "I assume you'll be here for dinner?"

"I'll be here for the foreseeable future, but that doesn't mean you have to feed me."

She pulls her head from the fridge and gives me one of those are-you-for-real looks. I've been the subject of one of those once or twice in my day and have learned the best way to deal with them is raise your hands in defense and retreat calmly. Which is exactly what I do, all the way to the couch, where I take a seat and am immediately surrounded by a handful of dogs, all vying for my attention.

"Oh my God. I haven't even taken those guys for a walk," Jillian remarks.

"Then grab your coat and we'll take them," I suggest. "And when we come back, I'll help you with whatever it is you were planning to throw together for dinner."

I let her go out the back with the dogs and tell her to wait, while I lock up the house behind her. Then I leave out the front so I can set the alarm before I join her in the backyard. None of the dogs are on a leash, but she has them well-trained, and they seem to stick close to her.

The moon is already out and reflecting off the snow cover, creating a blueish glow. It's crisp, probably not too much below the freezing mark, but the chilly air has a bite. Jillian is keeping her hands warm by having them tucked in the pockets of her short bubble jacket. Our arms rub as we walk side by side, and I find myself reaching for her hand, pulling it free and folding it in my larger one. She doesn't pull back but slightly adjusts the grip so we're palm to palm, her slim fingers woven with mine.

I haven't had the urge to hold anyone's hand since leaving my high school athletic dance with Kayla Masters, who the entire football team lusted after, and then only to stake my claim. No one is here to see me hold Jillian's hand, but this isn't for anyone else's benefit and I'm not worried about staking any claim. I just crave the physical connection to feel close to her.

We walk in silence—any talking we need to do can wait until later—and enjoy the night and each other's company.

"If you can make a salad?" Jillian asks when we return to the house half an hour later.

"Sure."

She hands me a cutting board and a knife, pulls a bunch of vegetables from the fridge, and sets them in front of me.

"What are we cooking?"

"Pesto chicken and gnocchi. It's fast and easy."

"Sounds good to me."

It *is* good; I end up cleaning out the pot after Jillian swears she's had enough. Then I insist on doing dishes while Jillian puts on the kettle for tea.

All this time we haven't once discussed what happened today, but the subject has to be addressed at some point.

"Do you want to tell me what happened today?" I ask when we take a seat on her couch.

She sighs deeply, but does not resist when I tuck her under my arm. Then she tells me about her encounter.

"He used your name?"

"Yes. My full name. I thought he might've been FBI at first glance, but he identified himself as a representative for Hayley's uncle. Claimed to have been sent to thank me for finding and attending to Hayley, but the whole thing struck me as odd, and I was eager to get away from him."

"Good decision. Stefano Puma is not a nice individual."

She tilts her head back to look at me. "You've heard of him?"

"The man has been around and on the radar for a while."

I don't bother going into detail about Puma's reputation. Back when I was still with the FBI, he was known to get his hands dirty, but I suspect by now he has his own army of enforcers. Jillian doesn't need to know she turned her back on a callous killer, although I have a feeling she's starting to realize the potential gravity of her situation.

"Yikes."

"Right. There's good reason why law enforcement felt it necessary to put a protective detail on you. You're lucky it's a job I've done a time or two, and I was happy to volunteer."

That earns me a smile. "You were, were you?"

"Absolutely." I cup the side of her face in my hand and

lean in to kiss her smiling mouth. "I don't know about you," I mumble against her lips. "But I think an early night is in order."

"Mmm, that sounds like a plan, but first I've gotta let the guys out one more time."

While she takes care of the dogs, I quickly place a call to Wellspring to make sure Mom is settled in. Then I start turning off lights and making sure the house is secure, before I follow Jillian down the hall.

She's already stripping off her clothes when I walk in, and for a moment I just stand here and watch.

"You're still dressed," she observes.

"I know, I'm busy enjoying the show."

She crooks her finger and beckons me over. "Come here and I can help you get naked."

I walk over and reach for her, but she swats my hands away.

"My turn," she insists, her hands making quick work of my belt and jeans.

I have to lock my knees and suck in a lungful of air when she drops down on her knees, frees my cock, and in one smooth move slides me into the wet heat of her mouth.

I'm not sure I can take another breath, but what a glorious way to go this would be.

Jillian's body is still draped over me when I startle awake sometime during the night.

I'm not sure what time it is—it's still dark out—so I grab for my phone, which is plugged into the charger. The screen shows two fifteen, and I notice my phone is only at thirty-five percent battery capacity.

Maybe I didn't plug it in properly.

I follow the cord to the outlet to make sure.

Weird.

Gently rolling Jillian off me, I lift my head to glance at the digital clock on her nightstand to find the display dark. Then I reach for the lamp and flick it on.

Nothing.

I'm immediately on alert, my ears prick up, trying to catch any sounds, but the house is quiet. Almost too quiet. I listen for a few beats when I hear what sounds like a soft click. To my surprise, there is no reaction from the dogs. When I got up to go to the bathroom around midnight, one of them was whining by the back door, and I let the pack out for a pee. I know every one of them came back inside.

And that's when the adrenaline starts pumping for real.

Sixteen

My eyes snap open when a large hand presses down over my mouth.

Even in the dark I recognize Wolff's face just inches from mine, his index finger pressed against his lips.

"Quiet. Someone's here," he whispers barely audibly.

Now I'm wide awake. He takes his hand from my mouth and backs off, so I can sit up. He's just wearing a pair of jeans and reaches for his gun on the nightstand.

Then I hear it; the soft creak of the loose floorboard by the front door. Emo sometimes lies on the mat in the front hallway, but I don't hear the telltale sound of the tags on her collar rattling when she moves.

In fact, I can't hear the dogs at all. If someone is in my house, why aren't the dogs alerting?

Something is very wrong.

But when I start to move, Wolff grabs me firmly by the shoulder and shakes his head.

"You…bathroom," he mouths, as he grabs for the sweats I stripped out of last night and left on the floor, shoving them at me. *"You hear anything, get out the window."*

The bedroom window is facing the front of the house, but the small bathroom window over the tub faces out the back.

"The alarm…the dogs…"

"I've got it," he says, handing his phone to me. Mine is in the kitchen on the charger. *"Get away from the house, hide, call 911, then High Meadow. Code is 1537 to unlock."*

"But—"

"Go. Now."

He's already reaching for the door when I dart into the bathroom.

My hands are shaking as I try to get my feet into the legs of my sweatpants. *Shit,* I don't have socks. By now, my heart is hammering so hard it's all I can hear. I shove Wolff's phone in my pocket and carefully climb into the tub. I use the wide windowsill to store my shampoo and body wash, and quickly remove the bottles, setting them on the floor.

Making every effort to be as quiet as I can, I manage to take out the screen, unlock the window, only to find the window stuck when I try to slide it up.

The next moment, an ungodly loud crash sounds from somewhere inside the house, followed by the sharp crack of a gunshot. The sudden surge of adrenaline has me shoving at the window, putting all my weight into it, and with a high-pitched squeak, it slides open.

I perch on the narrow ledge of the tub on my toes and pull myself through the small window opening. Not ideal to go headfirst, especially not when I realize the bottom of the window is at least six feet from the ground, but I don't have a choice.

More cracks of gunfire have me heave myself through, panicking for a moment when my hips get stuck, but with a good kick of my legs and a hefty push off the window frame with my hands, I launch myself at the ground below.

I'm grateful for the snow breaking my fall, but the impact still stuns me for a moment. Or maybe it's the cold hitting me all at once. Still, I scramble to my feet; I have to get moving.

I aim for the back of my yard, and duck behind the shed next to the dog kennel, already pulling Wolff's phone from my pocket. My hands are shaking so hard it takes me three tries to unlock it. Then I call 911. I give the woman who answers the basics, but when she starts asking asinine questions, I hang up and quickly dial the ranch.

Jonas answers, and it's clear I woke him.

"The fuck, Wolff. Something better be on fire for you to call at this hour."

"It's me, Jillian. Someone has broken into my house. Seventeen Terrace View Drive," I rattle off in a whispered voice. *"Wolff is still in the house. Shots were fired."*

"Where are you?" Jonas snaps.

"Behind the dog kennel out back."

"Stay there. Don't move. We're on our way."

Abruptly the line goes dead and a heavy silence settles in around me. I strain to hear noises that may be coming from the house, but if there are any, I'm not hearing them; the snow cover may be muffling the sound.

My body starts shivering to try and ward off the cold creeping up from my feet. Those are turning into ice clumps and I can't feel my toes anymore. In hindsight, I wished I'd grabbed a towel or something from the bathroom I could've wrapped myself in, but I wasn't exactly thinking straight.

The fear I've been able to keep at bay so far is fast taking hold, and my imagination runs away with me. Visions of Wolff lying in a pool of blood make it hard to follow through on Jonas's instructions to stay put.

What if he's hurt and needs help? I'm a nurse, I know mere seconds can mean the difference between life and death. I've done what Wolff asked of me, but I can't simply hide here like a coward when I could be making a difference. That's not my style.

Determined, I slip from my hiding spot and—sticking to the fence separating my property from the neighbor's—retrace my steps back to the house. There's no way I'll be able to get back in the house through that bathroom window, it's up too high for me to reach. My best option is to go around the side of the house and see if I can get safely in the front.

I keep my eye on the house as I approach but don't detect any movement. I carefully lift the latch on the gate when I reach it, but can't prevent the squeal of one of the hinges in desperate need of some oil. The sound cuts through the silence and I freeze for a moment, waiting for some kind of reaction. When I don't hear anything, I slip through.

With my back to the side of the house, I keep my eyes fixed on the front, inching my way forward, when I'm suddenly grabbed from behind.

A surprised yell is trapped inside when a large hand clamps over my mouth.

～

Wolff

. . .

I'm second-guessing myself the moment I slip from the bedroom.

Maybe it would've been better to keep Jillian close. There may well be more than one intruder. In fact, it's more than likely there are.

As I sneak down the hallway, I can feel chilled air coming toward me. I'm guessing the window or door they managed to come in through was left open. *Fuck*, I sent Jillian out in that cold.

I hear a rustle of clothes, moments before the narrow beam of a pen light comes into view. Someone is moving through the living room.

Pressing my back against the wall, I try to stay out of sight as I cautiously move toward the intruder, my gun in hand. My best chance is the element of surprise, so I have to stay out of sight until I can get a bead on them.

When I see the light move into the kitchen, I peek around the corner and take a step into the living area, my eyes fixed on the guy's back. I'm hoping I can sneak up behind him and put my gun to his head before he even knows I'm here. But as I inch up on him, trying to stick as close to the wall so I'm partially blocked by the fridge, I'm suddenly shoved from behind and slam into the side of the appliance.

I was afraid there was more than one.

By some miracle, I'm able to keep a firm grip on my weapon, and when a bullet whizzes by my ear, I'm able to return fire at the figure I'd followed into the kitchen. I immediately pivot around and fire a shot in the general direction of whoever it was that shoved me into the fridge, but that individual is already darting out the front door, which is wide open. When I turn back, the original shooter is rounding the island, trying to get a better shot at me, but I'm already on the move.

Harder for him to hit a moving target, and his next shot hits the fridge behind with a loud ping. But his action leaves him partially exposed and I quickly fire off a responding shot, hitting him in the shoulder. He immediately drops his gun and—clutching his shoulder—starts running toward the front of the house.

The temptation is strong to go after him, but then I remember the other guy didn't seem hurt and is already outside. Chances are good, I poke my head out the door, and someone's going to take a potshot at it. No thanks.

Instead, I stop at the front door and slam it shut, not that that'll do much. Then I turn and catch a glimpse of something I can't afford to take the time to investigate closer. I have to make sure Jillian was able to get away safely and beeline it back to the en suite bathroom. She isn't there and the window is open, so I assume she made it out. The only problem is, now the two intruders are out there with her.

Running into the bedroom, I grab my shirt and pull it on, then I rush to the front door to grab my boots and parka, before going out the sliding door in the kitchen to look for Jillian. I peer toward the tree line at the back of the yard to see if I can spot her, but she's hidden well. I don't see anything.

I'm about to head back there to find her when I hear the squeal of a hinge on the side of the house. Jumping off the deck, I rush toward the sound, peeking around the corner of the house. Halfway down I spot Jillian's red hair and sneak up behind her.

Her body freezes the moment I slip one arm around her

midsection and clamp a hand over her mouth for the second time. I'm positive I'll be paying for that at some point, but for now I don't want to risk alerting anyone at the front of the house any more than we already have.

I have no doubt whoever is here is looking for Jillian, but they'll have to go through me to get to her.

"Me again," I mumble against the shell of her ear.

She instantly swings around and burrows her shivering body against me. She feels cold in my arms and I immediately wrap my coat around her, lifting her off her feet. I only now notice those are bare.

"Wrap your legs around me," I softly instruct her.

She hops up, her arms around my neck and her legs clamped around my waist, hanging on like a child. At least this way my body heat and the down lining of my coat will keep her warm. She's not that heavy, and I have no problem holding her in place with one arm so I can aim and shoot with the other if necessary.

"There's at least two of them," I whisper as I carry her into the backyard.

My main concern is Jillian and I'm not about to go to the front of the house, where those guys might still be lingering around, with her in my arms. In fact, I don't want her near the house at all, in case they decide to return. So instead, I carry her to the trees in the back, where I thought she'd been hiding in the first place.

"Jonas is on his way," she tells me when I stop behind a cluster of trees. "And he said he'd make the 911 call."

I can still see the house, but I doubt they'd be able to spot us.

"Good. We'll just hang tight until they get here."

Jillian tries to push off but I hold firm.

"You have no shoes on," I remind her.

She stops struggling, but her eyes are panicked. "My dogs. What happened to my dogs?"

The sound of sirens approaching saves me from having to describe what I thought I saw in her living room.

At least for now.

~

"Drugged."

"How?" Jillian wants to know, sitting on the floor with Nugget's limp body in her lap.

"I let them out one more time at about midnight," I inform her. "They looked fine when I brought them in, but I didn't see what they were up to outside. It's possible they ate something."

Those guys could've tossed something in the yard to incapacitate the dogs. It makes sense. They would've waited until they were sure it took effect before making their next move, which apparently was to kill the power. That effectively disabled Jillian's house alarm, which is hardwired into the electrical and does not have an alternate energy source. After that it was a matter of getting inside, which turned out to be too easy.

Unfortunately, there was no sign of the two when the cavalry rolled in, but I felt some satisfaction when the sheriff's deputy was able to recover the gun the guy dropped when I winged him. There was also a blood trail they were able to follow to an empty house a couple of doors down. The owners have apparently gone south for the winter.

"JD is on his way with Doc Richards," Bo announces. "She'll figure it out."

Janey Richards is our local vet, who took over for Doc Evans when he retired last year. She's young, but she's already proven she knows what she's doing, looking after the horses at High Meadow.

Bo is sitting on the floor taking care of Hunter. He'd already been here working on the dogs by the time I figured it was safe enough to bring Jillian back inside. She'd surprised me, keeping a cool head as she went down to her knees by her dogs and asked Bo what she could do. Both of them have medical backgrounds and I guess when push comes to shove, some of the basic principles remain the same, whether dealing with people or animals.

Peanut, Emo, and Murphy—the three bigger dogs—are groggy but seem to be coming out of it. However, the two smaller ones, Hunter and Nugget, are not faring as well. Their breathing is shallow and neither of them are responding to stimuli.

Twenty minutes later, the two smaller dogs are sufficiently stabilized for Doc Richards to take them back to the veterinary clinic, where she plans to keep a close eye on them. If not for the other three still needing care, I'm sure Jillian would've insisted on going, but Janey convinced her she'd be more useful looking after the bigger dogs, and she promised to keep her up-to-date on Hunter's and Nugget's conditions.

"Let's pack up the dogs," I tell her after JD and Doc leave with the two sickest animals.

"What do you mean?"

Bo, Dan, Jackson, and Jonas already left, but the sheriff's department is still here waiting for the FBI to arrive. I would like to get Jillian out of here before they do, otherwise we'll be stuck here all night. The feds can wait until tomorrow, when we've had some rest and hopefully know Jillian's dogs are going to be okay. We won't be able to get that here with people going in and out all night.

"This place will be swarming with law enforcement, and we need to decompress and find a quiet space for the dogs."

For a moment, it looks like she is going to object before exhaustion slumps her shoulders and she shakes her head.

"Where are we going?"

"The ranch."

Seventeen

"No."

I cross my arms over my chest and stare down the FBI agent.

Like hell I'll be leaving my dogs behind, which is what would be expected of me if I volunteered myself into their protective custody.

Special Agents Bellinger and Cohen showed up half an hour ago to get our statements on what happened last night. Bellinger waited until the end to drop the protective custody bomb on me.

"Ms. Lederman..." he placates me. His tone is the equivalent of a pat on the head and has the absolute opposite effect.

"You have my answer. Unless you actually intend to take me into custody, we're done here."

I hear Wolff stifle a snort behind me. I'm surprised he hasn't jumped in, but he seems content letting me take the lead.

"It's safer for you," the agent insists.

"I'd rather you keep Hayley safe," I fire back.

"The girl? We have her safe," he assures me.

"Good. Focus your energy and manpower on keeping her that way. She has no one else looking out for her."

"Actually, her uncle is very concerned about her and is supposed to arrive in the coming days."

"Wasn't he stuck in Guatemala?" Wolff asks, putting his hand on my shoulder in a possessive gesture.

Bellinger closely observes the move before lifting his eyes to his former colleague.

"Not for much longer. With the help of embassy personnel, he is currently being transported to Mexico, where we have resources waiting to fly him here."

Thank God. Having family here will be good for Hayley. Maybe it'll be a start for her to begin processing and healing from the trauma she endured. Nothing worse than feeling utterly alone in the world when you have a heavy burden to bear.

"Any luck tracking down the guys who paid us a visit last night?" Wolff pushes for more answers.

"We're working on it. We're still processing the scene."

The scene. I'm assuming he's talking about my house.

"What would they want with me in the first place?"

Bellinger shifts his attention to me and shrugs.

"This would be speculation only, but it's possible they were hoping you could lead them to the girl. We were able to quietly move her from the hospital yesterday afternoon, but they must've found out she was gone. We suspect they had a contact in the hospital."

"Staff?" Wolff wants to know.

"Possibly. We're narrowing it down," Bellinger dismisses

him and addresses me. "But these people are dangerous, determined, and ruthless. They'll have no qualms going through you to get to the girl, and one failed attempt will not deter them for long. And next time you—or your dogs—may not be so lucky. You really should come with us."

He's dead wrong if he thinks that comment will sway me. All it does is piss me off, and I also think he's wrong.

"And what would that accomplish, other than point a giant arrow at my head? All it'll do is reaffirm the notion I have information they're looking for. Which, I'll remind you, I don't."

Wolff squeezes my shoulder as he throws in his two cents.

"She has a point, and you know it." Then he adds more aggressively. "Unless, of course, that is exactly what you're counting on. Were you hoping to use her to draw them out?"

"Don't be ridiculous," Bellinger blusters, but I can tell by the reaction of Agent Cohen—who has lingered in the background—Wolff hit a mark.

Angry now, I slip from Wolff's hold and march to the door of his cabin, flinging it wide open.

"I believe you've overstayed your welcome," I bite off, trying with all my might to hold on to my temper.

Bellinger opens his mouth to say something but, wisely, thinks better of it as he starts walking out, his partner in tow. As soon as Cohen steps out on the porch, I fling the door shut with a bang. Wolff nods his approval when I turn to face him.

"They were gonna use me as bait," I grumble, still seething.

"Yup."

"Is that normal FBI practice?"

"I wouldn't say normal, but it's not uncommon," he answers cautiously.

"Assholes," I vent. "I can see why you left."

He doesn't stop me when I walk past him, heading for the spare bedroom where we left the dogs to sleep off the remnants of the drug in their systems. We still don't know what it may have been they were given, but as I understand it, samples of Nugget's and Hunter's blood were sent to the lab first thing this morning.

I was still in bed when the vet texted with an update on Nugget and Hunter. She'd put both of them on an IV and has been trying to flush the drugs from their systems. It's been more successful on Hunter, who is apparently awake and responsive, although still a little sluggish. Nugget is a little slower to perk up, but Doc Richards was cautiously optimistic. I want to go check on them with everything in me but, as Wolff pointed out before the FBI agents showed up, it's safer for me to stay put and trust my pups are receiving the best possible care.

Peanut lifts her head when I walk in. All three dogs are sprawled on the double mattress, having had to leave their own beds at home. They even made me leave their food and water bowls behind, which Wolff later explained would be standard protocol in the case of a possible poisoning. The only things I was able to bring were their collars and leashes.

I flop down on the bed and snuggle my pups. All three have their tails wagging, thumping the mattress. I gratefully receive kisses as I spoil them with attention.

"Do you guys need to go out for a pee?"

"I can take them," Wolff offers from the door opening.

"Are you trying to keep me locked in here?" I snap.

I immediately realize that was uncalled for and raise my hand in apology, as I scramble up from the bed.

"Nope," he replies calmly. "I just thought I'd offer. I was going to go out to check on a few things anyway, but you're welcome to come. We're keeping the gate to the ranch closed, and security is tight here. No one will be able to get close unnoticed, so you're safe as long as you don't wander off too far."

I walk up to him and loop my arms around his neck.

"I'm sorry," I mumble, pressing my mouth to his. "You didn't deserve that. And yes, I'd love to come with you. I could use some fresh air."

"Are you saying it smells in here?" he teases.

"No," I assure him with a smile. "I just need to clear my head."

~

Wolff

"Glad to see it, boy."

I just left the office and step out on the porch when I hear Thomas's voice.

He's sitting in his usual spot—the rocking chair—all bundled up with a blanket over his lap and a space heater by his feet. Jonas's father lived most of his long life in Texas, where he was a rancher, before Jonas coaxed him into coming to Montana. His favorite pastime is watching the ranch's activities from his perch on the porch, and nothing will deter him. Not even Montana's much colder winters.

I walk over and lean my hip against the railing.

"See what?"

The old man points his gloved finger at the corral, where I see Jillian playing with her dogs in the snow. She took them off leash, and even though they could easily slip through the fencing, they don't wander off.

"She's a pretty one. Dainty-lookin' but I bet she's made of stern stuff. Gotta be, doing the kind of work she does. Good with animals, smart, and...she's sweet on ya, boy."

Thomas calls everyone boy. He seems to have adopted us all and loves doling out fatherly advice. Whether we ask for it or not. He also has a romantic streak a mile wide and likes to play Cupid, given the chance. But the man truly cares, which is why I don't blow him off like I might have otherwise.

"I like her," I volunteer, earning me a bark of laughter.

"Always understated and aloof, aren't ya? You don't fool me though. I wasn't sure about you—thought maybe you'd be the one holdout in the bunch—but all it took was the right gal to come along."

"Fine," I concede. "I like her a lot."

His hoarse chuckle turns into a coughing fit, and I look on with a bit of concern.

"You can blink now," he finally says, catching his breath. "Ain't ready to croak yet."

"Good," I return. "Things would get boring without you."

"Yeah, yeah. You can mock an old man, but have a care with that filly; she's carrying deep hurt."

I don't know how he knows these things, whether he just guesses at it or what, but in this case, he is right on the mark. The truth is, if I had known how devastating and deep that hurt ran, I might not have risked getting involved with her.

Ah, who the hell am I kidding? I'd already had second and even third thoughts and still went ahead, because I couldn't stay away.

It's that simple.

"I'll have a care," I promise him as I push away from the railing.

Jillian looks up when she hears the crunch of my boots in the snow and greets me with a smile. Fuck, I like that. Even the pack seems happy to see me, sidling up to me for pats and ear scratches.

"These dogs certainly perked up," I point out.

"They did, didn't they? It's amazing what a whiff of cool outside air and a good run in the snow will do." She puts a hand on my arm. "Did you get done what you needed to do?"

All I did was talk to Jonas about my schedule and Ama about dinner tonight. Things are pretty slow at the ranch right now and, unless we get called out on a search, taking some personal time is not an issue, according to Jonas. Ama was already aware of the extra guest at the ranch and accounted for it in her planning of dinner, so that wasn't a problem either.

"I did. I got tomorrow off and was going to suggest heading to Kalispell. Maybe checking in on Mom at Wellspring? We could take Peanut, and I'm sure Jackson would be happy to have the other two hang out with him."

At least I'm hoping he will be. Since Jillian first arrived here, we've been trying to get Jackson—who suffers from PTSD—to let her find him a good emotional support dog, but so far he's been a bit resistant. Maybe looking after Jillian's two will open him up to the idea.

She glances at Emo and Murphy before turning those pretty green eyes back to me.

"Happy? That doesn't exactly sound like Jackson. You wouldn't be manipulating the situation now, would you?"

I point my index finger at myself. "Me? Manipulate? I don't know what you're talking about."

She grabs the front of my coat and pulls herself up on her toes, laughing in my face.

"You're an awful liar, but I appreciate the effort."

I slip my arms around her waist to hold her in place and drop my head so I can kiss the grin off her face. As every time my lips taste hers, the world disappears, and I don't even realize we're standing out in the open until a sharp whistle pierces the air.

When I look up, I see Thomas standing at the edge of the porch, hollering.

"Do I gotta put the hose on y'all?"

Eighteen

"We may need to postpone the trip to Kalispell."

I glance up from the amazing breakfast spread Ama put out in the kitchen.

She'd cooked dinner last night as well, which was scrumptious, so when Wolff suggested going to the main house for breakfast after finding only a stale box of cereal and a quarter gallon of questionable milk in his cabin, I was on board.

"Why?"

Wolff braces a hand on the kitchen island and leans in.

"Doc called. She's on her way here to check in on an injured horse and may have your pups in her truck."

The pressure balloon I've carried around in my chest these past few days pops, and all the worry for Hunter and Nugget drains in the form of unexpected tears. I'd wanted to go see them so badly, but recognized that probably wouldn't be smart, not only exposing myself but possibly drawing unwanted attention to Janey Richards. As hard as it was to stay away, I wasn't going to take that risk.

"Nice going, Lucas," Jonas's father grumbles when he shuffles into the kitchen. "What'd I tell you?"

Embarrassed, I hide my face in a napkin.

"Ease up, old man," Ama jumps to Wolff's defense. "I believe those are happy tears."

I lower the napkin to find Thomas intensely staring across the kitchen island at me.

"They are," I confirm.

He turns his attention back to Wolff. "Well, in that case, well done, son."

"More coffee?" Wolff asks me, pointedly ignoring the older man.

"Please."

I'm happy to return to my apple-stuffed French toast and bacon Ama served up this morning, and make a mental note to ask her for the recipe, if she's willing to share. I enjoy the rest of my breakfast in silence, as I listen to Ama and Thomas bicker like siblings. They're not related, and a generation separates them, but the love between them is obvious. At some point, Jackson walks in, closely followed by Sully, and before you know it every stool at the kitchen island is filled, and the supply of food seems never-ending.

It's a strange patchwork of individuals in this kitchen, but there is no doubt these people are family. I feel pretty lucky I'm being made to feel included.

I'm just shoving the last bite in my mouth when JD walks into the kitchen, his eyes on me.

"Doc's here," he announces.

I'm off my stool and beelining it for the front door. I didn't even thank Ama for breakfast. Janey is standing next to her truck with the rear door open, grinning widely as she steps aside for me to poke my head inside.

"Oh my God, you guys. Hey…"

Hunter leaps up from the back seat and attacks my face with her tongue, while her tail beats a tattoo against the leather seat.

"Hello, pretty girl. You're looking a lot better."

When I nudge her aside, I catch sight of Nugget on the other side of the back seat, whimpering softly. He lifts his head and his tail wags too, albeit with a little less enthusiasm.

"Who's my good boy?"

I quickly lift Hunter out of the truck and reach back in for Nugget, who is already crawling toward me. I gingerly pick him up, cradling him in my arms when I back out of the truck.

"He's still weak," Janey volunteers. "Much better than he was though. Given he has the smallest body mass of all the dogs, I think it's going to take some time for the drugs to get completely filtered from his system. But he's progressing, and I'm positive he will do even better once he's back with his pack."

"I don't know how to thank you."

"Believe me, it's my pleasure. Happy to see them doing better. Although, you may want to keep an eye on Nugget just for today. I think you'll see a great improvement in him with another day or so."

"Did you ever find out what they were given?" Wolff asks.

I hadn't even noticed him following me outside, I was too focused on my dogs.

"Yes," Doc responds. "I believe it was acepromazine. It's a tranquilizer often used as a pre-anesthetic. It would've been about forty minutes to an hour before it would've taken effect once in a dog's system and can last six to eight hours to wear off when properly dosed."

"They were probably given something when I last let them out before we went to bed," Wolff suggests.

The vet agrees, "That would be my guess."

I thank her again and ask her to send me the bill, to which she responds with a smile and a, "Sure." I have a sneaking suspicion I'll have to chase that bill down.

Once again, I feel that warm sense of community, of family. Something I've denied myself for too many years.

I carry Nugget as I follow Wolff, who leads Hunter to his cabin. The welcome from the rest of the pack is enthusiastic, and I have to caution my bigger boys to be gentle with especially Nugget.

"New plan for today," Wolff announces once the pack seems settled down.

"Which is?"

"You stick around here with the dogs. Give Nugget a chance to recover and maybe tomorrow he'll be good enough to come with us to Wellspring. Give the big dogs some exercise so they don't feel left out. And Jackson says he's sticking close by today," he suggests as he reaches for me.

I step willingly into his arms. Amazing how fast his embrace has become like home to me.

"And what about you?"

"I'm gonna head over to your place. The feds should be done with it by now, but they're not known for leaving things tidy. I'll do a bit of cleanup, maybe grab whatever perishables are in your fridge and freezer to bring back, and make sure the place is locked up tight. Anything you need that I can pack up?"

I squeeze his waist and tilt my head back. "A couple of the dog beds. Three dogs barely fit on your spare bed, all five of them would be pushing it. Nugget won't be able to jump up there by himself anyway."

He drops his head for a quick, hard kiss.

It's not until he grabs his keys off the coffee table, fits his hat back on his head, and aims for the door, I realize I only grabbed my toothbrush and one change of clothes when we left my house in a hurry.

"Wolff?"

"Yeah?"

He looks back over his shoulder, and it suddenly strikes me how incredibly handsome this man is. Not in any flashy way, he doesn't have JD's dark, cut, smoldering looks, or Dan's stacked physique, but I much prefer Wolff's swimmer's body and his calm blue eyes. I've even grown to love his longer hair, and nothing beats that little smile he seems to reserve just for me.

I think I may be falling for him.

"I forgot; I don't have any more clean clothes."

That smile makes an appearance. "That's okay, I much prefer you without."

I roll my eyes.

"That'll for sure get tongues wagging at Wellspring Senior Living tomorrow," I fire off in return.

Wolff throws back his head and starts laughing, his eyes crinkling and white teeth flashing.

Oh yeah...I've got it bad.

~

Wolff

. . .

It surprises me to find a sheriff's cruiser parked outside Jillian's place.

Billy Keegan, one of the deputies, who is sometimes partnered up with Sloane, gets out when I pull up behind him.

"The scene hasn't been released by the feds yet," he informs me when I step out of the truck.

"Still? What the hell do they think they're gonna find here?"

Billy shrugs. "They're supposed to be back to finish up. There was a task force meeting at our office earlier this morning, and it looks like some of the evidence they found links back to that Puma guy."

"Stefano Puma?"

"Fingerprints on the gun he dropped."

All right.

I didn't get a good look at those guys in the middle of the night. It was dark and I was working on instinct rather than sight when I confronted them. That said, I don't mind the idea I put a bullet in Puma—that piece of shit—although I have to say, I'm surprised he got his own hands dirty.

I hope he's hurting.

"What are you doing here?" the deputy wants to know.

"I was hoping to clean up a little, pick up a few things, and make sure the place is locked up," I explain.

"The cleanup will have to wait, we can call about letting you grab some things, and as for locking the place up, I'll make sure you're notified the moment the feds are done with the place."

I clap him on the shoulder. "That would be helpful."

Ten minutes later, after a bit of a runaround from SA Bellinger, I'm finally granted permission to go in the house.

Of course, with Billy Keegan looking on. As suspected, the place was left a mess, fingerprint powder everywhere, still smudges of blood on the kitchen floor, and just about every drawer, cupboard, and closet door left open.

Billy dutifully follows me around the house, but when he trails me down the hall to Jillian's bedroom, I stop him.

"Seriously? Her bedroom?"

He grins sheepishly. "Just following orders."

"Her bedroom is not part of the crime scene," I remind him. "You can wait out here."

No need for him to look over my shoulder when I go through Jillian's dresser drawers. I think she's been violated enough.

At least they left the bedroom door closed, but when I slip inside, it's evident the room didn't escape scrutiny. Clearly, sometime after we left early on Tuesday morning, her closet, her dresser, and the nightstand were gone through. Even the fucking sheets on the bed are gone. It looks like they've been in the damn bathroom too.

No way in hell I'll let Jillian see how badly her privacy was invaded.

I grab a bag from her closet and start shoving clothes and underwear in. In the bathroom, I add the obvious toiletries from the edge of the tub and the counter. Then I yank the door open, startling Billy Keegan, who is looking at something on his phone.

"Get fucking Bellinger back on the phone," I bark as I brush past him.

"No need," he says as he follows me to the kitchen. "I just got a message he's on his way with the sheriff."

Good. I'd rather look him in the face when I give him a piece of my mind.

I already have Jillian's bag, the dog beds, and the

contents of her fridge and freezer in a box in the truck, when the sheriff's cruiser followed by a black Ford Expedition turn on to the driveway. Perfect goddamn timing.

I'm waiting for Bellinger to exit the SUV, my arms crossed over my chest in case I'm tempted to throw a punch.

"Mr. Wolff, I was hoping to catch you here."

I notice Ewing walking up behind the agent, but my focus is on Bellinger.

"You took the fucking sheets?" I hiss at him.

He jerks back and I can tell he wasn't expecting a full-frontal attack. Well, too damn bad.

"I'm not sure what you're referring to," he skirts.

"The bedsheets. Off the bed Jillian and I were sleeping in. In the room that was never part of any crime scene."

"Ease up, Wolff," Ewing tries to moderate when I get into the agent's face.

But I'm pissed. I can't remember the last time I was this worked up.

"You already went through her goddamn underwear drawer. That wasn't enough of a violation of her privacy for you? You had to take the sheets off her bed?" I continue my rant.

"Now hold on a second. I guess you've been away from the Bureau a few too many years, so maybe you've forgotten standard procedure when processing a crime scene? Or has your judgment been clouded by the pretty little redhead?"

I'm surprised at Billy Keegan's strong hold when he wraps his arms around me from behind, pinning mine to my side. Just as I was about to throw a right hook in Bellinger's smug, fucking face.

"That's enough," Junior Ewing barks, stepping in front of me, waving a finger in my face. "Cool your goddamn jets, and don't you dare take that swing, or I *will* throw your ass in jail."

Then he turns his back and faces off with Bellinger.

"Standard procedure? Bedsheets?"

"Just being thorough," I hear the asshole respond. "If anything, we needed to rule out any possible involvement Ms. Lederman might have in this case."

"What?" I can't hold back my disbelief. "Are you nuts?"

"Surely, you don't believe that is even a remote possibility," Ewing expresses the same sentiment, except in milder terms.

"Look, we have the woman on camera talking to Stefano Puma in the parking lot of your hospital. There's no way to know what they were discussing. Hell, they may have greeted each other as old friends, there's no way to tell what was said, except for Ms. Lederman's claims."

"And she then turned around, told a sheriff's deputy, and made sure everyone's attention was drawn to the man?" I scoff, getting heated up again. "How does that even make sense? You think she willingly had someone poison her dogs? To what fucking end? What is her gain? You're reaching, Bellinger."

"He's got a point," Ewing offers his support as he steps out of the way.

I can see Bellinger, both his hands clamped at the back of his neck and his head tilted up to the sky. Then he drops his gaze and locks eyes with me.

"Look. We don't know, all right? All we know is these guys disappeared into thin air in the early hours of Tuesday morning. We don't know where they are, we're not even sure what they want, so yes...I'm going to fucking run down any and every possible lead, however thin or far-fetched it may appear. And I'm sorry if that offends you or your girl-friend, but I have an eleven-year-old orphan whose life may depend on me solving this case."

Just like that, the fire raging in me is doused.

He's right, it's easy to forget who this is really about, and the kicker is, Jillian would have volunteered her underwear drawer and her sheets if it meant getting closer to answers for Hayley.

Dammit.

Now I have to eat crow.

Nineteen

"No, no, no…"

I groan at the loss of him when he pulls out.

But then he flips me on my back, grabs my right leg behind the knee, and pushes me wide open. With a predatory grin on his flushed face, he drops his hips in the V of my legs and powers inside me.

My back arches off the mattress, and my hands find purchase on the globes of his fine ass as my body seeks release. He's been teasing me for what feels like hours, driving me to the brink only to withdraw, and leaving me suspended, my entire being thrumming with need.

He woke me up with his mouth when it was still dark out, and all I could see was the glint of his eyes between my legs. By now sunlight is filtering through the shades, reflecting off our sweaty bodies, and still, he is toying with me.

"Lucas, no," I warn him again when the first flutters of

what promises to be an epic orgasm make my core pulse. But despite my firm grip on his ass, he retreats again.

This time I don't let him go far and—wrapping my legs around his hips and hooking my feet to lock them in place—I surprise him by flipping him over on his back. Our connection never quite lost, I triumphantly plant myself on his rock-hard cock, and ride him hard with a singular purpose.

The orgasm shatters me, leaving me breathless and boneless, draped like a wet blanket over his body, which is still bucking with the power of his own release.

I'm not sure how long it is before I register a soft scratching on the bedroom door. My head shoots up and my eyes dart to the clock on the nightstand, which shows it's almost nine o'clock.

"Oh my God! Those poor dogs," I lament, scrambling off Wolff, who tries to hold on to me.

"I'll go," he volunteers, rolling on top of me and pressing me down in the mattress.

He drops his head and takes my mouth in a sweet kiss.

"Now that's a good morning," he mumbles against my lips.

"It won't be when you find the dogs have peed all over your couch," I warn him.

"It will have been worth it." He grins back at me as he gets out of bed. "And for the record, I like when you call me Lucas."

I flip over on my stomach and prop my chin on my hands so I can watch him in his full glory, as he grabs a pair of sweats from his dresser and ducks into the bathroom. Luckily, he doesn't waste too much time in there, and in minutes I hear him head outside with the dogs.

The next thing I know, I wake up from a slap on my ass and a cold, wet nose in my face.

"Come on, lazy bones," Wolff taunts me.

"Lazy?" I react predictably. "You barely let me sleep."

My grumbling only makes him smile bigger.

"Quit your whining. Didn't I just rock your world?" he teases, sitting down on the mattress beside me as he sets a cup of steaming coffee on the nightstand.

"You mean I rocked my own world, since you would still have been stringing me along," I complain ungraciously, even as I sit up and reach for the coffee he brought me.

He bumps my shoulder with his. "Jilly, honey, are you saying you don't like my mouth in the morning?"

I try to glare at him over the rim of my coffee mug, even as my well-used parts experience a tingle of new life at the memory. Just the thought of missing out on that has me blurt out, "I never said that."

"That's what I thought," he mutters smugly, before getting up and pulling me with him. "Let's get moving; we have a facility full of seniors eagerly awaiting their doggy licks and snuggles."

It's two hours later when we finally get on the road.

Given our early morning activities, we both desperately needed a shower. Then there was the issue of security, something I'd almost forgotten about the past two days.

It was Wolff's idea to borrow Jonas's dark navy Yukon. The rear of the SUV has dark tinted windows, making it difficult to see who or what is inside, so I was relegated to the back seat with both dogs. Wolff tucked his hair under his hat before getting behind the wheel.

To help throw off anyone who might be looking,

Jackson took Wolff's truck five minutes ago and drove toward Libby.

"Ready?"

"Yup," I confirm, catching Wolff's wink in the rearview mirror.

Flanked by two affectionate dogs snuggling up against me, I find myself dozing off every so often, making the drive feel short. Before I realize it, we're pulling into the parking lot of Wellspring Senior Living.

"Nice nap?"

He throws a quick look over his shoulder as he parks the SUV, and I stick out my tongue at him in response.

Trudy Wolff is sitting front and center in the community room, her arm in a sling, but a smile on her face when we walk in. I unclip Peanut, who immediately makes a beeline for Wolff's mother, and she laves her with attention.

"So glad to see you, Jillian," she directs at me with a smile.

"Nice to see you too. And great to see you up and about. I heard about your ordeal. How is the arm?"

"Much better than it was. You're so sweet for asking."

Behind me I hear Wolff clear his throat.

"Hello, Mom, what am I? Chopped liver?"

Wolff bends down to kiss her cheek. Trudy winks at me over his head, before she turns a smile on him.

"Well hello, dear. I didn't notice you there."

The expression on his face is priceless, and I stifle a snicker. The woman is a big tease, and I think it's hilarious she is giving him a taste of his own medicine.

"I'm six foot two, Mom. You didn't notice your own flesh and blood standing right here?"

"Now, now, Lucas, honey. Keep your shorts on."

It's impossible not to laugh, which I do heartily at Wolff's expense.

His mother is mercurial, and I think I love her.

Wolff

Mom is definitely on a roll today.

Despite being her favorite subject to poke fun at, I couldn't be more relieved to see she has her mischievous wit back. I know at her age it wouldn't be unheard of to come out of anesthesia with diminished capacity, but I'm happy she seems to have recovered just fine. At least mentally.

Mom doesn't miss a thing, observing closely as Jillian puts a hand on my arm and smiles up at me.

"I'm going to do the rounds with Nugget," she announces.

"So..." Mom drawls as Jillian walks over to a group of waiting seniors. "I see things have progressed?"

I drop my head between my shoulders.

Why is every old person around me determined to stick their nose in my business?

No use trying to evade the question because I know my mother, she's like the proverbial dog with a bone and won't let go until she has an answer that satisfies her.

"Yes," is my curt answer.

"That's all you've got?" she pushes for more, and I turn to her, exasperated.

"Mom, there's only so much detail you'll get from me on the subject, and *yes* reaches that limit."

When she presses her lips together to hide her smile, I

realize she's been pushing my buttons and enjoying every minute of it.

"I'm thinking I liked you better sedated," I tell her.

Mom lets out a peal of laughter. It is music to my ears, even though she's annoying me with her unapologetic probing. From across the room, I see Jillian look back over her shoulder, a smile on her face.

"So how is your arm?" I ask her, firmly changing the subject.

"Irritating. I can't even get myself dressed, and at breakfast I needed someone to cut my food for me. It's embarrassing."

My annoyance with her quickly disappears and is replaced with sympathy. I know how much Mom values her independence, which has been whittled away from her in increments over the past few years, but at least she had her mind and the use of her arms. Thank God her mind is still there, but she lost the use of her arm, and we'll have to wait and see how much of its function she can get back.

Getting older sucks. I've already started feeling the occasional pains and stiffness age seems to bring with it. Especially after the kind of activities I was performing early this morning.

It's bringing home the idea our time is limited. Our chance to experience life as we'd like to is limited. I use *our*, but really, I mean *my* time. I've been wasting it. Not so much with what I've done, but more in terms of what I've avoided.

My eyes are drawn across the room again, where Jillian is crouching down beside one of the other residents, laughing at something the man says. If I still harbored any ambivalence about getting involved with that woman; the events of a couple of nights ago, when her safety was at stake, made it abundantly clear I was already deeply invested. My feelings were well ahead, it just took my brain a bit longer to catch up.

Besides, if a woman like her—who has lived through one of the most devastating traumas someone could endure—has the courage to open up to new beginnings, what possible excuse could I have for not doing the same?

I freely admit, it's a little uneasy to let feelings guide my actions, but I'm sure that'll get easier with time. Life is too short to play it safe, and I've been playing it safe long enough.

"Is everything all right, Lucas?" my mother asks, putting a hand on my arm.

I turn my head and smile at her. "Yeah, it's all good, Mom."

But of course, it isn't, because there is still a significant threat out there; and Jillian is a target. Opening up to feelings means fear finds a foothold as well, and suddenly I'm in a hurry to get her back to the safety of the ranch.

"We could've stayed for dinner."

I glance over at Jillian, reaching for her hand and weaving our fingers together. She's sitting in the passenger side this time, wearing my too-large hat, her hair tied in a ponytail and tucked away underneath. I felt better having her within reach, rather than behind me where I wouldn't be able to keep a physical eye on her.

"There will be plenty of opportunities for shared dinners, once things settle down."

Settling down is a poor euphemism for neutralizing the

threat to her, but we've had a good day and I don't want to spoil it by highlighting the negative.

"Plenty?" she repeats in a teasing tone.

"I'd like to think so. Don't you?"

She nods, a smile on her lips as she concedes, "Yeah, that'd be nice."

I bring her hand to my mouth and press a kiss to her knuckles, feeling pretty pleased with myself as I focus my attention back on the road. It's already dark out, and it's not uncommon for wildlife to cross the highway and cause an accident.

In fact, that's just what I suspect happened when, half an hour later on a dark stretch of road between Happys Inn and the ranch, an impact suddenly has the Yukon's back end swinging toward the ditch.

My reaction is instantaneous; my eyes dart to the rearview mirror, and I brace my arm in front of Jillian, even as my foot slams on the brakes.

It takes me a moment to realize my mistake, but by then a dark SUV, similar to the Yukon, has blocked exit from my driver's side door. In the ambient glow of my headlights, I can just catch the reflection of a gun barrel aimed at the Yukon.

That was obviously not a deer or an elk that hit us.

"Get down," I manage to bark at Jillian, who is leaning over the back of her seat to check on the dogs, as I pull my gun from my hip holster.

I'm about to cover her with my body, when the passenger-side door is ripped open. I don't think, I react and take aim at the dark figure—face hidden behind a balaclava—who reaches into the vehicle.

The gunshot is loud in the confined space. So loud I don't even hear the second shot, I only feel the thud of the impact. I watch the figure crumple right outside the SUV and throw myself sideways across the center console. I'm trying to reach the passenger door, but Jillian beats me to it, pulling it shut and quickly locking it before ducking down again.

"Peanut, Nugget, stay down," she yells at her dogs.

I lean over to cover as much of Jillian as I can, while still able to monitor the threat coming from my side.

My gun is aimed at where the window in the driver's side door used to be.

"Are you okay?" I ask Jillian.

"I think so. You?"

I'm about to answer when the inside of the Yukon is suddenly lit up by headlights approaching us from behind. At the same time, I hear the revving of an engine and catch a glimpse of the dark SUV's roof as it pulls ahead and speeds off.

I cautiously sit up when the familiar face of Ira Nelson, a mechanic who works for Sully's wife Pippa at the Pit Stop, appears beside my door. The dogs both start barking in the back.

"You folks all right in here?"

I turn to Jillian. "Call 911 and stay put, I'm gonna check on the other guy."

Then I push the door open and ask Ira, "Got a gun on you?"

He pats his side.

"Never leave home without it."

"Good," I mumble, motioning for him to follow me.

I have no idea if the guy I hit went down permanently or is still alive, or perhaps even hiding in the bushes on the other side of the ditch. There'd been too many moving parts for me to keep my eye on the guy after I saw him go down.

So I move slowly as I round the hood of the Yukon, using the SUV as cover for as long as possible. I can feel Ira behind me, who seems to take his cues from me and is taking things seriously. When I carefully poke my head around the side, I immediately see the guy hasn't moved from where he fell.

A gun is visible only inches from his hand, and the first thing I do is kick it out of his reach. Then, with my weapon trained on him, I go down on a knee and feel for a pulse. It's faint. The bullet hit him mid-torso and he's losing a lot of blood.

"Jillian?" I call out.

She immediately opens her door and catches sight of the injured man. She has her phone pressed to her ear.

"Oh shit," she mumbles. "Is he dead?"

"Not yet."

"We're going to need an ambulance too," she relays to whomever is on the other side.

Then she catches sight of me and shock washes over her face.

"Make that two ambulances."

Twenty

Jillian

"I am *fine*."

He's grumbled that same line several times over the past hour or so, and his irritation is starting to get on my nerves.

My body is shaking and tears threaten when finally, the dam breaks.

"What do you mean you're fine? You are *not* fine. You were shot and you have a gash in your head from flying glass."

"It's just a flesh wound," he counters predictably.

"A flesh wound? You're not Arnold Schwarzenegger. You could've been dead. So I want you to sit here, wait for them to stitch you up, and stop being such a damn *man*!"

He tries to grab the finger I'm poking his chest with, but I'm not done.

"Do you know how hard it is for me to be sitting in a hospital—again? To see someone else I care about bleeding? Do you realize how hard I am fighting not to run out of here, away from you, because the thought of what might have happened terrifies me so much, I'm not sure my heart can handle another hole."

Suddenly he's there, all around me. My face is pressed into his chest, as his arms surround me and his mouth is by my ear, mumbling soothing words while I completely lose my shit in the hospital emergency room.

"I'm sorry. Don't cry, Jilly. *Shit.* I'm so sorry."

Good God, what is wrong with me?

I'm mortified. Not only do I embarrass myself by going ballistic on an injured, bleeding man in full view and hearing distance of the entire emergency room staff and patients, but worse; I'm embarrassing him and making him feel guilty.

Jesus, I'm a basket case.

"Where do you think you're going?" he says when I try to worm out of his hold.

"I've gotta go," I sob.

Apparently, the wrong thing to say, because the next thing I know my face is once more buried in his shirt as I'm lifted off my feet, and hear Wolff grumble, "I need someplace private."

"Second door on your left," an anonymous voice responds.

It's not until I hear the click of a door closing, he loosens his hold on me. As soon as my feet touch the floor, I step out of his arms.

We're in a small treatment room with just a hospital bed and one stool. Wolff is blocking the only exit, his arms crossed over his chest.

"Just us in here, sweetheart. Let's slow down a minute and take a breath."

"I'm a mess," I blurt out.

"Well...so am I, so you're in good company," he confesses, taking the wind out of my sails.

"You? How are you a mess?"

"When that guy pulled open your door and reached in for you, I've never been so fucking scared in my life."

He unfolds his arms and runs his hands through his long hair.

His hat got lost in the shuffle, and is probably still somewhere in his truck, which we left at the side of the road when EMTs and Jonas—who'd arrived not long after first responders got there—insisted Wolff be taken by ambulance. I wasn't about to let him go to the hospital alone, and hopped in there with him after Jonas promised he'd take care of the dogs.

"Look," he continues, his head still hanging low but his eyes fixed on me. "I'm new at this...whatever is happening with us. I'm practical, normally lead with my head and operate on training, and feelings don't really come into play, but that's obviously not the case anymore."

"Obviously?" I echo. I have an idea what he is talking about but I want to be sure.

It takes him a moment to respond, and by the time he does, I'm squirming under the intense look in his eyes.

"I thought it was obvious I have feelings for you."

That is very direct, and leaves me searching for a response.

"Well...I...uh, I suppose. And I clearly have feelings for you as well, which is why I kinda flew off the handle earlier."

We're staring at each other across this small, nondescript hospital room, and the air crackles between us. I'm not sure who makes the first move, but the next moment his hands cup my face and his mouth covers mine in a searing kiss.

"Oh, excuse me..."

The voice belongs to a young man in blue scrubs who pokes his head in the door.

"I'm looking for Lucas Wolff?"

"You found him," Wolff rumbles, slipping his good arm around my shoulders.

"Ah. I believe you need some stitches. I'm Dr. McDougall."

He walks in, a nurse behind him wheeling a cart, which she parks beside the bed. The doctor looks young, barely out of his teens, although I'm sure he'd have to be late twenties at least to have finished the required schooling to call himself doctor.

Wolff turns his head to me and mouths, *"Doctor?"* I swallow a chuckle.

"Why don't you hop on the bed? We'll get this done and have you out of here in no time."

First, he tackles the nasty gash on Wolff's forehead, which is right at the hairline. It requires twelve tiny stitches the doctor assures him won't leave much of a scar.

Next is the bullet wound, which is more of a deep groove through the muscle of his upper arm than it is a hole. Work on that takes a little longer, but eventually that wound is closed as well, and we're sent off with an appointment for Wolff to come back in ten days to remove stitches, and a sheet of care instructions he promptly crumples up and stuffs in his pocket.

A few people gawk at us when we walk through the ER waiting room, and I realize it's because both of us still have bloodstains on our clothes. Wolff grabs a firm hold of my hand and guides us to the sliding doors.

When we get outside, two sheriff's cruisers are parked in front.

Sloane and Sheriff Ewing are standing next to them.

"I take it you're our ride?" Wolff guesses.

"Yeah," Ewing confirms. "You okay?"

"As okay as you'd expect someone to be with a bullet hole and a couple of dozen stitches in their body," I snap in a knee-jerk reaction.

Wolff squeezes my hand he is still holding.

"I was lucky. I should heal up fine," he shares.

Ewing nods, already having dismissed my snarky comment, but Sloane is still looking at me, a smug grin on her face.

Whatever.

~

Wolff

"We towed the Yukon to the sheriff's department. We didn't want to mess with it in the dark on the side of the road," Ewing volunteers.

"That's fine. I'll tell Jonas. It's his vehicle."

Fucking hell.

I'm sure he's going to be glad he decided to lend the Yukon out to me. Hopefully, the only damage is to the driver's side window. I didn't really look that closely; I'd been too busy making sure the threat was neutralized and Jillian was safe.

"And my dogs?"

"Jonas took 'em back to the ranch as promised," Junior answers Jillian's question.

She took the back seat in the sheriff's cruiser and insisted I take the front seat. Sloane is following behind in her cruiser as a precaution.

"Any updates on the guy I shot?"

The guy had a faint pulse, and we did our best to staunch the bleeding from the hole I put in his body until the EMTs finally arrived. I'd like to say I don't give a flying fuck if he lives or dies—he was trying to harm Jillian—but I'd be lying.

I do care. I'd been forced to shoot a man in the line of duty once, and it was an experience I do not care to repeat. There is nothing redeeming about taking another man's life, I don't care how bad the man or how just the cause. I carry that man's death like a dark stain on my soul.

I'm not looking to add another.

"He's in surgery and I should be notified when he comes out," Ewing informs me, glancing over. "For what it's worth; from what we've put together, it was a justified shooting," he adds.

I nod and grunt my appreciation.

"As for the other guy; Ira had the presence of mind to memorize the license plate. Bellinger was on that as soon as he got to the scene. I'm sure he's gonna want to talk to you at some point, but for now he's trying to chase down the second guy." He glances over his shoulder at Jillian. "He also asked me to check whether you'd changed your mind about FBI protection."

It's quiet in the back seat, and I'm wondering if maybe what happened this afternoon did change her mind. I can't really blame her if it did.

"Maybe you should think—" I start, but as I turn around, I catch sight of her angry face.

"No. Not even discussing that," she says stubbornly. "It's not an option."

"Figured you'd say that," Junior announces beside me, a smirk on his face. "Even told Bellinger as much."

We're about to pass the road to Jillian's place, when we catch sight of flashing lights on the opposite side of the road up ahead, turning off toward Libby's small regional airport.

Ewing immediately steps on the brakes and pulls off on the shoulder, stopping even with the turnoff. In the side mirror, I can see Sloane pulling up behind us.

"Unmarked. Feds?"

"Looks like it," I confirm, counting three in total.

Typical dark SUVs with grill and dashboard lights.

The sheriff rolls down his window and gestures for Sloane to follow him. Then he waits for an opening in traffic, and cuts clear across the lanes, taking the exit toward the airport.

"What are you doing?"

Ewing darts a glance at me before returning his focus on the flashing lights up ahead.

"My wife works at the airport," he clarifies.

I guess that would explain why he's driving us into what could be a possible volatile situation. I glance over my shoulder at Jillian, who bulges her eyes at me. I shoot Ewing a pointed look and when the airport buildings come into view up ahead, he pulls the cruiser onto the shoulder.

"You guys wait here. I'll leave the engine running; get yourselves out of here at the first sign of trouble," he orders as he gets out of the vehicle.

I get out as well, in time to watch him jog over to Sloane's cruiser stopped behind us, and get into the passenger side. As they speed off, I round the hood and get into the driver's side.

"What is going on?" Jillian wants to know.

I lean over the steering wheel, peering at the cruiser's taillights as it makes a left onto the airport grounds. Farther to the left, closer to the runway, I can see the flashing lights reflecting off the night sky. It doesn't look like they are still moving, but it's hard to tell.

"I'm not sure. We know they're looking for the shooter and the vehicle, so it's a pretty safe guess they have reason to believe he's here somewhere. They may be looking for him in the hangars."

Despite the cold night air, I roll down the window to see if I can hear anything, but it's surprisingly quiet. I can't see any movement either. I'm concentrating so hard on what might be happening outside, I almost have a heart attack when the radio crackles to life.

"Wolff, come in..."

I grab the mic and depress the button to respond.

"Wolff here."

"Blue pickup heading your way. Don't let him pass."

Don't let him pass? And how the fuck am I supposed to do that? I had to hand over my weapon before I was taken by ambulance.

While I'm still debating my options, I catch sight of a vehicle coming down the road toward us. No headlights, that's got to be him. He's going at a good clip too. Behind the truck I notice several vehicles in pursuit.

"Is that him?" Jillian asks from the back seat.

"Yeah. Make sure you're buckled in."

When the truck gets within a couple of hundred yards, I turn on the cruiser's headlights, hoping to blind him, maybe force him to slow down. Unfortunately, it seems to have no impact, and with time running out, I only see one option left.

"Brace," I warn Jillian, as I shift the cruiser in drive.

Then I slam my foot on the gas and jerk the steering wheel to the left.

The truck never slows down, and the enforced grill

guard of the sheriff's cruiser hits it broadside. The impact is bone-jarring, throwing me forward against the restrains of the seat belt. Over the sound of grinding and squealing metal, I can hear Jillian scream behind me.

The next thing I know, bright lights shine in my eyes and I'm a little disoriented as I hear voices yelling outside the vehicle. Then a cool hand touches the side of my neck.

"Lucas? Are you okay?"

I lift my own hand to cover Jillian's.

"Yeah. You?"

"As far as I can tell," she replies dryly. "Except my heart is still lodged in my throat, and I think I've had enough excitement for one night."

I take her hand and turn my head so I can kiss her knuckles.

"Fair enough."

Suddenly, the door beside me is yanked open with a loud metal groan, and Junior Ewing sticks his head inside.

"You are one crazy motherfucker."

"You're the one who told me to stop him," I fire back, unclipping my seat belt and heaving myself out of the mangled vehicle.

Ten feet from me, FBI agents are slapping cuffs on whoever was driving the truck. He's down on the ground so I can't see his face, and right now all I need to know is that he's secure, so I can get Jillian from the back of the cruiser.

She's already out of the seat belt when I open her door, and I barely have time to open my arms before she launches herself at me.

"God..." Her voice is muffled by my shirt as she pounds a fist against my chest. "I wanna be so angry at you for that harebrained stunt you just pulled, but I'm just too damned relieved it is over."

Her head abruptly pops up and she seeks out Ewing.
"It *is* over...right?"

Twenty-One

"Your daddy is crazy."

Aspen agrees, nodding her head and bouncing on her toes as she hangs on to the porch railing.

Dan was off on an errand and Sloane asked me to look after the little one for a couple of hours while she went for her doctor's appointment. I ended up taking the little one out on the sled and dragged her around the paddock and to the barn and back, when Ama called us over to join Thomas on the porch for some hot chocolate.

"That boy is as smitten with that little girl as he is with her momma," Thomas contributes.

"I'm not sure how far that's going to fly with Sloane right now," I point out.

Sloane, who returned to the ranch after her doctor was called away for an emergency and her appointment post-poned until next week, spotted Dan unloading the surprise gift he picked up for Aspen's birthday. Never mind the girl doesn't turn one until April, still almost two months away.

From what I've been able to pick up from my perch on the porch, the cute little black-and-white Shetland pony had been well-trained and the price a steal he couldn't pass up, but apparently Dan didn't clear his plans with the baby's mama first. In fact, I have a sneaking suspicion his timing to pick up said pony while Sloane was supposed to be at her appointment was not an accident.

"What were you thinking?" I hear Sloane raise her voice at him. *"She's only one, she can't look after a pony, so guess who's going to be doing that?"*

Dan says something in response, but I don't hear more than the faint rumble of his voice as he obviously tries to calm her down.

"And what about when the team gets called out and you're gone for days at a time? I'll not only have a toddler and a dog, but also a newborn to look after, and now you're adding a damn pony?"

We've gone from angry to emotional, and I have a feeling Sloane has just shed a light on what really has her freaked out. It has less to do with the cute little Shetland and more with the fact she is pregnant.

"Hormones," Thomas mutters.

He's not wrong, but he'd better not say that to Sloane's face or she might lose it altogether.

From what Sloane told me, Aspen's father decided parenthood wasn't for him when the baby was only a few months old. I could see how she could worry history might repeat itself. Of course the rest of us can see Dan would never be that guy, but given Sloane's earlier experience, it may not be as obvious to her.

I have a feeling Dan may have clued in to some of that as well. I watch him take Sloane in his arms.

"What's going on over there?" Wolff asks, coming up the porch steps.

He'd been out on the ranch with JD this morning, carting hay to some of the outer pastures. We'd had our own argument about it earlier, since I didn't think the doctor's, "Take it easy for a few days," translated into going out on an ATV and hauling bales of hay. Wolff argued he would be careful but had to burn off some energy.

It wasn't until after he'd taken off, I found out from Sloane the second guy—the one Wolff had shot—did not survive and died last night. The sheriff apparently informed Wolff this morning, but he never told me. I suspect that may have been the reason he insisted on going out, needing some space—some fresh air—to process the information. I'm still trying to wrap my head around it myself, and I wasn't the one holding the gun.

"Nothing they can't resolve," I tell him, walking up and slipping my arms around his waist. "Are you done or do you have to go out again this afternoon?"

When he aims his blue eyes at me, I can see the fresh shadows there.

"We got done what needed to be done."

"Good, because I was hoping maybe you could drive me back to my place this afternoon."

"Wow. You're not wasting any time," Wolff scoffs, taking a step back. "Sure, I'll drive you home."

As I register his response may have been a little abrupt, he's already down the porch steps and disappearing toward the cabins.

I turn to Thomas, a little confused. "What just happened?"

But he just shakes his head. "Other than that communication seems to be a lost art? Heck if I know; must be something in the dang air."

Before I have a chance to react, Aspen suddenly starts crying.

"What's wrong, little one?" I coo, picking her up from her spot at the railing.

"Mama…"

I guess she saw Sloane, because she's twisting her little body in my arms to keep her mother in view. Of course her cries have not gone unnoticed, both her parents are already making their way over. Dan has the pony by the lead.

"Hello, sweetheart." Sloane plucks Aspen from my arms. "Want a sneak peek at what your silly daddy bought you for your birthday?"

"Isn't her birthday yet," Thomas contributes.

"Not like she'd know the difference," Dan calls back.

"Corn bread out of the oven. Chili is on the stove," Ama announces, sticking her head out the door. "Thomas, get your bony butt in here before the young 'uns descend and eat it all."

"They better not if they know what's good for them," he grumbles, tossing his throw blanket aside, and pushing himself up out of his rocking chair.

I grin and shake my head. These guys are like one big patchwork family.

"Where's Wolff?" Ama aims at me.

Right. I should probably do some damage control there.

"I'll go get him."

❧

Wolff

Fuck it.

If she wants to rush back to her place, let her.

I don't know why it pisses me off anyway.

The moment I open the door of the cabin, her dogs are all over me. They've only been here a couple of days but greet me with almost as much enthusiasm as they do Jillian. It'll be quiet here if she goes back home. *When* she goes back home. Only a few days and already I know I'll miss them. All of them.

So maybe I do know why. I like having her and her dogs in my space, but it seems evident she's not enjoying it as much, or she wouldn't be in such a hurry to leave. Hell, maybe it's better she does, I'm in a foul mood and not up to being social anyway.

Maybe I need to take Judge for a nice long ride, clear my head. He hasn't had much exercise since the search for the plane. It's a nice day and as far as I know, there's no bad weather in the forecast.

I change my muck boots for my riding ones, and step outside to head to the stables, when Jillian comes walking up.

"I was just coming to get you," she indicates. "Ama has lunch ready."

"That's okay, I'm not particularly hungry. I'm gonna head out for a bit, I'll grab something when I get back."

The expression on her face is a combination of confusion and maybe some hurt, but she forces a smile on her lips.

"Yeah, sure."

But when I start walking past her, she grabs my hand.

"Hey, listen. I hope it doesn't have anything to do with what I said earlier. I should've worded that differently."

I retrieve my hand from her hold and wave it dismissively.

"Nah. I just need to clear my head, that's all."

"Of course," she responds immediately.

For some reason, her look of understanding makes me feel guilty as hell. It doesn't stop me from going to the barn and getting Judge saddled up. I need some air and a bit of space to get my head straight, because I'm not myself.

Leading Judge out of the barn, I hear Jackson behind me.

"Hold up, will ya?"

I wasn't paying a lot of attention to my surroundings and hadn't noticed Jackson inside. He walks out behind me with his horse, Banner.

"What are you doing?" I ask as I mount Judge.

"Going for a ride, I guess," Jackson returns, swinging into the saddle himself.

I nudge my horse toward a trail that runs behind the barn and up into the mountains. Jackson follows close behind.

"I don't need company."

"Just pretend I'm not here," the asshole persists.

Whatever. If he wants to follow me around, I can't stop him.

To his credit, he doesn't say anything until I stop to take a break at the highest point on the trail. It's at the top of a rock face overlooking the ranch and the Fisher River beyond. From this vantage point I can even make out the roof of Dan and Sloane's place, which was only finished the fall of last year.

I loop Judge's reins around a low branch and find a rock to sit on. Stretching my legs out in front of me, I settle back to take in the view in peace. Jackson has a different idea as he joins me and hands me a can.

"Seriously? Beer?"

He shrugs. "Found them in the bar fridge in the tack room. Call it lunch."

It's still cold, and a sharp hiss escapes when I crack the tab. The beer goes down smoothly.

"Thanks," I mutter.

"You're welcome."

He cracks his own beer, takes a good drink, and belches when it goes down too fast.

"Charming."

He darts a glance my way. "Nobody here but us."

I know what he's suggesting but choose not to bite. Instead, I take another drink, but Jackson is ready to make a point.

"Most people think I attempted suicide because of this." He raps his knuckles on his prosthesis.

I'm surprised he brings up his attempt, it's not something he's talked to me about before.

"It isn't?"

I guess I'm "most people." I figured it was the trauma of the ambush that lost him his friends and his leg that had him swallow a cocktail of medications last year.

"No, that wasn't it. Do you know what I did in service of our fine country?"

I shake my head. I know—like the original High Mountain Trackers team—Jackson was special ops, which means what he or any of the others did, isn't exactly common knowledge.

"I was a sniper. A sanctioned killer."

I must've made a face, because he calls me out.

"What? Too harsh? It's what I was called in to do; eliminate targets. At some point you stop counting, after all, they're no more than a speck through your scope. Something abstract. And all of it is justified. Enemies to our country."

He takes another drink from his beer, and I wait him out, unsure what to say at this point anyway.

"Then one day your unit becomes the target, and you become the speck in someone else's viewfinder. Someone who believes wholeheartedly in their cause, whose actions were justified in their defense of their existence. Then by some stroke of luck, you wake up in a hospital and realize your leg is missing but at least you still have your life." He nods and glances over at me. "Suddenly those specks you saw through your scope become as real as you are."

He rubs a hand over his face and turns back to the view, taking another drink before he continues.

"For months after, you're encouraged to talk about the loss of your limb, of your friends, about what was done to you. Yet, no one asks about what *you* have done, and that is what has you waking up in the middle of the night, screaming. And keeping it in, not sharing what is really eating at you, can do a lot of damage."

It takes me a few moments to process all that information. I've got to admit, his story stirs something in me. As much as I don't think our experiences are necessarily the same, I can't deny I've been shoving down the news I caused another man's death.

"He wasn't my first," I confess. "But you're right, I don't like talking about it. What's there to talk about? I had no choice."

"It's not about that. It's about the taking of a life. That was someone's loved one, someone's friend, someone's family."

I wince at that. He just put into words what I don't allow myself to linger on, but that doesn't mean it's not on my mind.

"Look," he continues. "I'm not the only one, there are at least four other members of our crew who've at one point or another struggled with this. All you've gotta say is you're struggling, and any one of us will follow you to a quiet spot with a beautiful view and have a beer with ya."

Good to know. Real good to know.

"I don't recall asking you though," I kid, in an attempt to lighten the mood.

"No, you didn't, but listening to you blow off your girl-friend like that was an obvious cry for help."

Fuck. Jillian.

I took my bad mood out on her by getting pissed over something that could have probably been resolved with some clarification. Instead, I used it to distract from what's really been eating at me since this morning.

Throwing back the dregs of my beer, I crush the empty can and toss it at Jackson, who deftly plucks it from the air. Then I get to my feet.

"I should be getting back."

He grins at me. "Got some groveling to do?"

I adjust the hat on my head. "Something like that."

"You better get to it then. Looks like you've got a good thing going." He leans back, folds his hands behind his head, and crosses his ankles. "I'm gonna enjoy the view a bit longer."

I take Judge's reins, grab the horn, and swing myself back in the saddle.

"You know, that offer of a quiet spot and a beer goes both ways."

Jackson throws me a mock-salute.

As soon as Judge and I hit level ground, I give him my heels, and we head for the ranch at an easy canter.

Jillian is sitting on the couch with her stuff all packed up and waiting beside her when I get home. But before I can get to any of the things I thought up to say to her, she beats me to the punch.

"What I meant is that I should get home for the dogs, not because I don't like being with you, because I do. Even if the circumstances weren't ideal. But the dogs need their space, they need proper exercise and continuous training," she rambles. "And my business; I haven't looked at my emails in days, so it's about—"

I easily silence her with a hard kiss. While she's still recovering from the shock, I grab my opportunity to say something.

I decide to go with the simple truth.

"I'm sorry I was an ass. I took my bad day out on you. Thank you for clarifying your reason for wanting to leave, it makes it a little easier to let you go."

Her beautiful mouth stretches into a grin.

"You're always welcome to pack a bag of your own and come with me."

Twenty-Two

Jillian

"Do you want more of this?"

I point at the cast iron pan with the leftover spicy scrambled egg, sausage, and potato skillet.

I may have gone a little overboard with breakfast today. In fact, I've been overdoing it with the cooking in general since we got here the day before yesterday.

Maybe I'm trying to compensate for what he is missing out on in Ama's kitchen, because I want him to stay. Or at least make him want to come back. It's silly, and I'm well aware of that, but I can't seem to stop myself. I really enjoy having him in my space, and that is saying a lot for someone who has consciously lived alone for the past eight years.

"Sure, I'll finish it off if you don't want it."

I pile the rest of the food on his plate and turn to the sink to run hot water in the pan. Always better to clean right away before food residue hardens on the cast iron surface.

"Hey, you cooked; I'll do dishes," Wolff announces.

"I'm just doing this pan."

This is the way it's been since we got here; easy, relaxed, and uncomplicated. I fully expected to spend some time cleaning up, given that blood was spilled, and an army of FBI agents went through the place. However, someone beat me to it and the house was spotless. The company that cleaned it left their calling card on the kitchen island.

Wolff denied it was him, and he seemed genuinely surprised, so I'm inclined to believe him. Which leaves Sloane, who hasn't yet returned my message on the subject. In all fairness, she may be a bit preoccupied with the latest addition to her growing family, but I'll get the truth out of her at some point.

With cleanup taken care of, that left me to put away the dog stuff and my clothes, run a load of laundry, and hit up the grocery store to restock my fridge. The rest of the weekend was spent relaxing, taking the dogs for long walks and putting them through their paces, and most importantly, getting to know each other better, in every sense of the word.

He isn't a natural talker, but he opened up a bit, and the more I learn about Lucas Wolff, the more I like him. In a lot of ways, he's what you would expect of a federal agent, with a clear focus on justice, strong discipline, and an inherent desire to abide by the rules. The big difference with Wolff is his moral compass proved to be stronger than his willingness to toe the Bureau line at all cost.

The man is back to work today, heading to the ranch shortly, which is why I got up at five thirty to get breakfast going. A large part of me would really like him to come back tonight, but it may not be a bad thing to create a little breathing room. Things have been moving fast enough, and perhaps slowing it down a bit will give us a chance to get a handle on where this seems to be heading.

I end up tidying up a bit, putting stuff back in the fridge, rinsing out the coffeepot, and cleaning off the counter. I'm about to tackle the stove when Wolff comes up behind me and reaches around to snatch the sponge from my hand.

"That's my job," he mumbles, his lips brushing the shell of my ear and sending the tiniest of shivers down my spine.

"Fine. I'll get cleaned up."

When I return to the kitchen after brushing my teeth and throwing on some clothes so I can take the dogs out for a run, I catch Wolff on his phone. His eyes meet mine.

"If you wouldn't mind loading up Judge for me. I'll be there in ten."

He ends his call and slips his phone in his pocket.

"You have to go."

"Yeah. Jonas got a call from the ranger station in Libby. We've got a few hikers missing up on Sheldon Mountain. They were winter camping at the trailhead, going for day hikes, and were supposed to report in to the ranger yesterday, but never did."

"That doesn't sound good. It was cold out last night too."

He steps up and slides his hands over my hips to the small of my back.

"Which is why we're hustling this morning." He bends his head for a kiss. "I'll be in touch, and if you need anything, call the ranch."

I grin at him. "How ever did I manage without you for thirty-nine years?"

"Smart-ass."

Another hard kiss later, and I'm watching him walk out the door.

Then I turn to the living room where the dogs are sprawled all over the floor and the furniture.

"All right, guys...who wants to come with me?"

I take them for a nice, long walk. The gang is happy to be off leash, with full freedom to explore. At the ranch their free movement had been limited to the corral, mostly for their own safety. They're not really used to being around horses and could easily get trampled.

Of course, I end up carrying Nugget most of the way, but he enjoys these walks as much as the others; whether it be under his own steam, or mine. It does mean by the time we reach my backyard and I put him down, my arms feel like lead. Not just a good workout for the dogs, but me as well.

As soon as I unlock and start opening the back door, the dogs force their way inside and head straight to the front door, barking.

"Guys! Quiet!"

I wrestle my way through the dogs to get to the door and check the peephole. Coming up the steps are Special Agent Bellinger and a man I don't recognize. I'm not a fan of Bellinger and curse myself I yelled at the dogs earlier, now I can't pretend no one's home.

"Back away, guys."

Nudging the dogs out of the way with my legs, I open the door.

~

Wolff

. . .

"Husband and wife, Rick and Kelly Greenbaum, and her brother's name is Shaun McInnis. All from Missoula, all experienced hikers."

I tighten the cinch and give it a tug, making sure it's secure before leading Judge a few steps away from the trailer. Then I put my foot in the stirrup and swing myself in the saddle. The others are already mounted and listening to the ranger give details on the missing trio.

"They missed their check-in yesterday so when I went to check first thing this morning, their vehicle was still parked here." He points at a green Ford Bronco Sport at the far end of the parking lot. "I walked over to their site, found their camp still up, but it didn't look like anyone had been there for at least twenty-four hours. The ashes in the firepit were stone cold."

"No satellite phone? Two-way radio?" JD asks. "PLB?"

A PLB is a personal locator beacon, often carried for safety by wilderness adventurers who like to wander far off the beaten track. It's a device that can be activated to send out a distress signal and your location.

The ranger shakes his head. "Nope, and cell phone reception is bad here, but pretty much nonexistent once you move away from the road."

It happens all too often; people don't think they need the extra precautions as long as they stick to trails and are not that far out in the boonies. The sad truth is, especially in winter, it's very easy to get disoriented in these mountains. It wouldn't be the first time we found lost hikers less than a mile from either the trail they wandered away from, or a road to civilization.

"Okay, guys," James calls. "Let's move out."

There are four of us on horseback. Dan, JD, his father, James, and me. Jackson is manning basecamp and flying the

Matrice, our state-of-the-art drone with Sully. The cold weather has an impact on Jackson's stump and on his prosthetic, which is why he doesn't ride with us until the weather warms up. It's not that he can't ride, it's that we have no idea how long we'll be out there, and—as harsh as it sounds—we can't afford to have anyone slow us down. We can't waste time when looking for lost individuals in this environment, especially in winter.

JD is leading. Like his father, he's a great tracker. Most of the time we move in a single line, so the person leading needs to be attuned to the smallest details. Riding at the back of the pack means keeping an eye on the big picture. Scanning the terrain, looking for anything unusual that might be a clue.

It isn't hard to follow the hikers' tracks, which basically follow the set trail and is supposed to be a fifteen-mile hike that loops around a small lake before returning to the campground. It becomes tricky when the trail crosses a dirt road meandering up the mountain. The trail isn't marked on the other side of the road, and it looks like the group mistook a much narrower game trail for the hiking trail and started veering off.

Overhead I hear the hum of the Matrice, as the drone flies past us, zigzagging back and forth to cover a wider area. Up ahead JD holds up a hand to stop us.

"I think this is where they realized their mistake."

He points to one set of footsteps changing direction and heading into the trees.

"And they made another," Dan concludes.

They split up, which is never a good idea. There may have been an argument about how to proceed. Two of them stuck with the game trail, maybe thinking it would lead to the small lake where they might pick up the hiking trail again. The one who veered off might have reasoned if the two trails run parallel, they could cut through the woods and find the hiking path that way. The smart thing to do would have been to follow their own tracks back to the road, but nobody did, and now we have two trails to follow.

"Dan, you and JD follow the game trail. Wolff, you and me are following this single track," James indicates.

As we quickly discover, the path this hiker chose is not as straightforward as they might've been thinking. For one, the game trail runs farther up the mountain than the hiking trail does, so at the point the hiker decided to cut across, there is a fairly dramatic difference in elevation. Secondly, since there is no path, terrain would dictate which way to go, and unfortunately for the hiker, a steep ridge that appears to run between the two trails prevents him from reaching the hiking loop.

To make matters even more challenging, in areas along the drop-off, where there is little or no tree coverage, the snow is thicker. Unfortunately, with the weather hovering around the freezing mark—warming up during the day and dropping substantially at night—the snowpack becomes less stable. An ice layer forms on top of the snow which can move and slide, becoming a hazard.

Especially near a drop-off, the ice could create an over-hang—a shelf, if you will—that wouldn't necessarily be noticeable when you're on top of it. One misstep and a piece of the shelf breaks off. It can be very dangerous, so we make sure to steer well clear of the edge.

My radio comes to life with the sound of static before I hear Jackson's voice checking in. Up ahead James comes to a halt and pulls out his radio.

"Jackson, what's up?"

"We spotted something about half a mile north of where you are."

Fifteen minutes later, we find a large section of an ice shelf broken away. The tracks we're following seem to head straight for the edge. Two abandoned hiking packs were left at the base of a lone tree about six feet back from where the ice shelf appears to have snapped off.

"Two backpacks?"

"I notice that," James states.

It seems unlikely one person is carrying two backpacks. I dismount and start toward them to have a closer look, but James holds me back.

"We're not doing anything without a safety line."

I nod my agreement and get a safety harness from my saddlebags. James is in the process of securing a rope to a large tree trunk, when we hear horses approaching. The sound of snorting, leather creaking, or the occasional clanking of a bit gives them away.

"What are you guys doing here?" James asks, when JD and Dan appear from the trees barely fifty feet from where we are tying the safety line.

"Followed the tracks here," Dan explains. "One minute they were following the game trail, the next they turned into the woods."

"Tracks show they were running," JD adds. "Look."

We walk closer to where he's pointing at the snow. I can easily see what JD means; the toe of the print is deep, the heel virtually invisible, and a trail is left pointing to the heel as forward motion pushes the toe of the foot back.

Judging from the prints, it looks like these two individuals stopped by the single tree to take off their packs, and from there they appear to walk straight off the cliff.

James hooks the safety line onto my harness and I walk

as close as I dare to the edge, before dropping down on my stomach and carefully inching the rest of the way.

I spot one of the hikers right away at the bottom of the drop. I'm pretty sure it's the hiker whose tracks we've been following. He's lying face down, still wearing his backpack. Judging from the substantial amount of blood around the body, it seems a safe guess we're dealing with a recovery and not a rescue.

"I've got one recovery," I call back to the team.

Then I start scanning the drop, looking for the other two hikers. I find them a third of the way down. The woman's upturned face startles me; her eyes are open and fixed on me, and her mouth is moving, but I don't hear any sound. She's sitting on a rock plateau, her back against the wall behind her, and she's cradling the upper body of the third individual in her arms.

"And one, possibly two rescues," I update the guys, before yelling down. "Kelly? Hang on tight. We're coming for you!"

It's midafternoon when we find them, but it's another almost four hours before Kelly Greenbaum and her husband are finally pulled to safety and handed off to waiting EMTs. It took that long to get the necessary equipment and enough manpower up here.

Apparently, it was Kelly's brother, Shaun, who decided to go off the trail. The couple heard him screaming and ran toward the sound, not realizing how unstable the ice shelf they were standing on was. Rick landed poorly and broke his leg, but Kelly only suffered bumps and scrapes. They likely survived by sharing their body heat, although they both suffered from severe hypothermia by the time we got to them.

After they are on their way to the hospital, we still have

to retrieve Shaun McInnis. By the time the county coroner's van drives back down the bumpy dirt road—his body on board—it's nighttime. We load our equipment on the truck Bo and Fletch drove up here, and ride the horses down the mountain.

It isn't until I'm in the back seat of the truck on the way back to High Meadow, I have a chance to send off a message to Jillian.

Just heading back to the ranch now.
Hikers found.

Catch up in the morning?

I wasn't expecting a response, since it's already late, so I'm surprised when one appears just seconds later.

Sounds good. Get some rest.

Twenty-Three

Eleven hours earlier

"What do you mean she hasn't been eating?"

The man introduced to me as Agent Williams, an FBI EMT who apparently had taken over the care for Hayley, looks sheepish.

"Are you kidding? She's been in your care since last week; are you telling me she hasn't had anything since then?"

I'm pissed. Beyond angry they would let this carry on for so long.

"According to Dr. Chahal, she'd been eating at the hospital, but since we moved her to the safe house on Wednesday, she barely even picks at her food, no matter what we put in front of her."

"And you didn't think perhaps to move her back to the hospital?"

"We contacted Dr. Chahal; it was her suggestion to get in touch with you. Apparently, you built up a rapport with the girl."

"Her name is Hayley," I snap, upset these people seem to care so little. "And clearly she should've been returned to proper medical care."

This time it's Bellinger who answers.

"We didn't feel it was safe at the time, we were able to apprehend a nurse who appeared to be the leak at the hospital, but can't be sure she was the only hospital employee on the Ovando family payroll. And now the girl's uncle is scheduled to pick her up tomorrow, and we haven't been able to interview the girl. She still isn't talking."

I narrow my eyes at him.

"You sound more concerned about getting information from her before her uncle takes custody of her, than you are about the fact she hasn't eaten a proper meal in almost a week?"

Agent Williams is clearly uncomfortable with my accusations, but Bellinger's expression doesn't waver. The man exudes arrogance and clearly feels entirely justified.

Suddenly the picture becomes clear.

"You want me to help get her talking and are only using the fact she's not eating to get my attention, aren't you?"

He shrugs. "This is still a very active investigation, the girl is a potential witness, and you are the only one she's spoken to, from what I understand. I'm only doing my job."

Only doing my job, my ass.

As much as I want to slam the door in his face, I can't turn my back on a starving young girl who is traumatized, scared, and alone, when I may be able to help her. With a little help from Nugget, of course.

"Where is she?"

I curb the urge to swipe that smug grin off Bellinger's face.

"We'll drive you there."

I plant my hands on my hips. "I don't think so. I can drive myself."

I'm getting the feeling everything with this man is a power struggle, as he tries to stare me down. Not sure what he thinks he'll achieve by doing that, since it only makes me dig my heels in.

"I can't simply give out the location of our safe house," he finally sputters.

I bark out a laugh at that.

"Are you serious right now? Unless you propose I communicate with Hayley telepathically, I have to know where she is."

"She's got a point," Williams, who has stayed quiet and in the background for most of this exchange, volunteers.

It earns him a dirty look from his colleague.

"Besides," I add. "I need to know whether I'm going to be two hours from home or five minutes so I can make appropriate arrangements for my animals."

"Fine. It's in town. You can follow us," Bellinger concedes, already walking down the porch steps.

"I just need a few minutes to get ready," I call after him.

"Williams, you drive with her. I don't have the time to wait," he orders without even turning around.

As Bellinger drives off, I invite Williams inside to wait while I feed the dogs, clean up, and pack a few things in my backpack. The dogs give him a good sniff down, but to his credit he tolerates their, at times, invasive scrutiny.

"Do you have dogs?" I ask on a hunch as we walk to my SUV.

"I do. Well, technically my wife does. They came as a package deal," he explains, a faint smile on his face. "Gibson is a twelve-year old chocolate Lab and spoiled rotten."

I instantly revise my initial impression of the man to one a bit more favorable. After all, he clearly cares for his wife and the dog.

He directs me toward Libby, but I'm surprised when he tells me to turn left on Break Road, only a few miles north of my place. I can see why they picked this location; it's the last house on a dead-end street and far from prying eyes.

The SUV Bellinger drove off in is parked outside, but when we enter the house there is no sign of him. A woman is getting up from the kitchen table when we walk in.

"Any luck?" Williams asks her.

The woman shakes her head. "Only a few sips of milk and one bite of toast. She went back up to her bedroom."

"This is Ms. Lederman."

"Jillian, please," I correct him as I face the female agent.

She offers her hand and I take it.

"Stephanie Kramer," she introduces herself. "I hope you have more luck with Hayley than we've had."

I hope so too, but I'm afraid what little gains I had made with her in the hospital will need to be rebuilt, if that's even possible. I can imagine Hayley might feel like I abandoned her and I may have to earn her trust again. That takes time. Time I may not have.

"I want to be realistic," I caution her. "I understand from Agent Bellinger, her uncle is to pick her up sometime tomorrow. That's not a lot of time for me to gain her trust, let alone get her to talk to me."

"We're trying to delay him as best we can under the guise of security, but Mr. Vallard is getting very impatient."

She leads me up a set of stairs and stops outside a door, knocking softly.

"Hayley? There's a visitor here for you." Then she turns to me and whispers, "Good luck," before heading back down the stairs.

I open the door a crack and see the girl lying on her side on the bed, her back to the door. My heart breaks for her; she must feel so alone.

"Hayley?" I alert her. "Can we come in? Nugget really wants to say hello."

The moment I mention the dog's name, Hayley turns her head and shoots up in bed.

"Nugget?"

I open the door farther so she can see the dog I'm carrying, but I have to steel myself when I get a good glance at Hayley. She looks gaunt, her beautiful copper-colored eyes dull and sunken, her skin pasty, and her hair looks greasy and stringy.

When I ease into the room, I notice she scoots with her back against the headboard and grabs one of the pillows, cradling it in front of her like a shield.

Everything in me wants to run up and gather this child up in my arms, but I don't think she is ready for that. If she ever will be. Instead, I put Nugget down at the foot end of the bed and mentally cross my fingers he can work his magic again. I swallow hard when she lowers the pillow as he scoots up the bed toward her.

When I last saw her in the hospital, she'd still been confined to her bed hooked up to an IV and monitors. She'd been limited in her movements, but not so today. The pillow falls to the side as she scoops Nugget up in her arms.

But I know I shouldn't be cheering just yet when she throws an angry look my way.

Nugget may be forgiven, but I'm not.

I glance around the basic guest bedroom. There's not a hint of personality in here, just a bed, a dresser, and a small desk holding a few old copies of Nancy Drew books and a pen and notepad, and I get angry all over again. No computer, or even a tablet, no pictures on the wall, nothing to make this a welcoming room for a young girl.

The only redeeming feature is the view. Her window faces the rear of the house and has a clear view of the Big Cherry Creek, and the mountains beyond.

"Oh wow. Your view is almost the same as the one from my house. Same creek too. My place is not that far from here." I pull out the desk chair and take a seat facing her. "In fact, I was walking the dogs along the creek earlier this morning. If I'd known you were this close, I'd have walked a little farther. I could've waved at you, and you could've seen my other dogs."

She doesn't look at me—her face is buried in Nuggets shaggy coat—but I can tell she's listening to every word.

"You see, I would've loved to have stayed in touch, but the FBI felt it was safer for you to be brought here and keep your location a secret. Even from me. I didn't even know you were still in town, Hayley."

When her eyes lift to mine, I'm afraid to breathe. It feels like the silence stretches forever, but it's worth it when she asks me a question.

"How many dogs do you have?"

I have to swallow the lump in my throat before answering.

"Five, including Nugget. He's the smallest of the bunch though."

I go on to tell her their names, breeds, how I got them, and the kind of work they do, although I don't mention Emo is a cadaver dog. That's probably information she can do without. She seems to listen with interest, even occasionally asking a question.

I hesitate to ask her questions though, afraid it might either remind her of what she lost, or send her back into the silence I just lured her out of. However, I do really want to get her to eat, but I have to be careful how I approach that.

"I'm getting hungry," I announce, rubbing a hand over my stomach. "It's gotta be close to lunchtime." I lean forward and lower my voice conspiratorially. "Do they have any decent food here?"

She shrugs. "I dunno."

"Okay, well, if you keep an eye on Nugget for me, I'll go see if I can scrounge something up for us."

I get up and move to the door when I hear her behind me.

"You're coming back, right?"

When I look over my shoulder, I catch a look of concern on her face.

"Of course I am. I'll just be a few minutes."

Bellinger has made an appearance and is in the kitchen with Agents Williams and Kramer. All three of them are looking at me expectantly.

"And?" Bellinger prompts. "Is she talking?"

"I've been here all of an hour. I'm not a magician," I tell him. "My first concern is to regain her trust, and to get some food into her. What have you got?"

A few minutes later I head back upstairs with a tray holding a few Pop-Tarts, a banana, two small containers of yogurt, a piece of cheese for Nugget, and two bottles of water. Hayley's eyes zoom in on the tray the moment I walk in. Instead of going back to the desk, I slide the tray in the middle of the bed and take a seat at the foot end.

"Unless you want that piece, Nugget happens to love cheese," I tell her casually while I grab a spoon and start on one of the yogurts.

From the corner of my eye, I see her reaching for the cheese, breaking off a piece to feed my dog. I don't let on I'm watching her every move, and pretend to be focused on eating. But it's not until I rip open the package of Pop-Tarts, I see a reaction to the food when she furtively licks her lips. I fish one pastry out of the package and leave the rest on the tray. Then I take my Pop-Tart and walk over to the window, looking out at the view while keeping an eye on Hayley in the reflection.

"Did you know there's a herd of elk that sometimes comes down to the creek?"

"Isn't the creek frozen?" she asks from the bed.

"It is, but they seem to like to eat the fresh snow off the rocky shores. I guess that's how they keep up their water intake in winter."

With my back turned, I ramble on about other wildlife and tracks I've seen on my hikes along the creek, while I watch her lean forward toward the tray of food. I keep talking even when I see her hand tentatively reach for the second Pop-Tart I left in the package.

It's hard not to get excited when I see her take her first bite, but I don't want to make this a big deal. I feel it would likely backfire and we'd be back where we started. So, I'm not going to focus on it, and instead hop onto a different subject as I casually turn around.

"So do you like dogs?" I catch her with her mouth full, looking guilty, but I ignore it. "Because if you do, maybe next time I visit, I could bring Peanut along as well."

"I like dogs," she mumbles, her hand covering her mouth.

"Good. Peanut will love it. Word of warning though, she likes to cuddle as much as Nugget does, but she's the size of a calf and partially blind, so at times a bit clumsy."

"I'm used to big dogs," she volunteers. "We used to have a Great Pyrenees. His name was Max, but he died last year."

It's like a switch is flipped. She claps a hand in front of her mouth as her face crumples, and her eyes well up. All of a sudden, the stubborn and resilient mask falls away, revealing the devastated and scared little girl underneath.

This time I don't hesitate. I shove the tray out of the way and climb on the bed, pulling her rail-thin body into my arms.

"I've got you. Let it out, sweetheart, just hold on to me."

Her sobs, quiet at first, turn into deep guttural wails, as the full force of her pain and trauma seem to be ripped from her innocent soul. All I can do is hold on as her body shakes and heaves with the violence of it all. During the worst of it, the door opens a crack, and Agent Kramer sticks her head in, alarm on her face. I give her a light shake of my head and she slowly closes the door again.

At some point, I manage to move us in the bed, so I'm a little more comfortable with my back resting against the headboard. Hayley is plastered to my side, her head against my chest, while Nugget presses up against her back, anchoring her.

I don't really know this girl, but my heart is open, and will every ounce of love I have in me to surround her. It takes a while, but eventually the storm of grief wanes and is replaced by sniffles and occasional hiccups.

She never moves in my arms, and I'm not sure how long we sit like that. At some point I may even have dozed off, but then I notice—glancing at the window—the sun is sinking lower in the sky already. I have four dogs I need to get home to, but I hate leaving her here.

She's asleep when I carefully ease myself out from under her. I set the tray on the nightstand so it's right there for her, and write her a quick note.

Then I tuck her under the covers as best I can, lift Nugget under my arm, and stick my note under the corner of the tray, so it's the first thing she sees.

> Hey, Sweetheart, I had to run home to look after the dogs (I'm afraid their bladders are about to explode), but I PROMISE I will be back in the morning, and will bring Peanut too!
>
> If you need me for any reason, my number is 406-554-3911.
>
> See you in the morning.
> xox Jillian

I take one last look and slip out the door.

Twenty-Four

WOLFF

"You're up and about early."

Nella walks in from the kitchen area with a tray of pastries, a welcoming smile on her face.

Fletch's wife does all the baking for one of our local coffee shops, Bean There, which is why I stopped by extra early this morning.

"I didn't want to miss the boat like last time."

If you stop in too late in the morning, chances are all the good pastries are gone, as I discovered at eight thirty in the morning a few months ago when I was looking for some fresh croissants.

"Are you picking up for the ranch?"

I shake my head and clarify, "I'm taking someone breakfast."

"Ah, the woman who made you whistle."

Nella smiles, but doesn't ask any nosy questions. Fletch obviously shared. Bunch of old maids.

I watch her fold together a good-sized box and grab a pair of tongs.

"So what would you like?"

"I was just going to grab some croissants."

"You should give them a choice. Add something sweet, maybe something savory," she suggests, pointing at the display case which is overflowing with baked goods.

"Sure. What would you recommend?"

Ten minutes later I walk out with two designer coffees I don't much care for, and a massive box of croissants and assorted pastries I can't remember the names of.

When I pull up to Jillian's house, it's still pretty much dark outside. It's only seven; sunrise won't be for another twenty minutes or so. The house looks dark too. Dammit.

I may be a little early.

In my defense, I come bearing breakfast AND coffee.

A few moments later I see lights go on in the house, including in the front entrance. By the time I walk up the steps, the front door swings open.

Jillian is wearing a pair of leggings and an oversized sweater about ten sizes too big for her. Other than that, she looks like she just rolled out of bed, the creases of her pillow still imprinted on her cheek.

I bend down for a kiss but she has other ideas, snatching the tray of coffees from my hand.

"Bless your soul," she mumbles, carrying the coffees into the kitchen like precious cargo.

I shut the door behind me and kick off my boots. Then I join her at the kitchen island and set down the box before giving the dogs the attention they're begging me for.

"Have they been out?"

She shakes her head, her eyes closed and humming with one of the coffee cups at her lips. I wrestle my way through the pack to get to the sliding doors and let them out.

"Good morning."

Her eyes snap open and zoom in on me. "Morning, Lucas," she returns, an apologetic smile on her lips as she sets down her cup and approaches me.

"Ohh, suddenly she remembers my first name," I tease her.

She leans into me, her hands on my chest as she lifts up on her toes, and brushes my lips with a kiss.

"I like saving it for special occasions."

"And this is a special occasion?"

She opens her eyes wide, pretending to be shocked.

"Why, of course it is; you brought me a caramel macchiato."

"I see. So...does that mean there is gratitude involved?"

"Depends on what's in the box," she goads me.

I band my arms around her waist and lift her off her feet, kissing her deeply. She tastes like sweet cream and coffee, and I can't get enough of her. I'd like nothing better than to carry her straight back to bed.

The dogs' barking to be let in puts a halt on those plans, because the moment I set her down on her feet, she rushes to the box I left on the island, and lifts the top.

"Oh my God..."

She grabs an almond croissant dusted with powdered sugar, which promptly sticks to her face when she takes a huge bite.

"Decadent," she groans with her mouth full.

Decadent? That certainly sounds like it deserves gratitude.

"Have you met Fletch's wife, Nella?" I ask her, taking the second coffee and giving it a sniff.

"No. I haven't."

I'm a little distracted when she pops her thumb in her mouth and licks off the powdered sugar.

"Why?" she has to prompt me.

"She makes all of those." I point at the box of pastries. "She used to be a librarian at a university in British Columbia, but she started baking for a local coffee shop when she moved here."

"Is she the sister of Sloane's aunt, Pippa?"

"That's her. Anyway, I went to grab a few croissants for us—Nella's are the best—but she insisted I needed to bring a selection, hence the box."

"I wish I could eat all of them," she announces. "But maybe I could take one of these almond croissants for Hayley?"

"Hayley?"

"That's right too, you don't know. I went to walk the dogs after you left yesterday morning, and when I got back, Bellinger and another agent were coming up my steps."

She proceeds to fill me in on her conversation with them, and the only thing holding me back from giving the special agent in charge a piece of my mind is Jillian's description of Hayley's condition. Then—while we eat breakfast—she recites the events of the day, after discovering the safe house they were keeping the girl at is only a few minutes up the road.

"Good for you," I compliment her when she finishes telling me how she not only managed to get her to eat, but finally broke through Hayley's protective shell. "So you plan to go back today?"

"Yeah, but first I want to hear about your search yesterday, how did it go?"

I know as soon as I get into that, any chance of some morning loving goes out the window, so I give her the basics only.

"Found all three."

It's clear from the expression on her face, my answer doesn't satisfy her.

"What happened?"

I'm not used to sharing experiences with someone. A hangover from my Bureau days, when almost everything was considered confidential, I guess. Or maybe I was never much of a sharer to begin with, aside from the fact I never really had anyone to share things with.

Not someone like Jillian, who is made of sterner stuff than most. The woman has a cadaver dog; she searches for dead people. She's tough as nails, as she proved last year when she and Emo found a boneyard full of murder victims.

She's probably the one person I could—and should—share with.

"They got caught on an ice shelf over a cliff. One went down and ended up at the bottom, dead, but his screams got the other two running. Their combined weight broke more of the ice shelf off, but they survived the fall when they landed on a ledge a third of the way down. They were barely hanging on by the time we got to them."

"Tough rescue?" she asks, her voice warm with understanding.

I'm remembering the recovery of the body from the bottom of the canyon. It hadn't been pretty.

"The couple came out alive, so I guess that's a positive, but the dead guy was the wife's brother, and we had to virtually scrape him off the rocks."

She winces at my crass description, but rallies with a smile right away.

"Have you had a shower yet?" she wants to know.

"Had one last night before I rolled into bed. Why?"

Her smile goes from sweet to calculating. "Wanna have one with me?"

That would be a *hell* yes.

My body is already perking up in response before the words make it out of my mouth.

"Fuck yeah."

❧

Jillian

I catch a glimpse of myself in the mirror as I get dressed.

The flush on my cheeks is probably from hanging upside down while I blow-dried my hair, but the stupid smile on my face was definitely put there by Lucas Wolff.

The man has skills he put to good use in my cozy little shower earlier. He's bossy too, which I find I don't mind at all. He even offered to take the pack for a walk along the creek while I got myself ready for the day.

I'd intended to get an earlier start—it's almost nine now —but I don't regret a single minute of how my day started. I could get used to that. Although, if it includes a box of baked goods every morning, it might start impacting my flexibility, which—as I've discovered—is much appreciated by Wolff.

Stopping in the bathroom, I run a quick final brush through my hair before heading to the kitchen to pack up a couple of pastries for Hayley. Wolff should be back with the dogs soon. I glance out the kitchen window to see if there is any sign of them, when I'm surprised by a knock at the front door.

Seriously? Two days in a row?

I walk up to the door and check the peephole. Not Bellinger this time, but two men I don't know, although I recognize one of them from pictures I found researching the Vallard family online.

Grant Vallard.

Except he doesn't look anything like the suave, debonair businessman those images depicted. This man looks disheveled and his face is a mask of grief. Not what I expected.

"Please, Ms. Lederman, I need your help. Agent Kramer gave me your address."

Stephanie? A rush of fear something might have happened to Hayley has me open the door a crack. Whatever reservations I had disappear when the man in front of me bends over, his hands on his knees as he blows out an audible sigh of relief.

"Oh thank God, you're home. My name is Grant Vallard and I need your help. My niece is missing."

Alarm has me throw open the door.

"Missing? What do you mean, missing?"

His eyes are red-rimmed like he hasn't slept in days when he looks at me.

"She wasn't there. They don't know where she is."

I'm about to question him in more detail when the barking of dogs announces Wolff's return. As soon as he comes in the back door, his attention is aimed this way, his eyes locked on the man in front of me.

"What is going on here?" he inquires sharply as he makes his way through the house.

He crowds in behind me and anchors me to him with a protective arm around my midsection.

"Hayley is missing," I quickly clarify before Wolff starts growling or something. "This is Grant Vallard, her uncle."

"I know who he is. What the fuck happened?"

"That's what I'm trying to find out. When I left her last night, she was sleeping in her bed."

"Agent Kramer said she went to check on her but she wasn't there," Vallard volunteers.

"What time was that?"

"Four fifteen this morning," the second man states.

I've been so focused on Vallard, I barely paid attention to the other guy, until now. I'm guessing he's in his forties, maybe former military with short-clipped, dark hair with a little hint of silver, and the physique of a bouncer, from what I can detect under the heavy parka.

"Four fifteen?" I echo, quickly calculating she's been missing over four hours already.

"And who are you?" Wolff barks from behind me at Vallard's friend.

I give him a little nudge with my shoulder.

"Jeff is with me. He's my private security detail," Vallard answers Wolff before dropping his eyes to me. "They've been searching for her, and when I suggested they call you since you found her once before, whoever that special agent in charge is said they didn't need help. Agent Kramer slipped me your address, so I came here to beg for your help. I'll pay you. Please...help me find my niece. She's all I have left."

"Of course," I find myself responding, worried sick for Hayley.

The next moment I'm pulled inside by Wolff, who kicks the door shut. I immediately twist out of his hold.

"What the hell are you doing?"

"Stopping you from jumping in with both feet."

Fueled by anger and disbelief, I get up in his face.

"In case you missed it, Hayley is missing."

He puts his hands on my shoulders and holds on tight when I try to shake him off.

"Stop for a minute. You're blindly going to believe some guy who walks up to your door; a man you've never met before?" he calmly reasons with me.

"I know who he is," I argue. "I've seen his picture."

Wolff nods, but persists, "I've seen his picture too, but I still don't know him. Let me at least verify his story."

My adrenaline is pumping and I'm eager to jump into action, but I have to admit he's right. The personal connection I've formed with Hayley is clouding my judgment.

"Fine, but at least explain to Vallard why you slammed the door in his face," I suggest. "I'll quickly feed the dogs."

Especially Hunter and Murphy are going to need their energy. I'm going to need something of Hayley's for them to track.

Wolff slips back out onto the porch while I start filling the dogs' bowls, my mind already in preparation mode. I'll have to change into thermal underwear, fill my pack with water and energy bars, and get my snowshoes from the SUV. I'll probably take Hunter first this time, since she found Hayley last time and may be more motivated. Dogs have amazing scent memory.

"Here you go, kids," I mumble at my pack, setting down their bowls in their designated places.

They know not to touch each other's food, but that doesn't mean some of them—I'm eyeing Murphy in particular—don't try to sneak a bite given the opportunity. With each of them having a designated spot to eat, it's easier for me to catch them before they can offend.

When the front door opens and Wolff steps inside, I happen to glance out the front window and notice Vallard and his bodyguard getting into their vehicle.

"Where are they going?"

"I told them to go back to the safe house and wait for us there," he clarifies, pulling out his phone. "I'm gonna make a few phone calls."

"Okay, and I'm going to get ready."

I rush into the bedroom and dig my thermal undies from the basket of clean laundry I haven't put away yet. After I put those on, I add two pairs of socks, a pair of lined cargo pants, and a long-sleeved shirt. Then I shove my arms in a zippered fleece sweater, quickly fasten my hair in a single braid, and head back to the kitchen where Wolff is just ending a call.

"And?"

"She's gone," he confirms. "Bellinger's team has been out searching since they discovered her missing. Sounds like he held off on calling in any help, hoping they'd get her back before her disappearance became public knowledge. His job may be on the line."

"So then, who did you talk to?"

"Bellinger didn't answer, so I called Stephanie Kramer. She's an agent I worked with before."

"I met her yesterday," I share. "She seems nice."

"A good agent. She normally doesn't work with Bellinger but was added to the detail because they wanted a woman close to Hayley. She suggested you come to the house and she'll walk you through what happened."

"What about you?" I ask him.

"I'm going to run to the ranch and hustle up the team, can't have enough people looking for her. But I'll be right behind you. In the meantime, I have a two-way radio in the truck I'm gonna give you so we can stay in touch."

A hard kiss on my lips, and he's back out the door while I shove a few supplies in my pack and put the leash on Hunter.

A few minutes later I'm in my SUV, heading up the road to the safe house. My heart is in my throat and I'm struggling to keep my growing fear for Hayley at bay.

I have to find her.

Twenty-Five

"No."

He looks surprised at my outright refusal.

I don't think he's heard *no* much in his privileged life.

"I should've taken her last night. She's my niece, and since I'm paying your bill, I'm coming." he states firmly, completely disregarding my boundaries.

"I don't know anything about last night, but no one is paying me, and I work alone." I can already tell he's going to try and wear me down, wasting valuable time, so I add, "Your presence could throw off my dog's scent trail, and if you decide to follow me anyway, I will make sure the world knows you are responsible if we don't find your niece in time."

I watch Vallard's eyes dart toward Agent Kramer, who has been listening in on the conversation, gauging if he can count on her support. The look she spears him with speaks volumes, and he wisely chooses to let the subject drop.

"Walk me out the back?" I ask the agent, wanting a word with her in private.

I'd barely had a chance to speak with her alone, since Vallard had been hovering from the moment I got here.

The first thing I'd asked was to see Hayley's bedroom. Stephanie took me upstairs and told me how they'd found the window open and her sheets together and used as a rope to lower herself to the ground below. The sheets hadn't quite made it all the way, but the drop wouldn't have been that far. Bellinger had insisted the sheets be removed. When I noticed the comforter that had been on the bed last night was missing as well, Stephanie suggested Hayley may have taken it. She had also apparently taken most of the clothes the FBI provided her with.

But when I asked about the note I left the girl, the agent said she hadn't seen any note. That's when I first had a hunch Hayley may have gone south, following the creek.

The agent had mentioned Bellinger was convinced Hayley would be running scared and end up heading for town, looking for populated areas where should could find help, or at least shelter. I disagree with the man's assessment. I think he grossly underestimates what that girl is capable of. I've seen firsthand how smart and resourceful and courageous she is.

Stephanie follows me out on the deck and slides the doors shut before joining me at the railing.

"Okay, so you're sure they're focusing the search north of here, toward town?" I confirm with her, keeping an eye on the house.

"Positive."

"Have any efforts been made to pull in more resources for the search?"

The woman winces, clearly feeling uncomfortable as she shakes her head. I put a hand on her arm.

"For now, it's probably better. You know there is nothing worse than an unorganized search, and this already has FUBAR written all over it."

"I know," she agrees.

"Okay, just so *you* know, I'm coordinating my search for Hayley with your former colleague, Lucas Wolff. He is pulling together his search and rescue team, and our focus is going to be south of here."

She nods her understanding and I turn to Hunter.

"Okay, girl. Are you ready to work?"

I open the Ziploc bag and let her sniff Hayley's pillowcase, then I lead her to the shrubs under Hayley's window. She sniffs around the bushes and the patch of grass immediately in front of it. Then she sticks her nose in the air, and takes off toward the back of the yard. I turn and give a thumbs-up to Stephanie before following my dog into the tree line.

As soon as I'm out of sight, I pull out the two-way radio Wolff handed me and put in a call.

"Wolff, come in."

Within a few seconds the radio crackles to life.

"Go ahead, Jilly."

His nickname for me puts a smile on my face. Call me a sap, but I like he is the only one who calls me that.

"Remember that note I told you I left Hayley?"

"I remember."

"She took it. Bellinger is convinced she headed toward town, but I don't think so."

"You think she's trying to find you," he clues in right away.

"I could be wrong, but I have this gut feeling."

"Good enough for me. Where do you want us to go?"

"Is there any way you could come up the creek toward my place?"

"Yeah, there's a cross-country trailhead about two miles south of you, which should give us access to the creek. We've just loaded up the horses and are ready to roll."

"Perfect. Over and out."

I'm pretty sure I mentioned the dog run and kennel at the back of my yard when I was trying to get Hayley to respond to me, but even if she misses my house for some reason, I don't think she'll go that much farther before she realizes that. There aren't that many residences with a clear view of the water, and there isn't much at all along the creek south of my street.

Hunter doesn't hesitate when we get to the creek, and follows her nose to the left. South. I guessed correctly so far, and the more I think about it, the more convinced I become Hayley is trying to find me.

I'm going to make sure she does.

Wolff

"Two by two, on either side of the creek. It's possible she crossed the ice."

I personally don't think it's likely, but I'm not going to argue with Jonas, who wanted to come and is leading this search.

"Yeah, we don't want to scare her off either," I add. "Four men on horseback will likely just send her deeper into hiding. Let's not forget, Hayley doesn't want to be

286

found. Right now, the only person she seems to trust is Jillian."

I also voted against putting the drone up when Sully offered, basically for the same reason. If she spotted it, I could see her get spooked which would only make her harder to find.

"Right," Jonas affirms. "You guys get rolling and stay in touch."

Judge automatically follows Santiago, JD's ride. We're often paired up; the horses work well side by side, and JD and I make a decent team. James is riding with us this morning, and he is teamed up with Jackson, who insisted on joining us on horseback this time. He is still learning, and there isn't a better teacher when it comes to fundamental tracking than James.

It's almost ten thirty already by the time we get to Big Cherry Creek. This isn't a run-of-the-mill type of creek. There are large portions where the creek splits off into meandering streams of water that rejoin farther up into one single flow. The water is frozen, so it wouldn't have been hard to cross any of these smaller tributaries.

James and Jackson cross to the west side of the creek and all but disappear into the trees on the far side. JD and I stick to cover as much as we can as well. We want to locate Hayley without giving her a chance to see us coming. That might be a tall order, given that we're a bunch of large men on big horses, but we can move pretty stealthily when we put our minds to it.

The sky is a bit overcast and I wouldn't be surprised if we were in for some snow later in the day. Not that anything was forecast when I checked the weather before we left, but if there's one thing you learn quickly in these mountains, it's the weather can change from one valley to the next.

"Does she know you?" JD asks as we make our way upstream.

"Hayley? When we first found her, I carried her back to camp, but I'm not sure she'd remember much. I haven't really had contact with her since, that's all been Jillian."

"Any idea what made her run? I mean, she'd been in the care of the FBI for a while already, hadn't she?"

"About a week, yeah. I've been thinking about that too. The only thing I can come up with is Jillian told me she'd had some kind of breakthrough with Hayley yesterday. She'd been closed off and mostly silent up until then, and according to Jillian, it was like an emotional dam breaking. Maybe that triggered something," I suggest.

JD hums once before silence returns, and we focus on the search. Every so often JD will signal for me to stop as he takes a closer look at something that draws his attention, only to dismiss it as not relevant. Search and rescue can be tedious and long at times, and our biggest struggle is to stay sharp and not start missing clues because of complacency. Patience and attention to detail are definite prerequisites for this kind of work, but every small trace we find renews our energy, and when a search comes to a successful end, there is no greater satisfaction.

Sadly, so far there have been no clues to find, and the closer we get to Jillian's neighborhood, the less confident I feel.

The burst of static on my radio is loud enough to startle even Judge, whose muscles tense at the sudden noise.

"*Wolff? Come in,*" I hear Jillian's garbled voice.

"Go ahead."

"*Hunter led me almost straight to my place, where are you?*"

"Maybe half a mile out."

~

Jillian

"Good girl."

I close the zipper on the plastic bag after giving Hunter another sniff at Hayley's pillowcase.

She didn't really need it—she's had the girl's scent since we left the FBI safe house—but I've been trying to slow down our progress to allow Wolff's team to catch up.

A little over a mile into the search, I started getting the sense I was being watched, and not long after I thought I heard some movement behind me, but I couldn't see anything. That happened a few more times since, and right before I radioed Wolff, I caught a glimpse of something moving in the trees about a hundred yards or so back.

It's a fair guess it would be one of two possibilities; either Grant Vallard ignored my warning and was able to slip away from under the FBI's scrutiny, or Bellinger returned and is hoping I find Hayley for him. I'm guessing the Bureau won't look kindly on him losing a witness under his protection—especially when the witness is a minor and the heiress to a vast fortune—so it makes sense he'd do anything to get her back.

Either way, I don't want to lead either of these men to Hayley's whereabouts until I have a chance to talk to her alone and find out why she ran. That's why I asked Wolff and his team to try and run interference, while I find the girl.

Pretending Hunter needed another sniff of Hayley's

scent bought the guys another few minutes to catch up with us.

"Go find her, Hunter."

There is no hesitation as the dog pulls on her leash and leads me toward the rear of my property. I have to resist the urge to constantly look over my shoulder and focus on my dog instead.

I can hear my dogs barking in the house the moment we step clear of the trees. They must've seen us coming. Hunter seems unaffected by the ruckus inside the house and instead aims for the dog run on the far side of the yard. Even from a distance I can tell the small door to the kennel is open a crack. I always make sure I keep that closed so other critters can't get in and make a house.

I'm so focused on the small building, it takes me a moment to realize the barking from inside my house has reached a fevered pitch, but by then it's too late.

"Where the fuck is she?"

The first thing I notice when I whirl around is the barrel of a gun aimed at my face.

Twenty-Six

My adrenaline has been pumping hard since Jillian's radio call.

I quickly raised James and Jackson on a different frequency to get them up to speed, before JD and I urged our horses ahead. The guys were going to continue on the other side of the creek to make sure we didn't miss anything, while we tried to catch up with Jillian.

We covered that half mile to her place in record time, even though it felt way too long. When I recognized how close to her house we were getting, I slowed down Judge and eventually dismounted. I'd prefer not to announce our arrival. I can much better control the situation when I keep the element of surprise.

We leave the horses tied to a tree and proceed on foot, JD falling into step behind me as I try to keep as low a profile as possible, using the cover of the trees. We're just able to catch sight of Jillian's green jacket disappearing through the trees. It looks like she may be heading for her own backyard, but my focus is behind her, where I hope to see a glimpse of whoever she thought might be following her.

"What are we doing?" JD whispers behind me when I stop and settle in behind cover of a wide trunk.

"Waiting to see who's on her tail."

But when nothing moves after a few moments, I start wondering if it's possible Jillian may have mistaken the movement of some wildlife for a person. I guess it's always possible—she never said she actually saw a *person* following her—but I'd rather be sure.

"Let's move closer," I suggest, but when we get to where I saw Jillian cut toward the houses, there is still no sign of any pursuer.

Part of me wants to go after her and make sure she's okay, but I can't simply assume she misinterpreted the situation. From experience, I know that rarely ends well.

"I can retrace her steps and see if I can find any secondary tracks," JD suggests, offering a solution to my dilemma. "Why don't you stick close to her?"

Giving him a thumbs-up, I don't waste any time and turn toward her yard.

I hear dogs barking when I'm about to step out from the cover of the trees. I can see the back of the house from here and notice Emo and Peanut, their front legs up against the sliding door as they bark furiously at something on the side of the backyard.

I see her before I see him, her hands up defensively, and when I realize why, my blood runs cold.

The gunshot is loud, and when I watch Jillian sink to her knees, my heart stops.

~

Jillian

"Where's the girl?"

The bodyguard?

"Obviously not here," is my prompt response, trying to throw him off.

I'm sure she is hiding nearby or Hunter would not have almost pulled my arm from my socket trying to get here, but I'm not about to draw this man's attention to that.

"Bullshit. Your dog led you here," he counters, waving his gun at Hunter, who is sniffing furiously at the chain-link fence around the dog run.

"Yes, she did, she followed her own scent and that of her pack to her own house. The search was too close to her own territory, too many familiar scents. She did what dogs do naturally, she found her way home, that's all." I gesture around me. "Look for yourself, Hayley isn't here. The house is still locked up tight, you're more than welcome to check," I bluff, eager to get him away from the kennel.

The next instant, he lowers the gun and for a moment I think the threat is over, but then, without any provocation, he fires at Hunter who is inches from my legs. At her yelp, I sink down to my knees.

"Useless fucking dog," I hear him mutter, but I only have eyes for my sweet girl, who is lying in the snow, a bloodstain spreading from underneath her head.

When a second shot sounds, I throw myself on top of her, using my body to shield hers. I vaguely register the barking from inside the house has gone frantic, as I wait for the next shot to hit me.

But there's no next shot, only what sounds like a physical struggle. When I dare a glance over my shoulder, I recognize Wolff and someone else, struggling with the man on the ground. Trusting Lucas to take control of that situation, I push myself off Hunter and press my gloves against the wound on her poor head.

"Are you okay?" I hear Wolff call out.

"Yes, but Hunter was shot," I yell back, hearing the panic in my own voice.

I already almost lost her and Nugget when they were drugged, and now this.

I'm almost in tears when a hand lands on my shoulder.

"Help is on the way," JD's quiet voice sounds beside me as he gently nudges me out of the way. "Let me take a look."

I reluctantly let go of her, and as JD calmly takes charge of the situation, I start noticing things I didn't see before. Like the fact Hunter's chest seems to rise and fall with deep steady breaths, and she's trying to lift her head.

"It looks worse than it is," JD reports, as he allows Hunter to sit up. "Part of her ear is gone, and she has a nasty gash from her ear to just above her eye, but the bleeding has stopped, and I don't think the bullet penetrated anything essential."

Suddenly I'm pulled up to my feet and enveloped in a familiar embrace.

"Christ, Jilly. That was another few years off my life," Wolff rumbles, his face shoved in my neck.

When he lifts me up in his arms and swings me around, my eyes catch on a pair of copper-colored ones, staring at me from the cracked door of the dog kennel.

Hayley.

~

Her body goes rigid in my arms.

"*Hayley,*" she whispers in my ear. "Don't turn around, but she's hiding in my dog kennel."

Poor kid. After everything that happened to her already, we can add a shooting to her trauma. Both the dog's, and my shooting of Vallard's fucking bodyguard.

I'm pretty sure he'll survive that first shot, but it makes me want to haul out my gun and shoot the bastard again.

He fought me for a bit when I tried to get his gun away from him, but I managed to struggle him to the ground. Since I'm not in the habit of carrying handcuffs on me, I had to improvise and ended up using my belt to secure his arms behind him, which can't be that comfortable, given that my bullet ended up in his shoulder.

When I glance over to where I left him on the ground, I see he's trying to get his feet under him. Behind him, I catch sight of Jackson and James walking into the backyard from the direction of the creek. Jackson takes one look at the bodyguard, who is just struggling to his feet and in one swift kick with his bum leg, knocks the guy right back on his ass.

"I see you've been busy," James comments lightheart-edly, but his eyes are serious as he seems to take in the situation. "Need me to make calls?"

"Already done," JD—who is tending to Jillian's dog—responds. "Jonas should be here shortly and he was calling emergency services, so those should be right behind him."

I glance down at Jillian, who is looking up at me with a plea in those sea-green eyes. I know what she's worried about, she doesn't have to say anything.

"Guys, maybe it's easier if we move everyone to the

front of the house," I suggest. "Any more people back here, and Jillian's dogs are going to come through that sliding door." Those dogs have not stopped barking. "JD, can you carry Hunter?"

"Sure."

James, who is more perceptive than any one of us, looks from me to Jillian and appears to catch her furtive glance at the dog kennel. Then he gives me the slightest of nods and walks over to help Jackson haul the bodyguard to his feet.

"How do you want to handle this?" I ask Jillian when the others start moving around the side of the house.

"Well, I can't leave her out here, but I'm not about to hand her back to the FBI. She needs my help; she came looking for me for a reason, and I intend to find out what that is before I do anything."

There is a note of challenge in her tone, daring me to disagree with her.

I don't. Hayley came here looking for a safe haven and that little girl deserves to find one. Even if it may end up being short-lived.

"Can you get in the back door?" I ask her.

"Yes."

"Good. I'm going to go out front and make sure no one comes back here, while you get her inside the house. As far as anyone needs to know, you're trying to calm down your dogs."

She nods, mouthing, "Thank you," at me.

"Go." I give her a little nudge in the direction of the dog run.

~

Jillian

298

I rush over to the kennel.

"Hayley?" I whisper when I can't see her face in the crack between the door and the frame anymore.

From inside the kennel, I hear a slight rustle of the straw I leave in there for my dogs. When I ease the door open, it takes my eyes a moment to adjust to the deep shadows inside. The first thing I notice is the colorful comforter from Hayley's bed at the safe house. Then I see her, her back against the far wall.

"The man you saw me hug? That's Wolff, he's my boyfriend. Maybe you remember he carried you all the way from that cave where we found you to the ambulance? Right now, he is making sure no one comes into the back-yard so I can get you safely inside my house, but we don't have much time."

I reach out my hand to her. For a brief moment I'm worried I may have no choice but to call in help to get her out of here, but then she grabs on to it.

"My dogs are barking like crazy and three of them aren't tiny like Nugget, but I promise they're all bark and no bite. You'll love them."

I babble on as I grab her comforter and wrap it around her shoulders, tucking her to my side as I hurry her through the yard to the back porch. There I have to let go of her to dig through my pockets for my damn house keys, hoping to God I didn't lose them somewhere. I find them in the zippered inside breast pocket of my coat, and I fumble to grab hold of the right key with my gloved fingers.

I breathe a sigh of relief as I finally manage to locate the right one and am about to slip the key in the door lock. The creak of one of the steps up to the deck has me holding up short and when I look up, I catch the reflection of a man wearing a balaclava coming up behind us. He is carrying some kind of pipe in his hand.

"Hayley, duck!" I scream, whipping around when I see him hauling back to take a swing.

She drops down instantly, the pipe missing her by a hair, but catching me full on the left shoulder. My teeth slam together at the explosion of pain, rendering my entire arm useless, as the pipe clatters to the deck. But that doesn't stop me when I see him reaching for Hayley, and I launch myself at him, wielding my keys in my right hand as my only weapon.

He's bent over and not expecting my attack, so even though he's larger than I am, I'm able to knock him off-balance and land on top of him. All I hear is the roaring of blood in my ears as I jab blindly at his head and face with my keys, and scream at the top of my lungs.

The only thought in my head is to keep him away from Hayley, so I fight with everything I have in me.

I'm still fighting when a pair of strong arms lift me off him.

"Easy..."

It takes me a moment to recognize the deep rumble in my ear as Jonas's voice. Jackson and a sheriff's deputy I don't recognize are making quick work of putting our attacker in handcuffs. When I turn my head to see if Hayley is okay, I see her cradled in Wolff's arms, her face pressed to his chest. His eyes are fixed on me as his mouth mumbles soothing words to her.

Only then do I feel the fight drain out of me, and I hang like a sack of potatoes against Jonas.

"You got him good, Jillian," Jackson comments.

I look to see what he's referring to when I notice blood

covering what little I can see of the man's face. When Jackson pulls the balaclava off, my stomach roils and I can feel the contents surging up my esophagus, but I'm not sure if it's because it looks like I took out one of his eyes, or because the mask was hiding Grant Vallard's face.

"Breathe through your nose, slugger," Jonas rumbles behind me.

I promptly drop the keys I was still clutching to the deck.

Twenty-Seven

"He refuses to give up the Ovando family, claims he doesn't know who we're talking about, but he's happy to spill the beans on Grant Vallard."

Stephanie Kramer stopped by to give us an update on the case. Apparently Special Agent in Charge Bellinger was taken off the case and shipped off to an unknown destination. The Bureau brass didn't hesitate after discovering not only had a minor witness gone missing on his watch, but Bellinger failed to make a report. He didn't take the appropriate steps and, instead of calling in resources to mount a proper search, took two agents on a wild-goose chase for hours, all in hope of covering up the fact he'd lost her in the first place.

So, Special Agent in Charge Bellinger was sent packing and Stephanie was asked to stick around to assist in finishing up the investigation. What she doesn't know is it was Jonas who spilled the beans on Bellinger to an old friend of his, who happens to be high-up in the Bureau hierarchy.

We retreated to Jillian's kitchen, since the dogs have taken over the living room. Hunter has earned the prime spot on the couch. She seems to be doing well after her ordeal, despite missing part of her ear. It doesn't seem to bother her much though.

It's been three days since the search for Hayley ended in such dramatic fashion. I've been kicking myself ever since. I should've made sure the backyard was secure before leaving Jillian and the girl unprotected. As a result, Jillian is wearing her arm in a sling, and will be for several weeks. Vallard's attack left her with a dislocated shoulder. It was set in the hospital and luckily didn't require surgery to repair, but it can take up to twelve weeks before she has full use of that arm again.

We were able to surmise Vallard had been hiding under the deck. There had been two sets of tracks following Jillian along the creek. Both sets were found cutting through her neighbor's yard and around the side of Jillian's place.

According to Stephanie, Vallard maintains his story that he was following Jeff Shapiro, his bodyguard, who he had become suspicious of. He apparently also swears he was trying to rescue his niece and mistook Jillian for Shapiro when he came at her with a metal pipe he'd found under the deck.

The only believable claim Vallard is making is when he points a finger at the Ovando family, suggesting his bodyguard must've been an agent for the family, and his objective was to finish the job of killing off the entire Vallard clan.

When confronted with the question of why they wouldn't have killed him off already, Vallard came up with the suggestion perhaps they needed him to take control of the company first. In his version, of course, he was another victim.

What Stephanie just finished telling us is the bodyguard sings a different tune. He was specifically hired by Grant Vallard himself to find and kill Hayley Vallard who is the rightful heiress to not only Vallard Holdings but the entire Vallard fortune.

I'm more inclined to believe the hired goon.

"His version seems more plausible," I volunteer. "Have you found any evidence this Shapiro is connected to the Ovandos?"

Stephanie shakes her head. "Nothing. I think you're right. I don't believe Vallard was ever in any danger and had no reason to need a bodyguard. The current consensus is that Grant was definitely in cahoots with the Ovandos to take out his family. We spoke with some members of the board at Vallard Holdings, who were able to inform us that Grant Vallard had been trying to push through a contract with a Bolivian manufacturer of soybean oil last year. This landed him in a major fight with both his mother and brother, who had done some research and discovered the manufacturing company was connected to the Ovando crime family. As a result of that falling out, Sarah-May Vallard, the family matriarch, had her youngest son written out of her will."

"Ouch, that must've stung," Jillian observes, as she gets up to grab the coffeepot. "Can I top anyone up?"

"Not for me," Stephanie declines.

I hold up my mug. "I'll have a bit more, thanks."

"Getting written out of the will sure makes for one hell of a motive though," Jillian states, returning us to the topic.

"Yes, it does," Stephanie confirms. "We also have means, albeit in the form of Puma who, along with his associate, we were able to place in Whistler at the same time the Vallards were there. When he was taken into custody after trying to get away from us at the Libby airport, we found evidence in the form of text messages between him and Grant Vallard; further proof Vallard may not have been in the country, but he was definitely in the driver's seat. From those messages we've been able to glean that as soon as Vallard heard his niece had survived the crash, he instructed Puma to make sure he finished the job."

"I just find it hard to believe Puma would even take orders from someone like Vallard," I point out. "I mean, the man is a died-in-the-wool criminal, and tightly connected to the Ovando family."

"Not that hard to believe when you think about the millions and millions of drugs the family could pipeline into the U.S. and Canada through Vallard Holdings. Grant was the key to that pipeline and without him the Ovando family has nothing. Puma was likely getting pressure from all sides, which is why he probably went after you..." She points at Jillian. "Thinking you'd be able to lead him to Hayley."

"Except Wolff foiled that plan," Jillian comments with a gentle smile for me.

Regrettably, it took killing a man, but I would do it again without hesitation to keep Jillian or Hayley safe.

"Right," Stephanie confirms. "And we know how that ended. Of course, Puma isn't saying a word, but we're still able to piece information together. I think the more we uncover, the more solid our case against Grant Vallard will be."

"Good. I hope the bastard never sees the light of day again," I grumble.

"Even if he does, it'll only be half with just the one eye," she fires back, immediately slapping her hand over her mouth. "Too soon?" she mumbles, her eyes wide.

Luckily, it's Jillian who starts laughing first, breaking the uneasy silence that follows. She's been struggling a bit with the knowledge she'd actually gouged the man's eye out with her keys. As justified as she was, fighting for her life, the responsibility still weighs on her. Gallows humor; if you're in law enforcement or the military it's an often-used coping tool to deal with some of the atrocities you encounter, but it can be off-putting for the regular public. I guess it's working for Jillian as well.

"Talking about a solid case; has she said anything yet?" Kramer asks.

I let Jillian answer that. When it comes to anything to do with Hayley, I defer to her. She fought like a goddamn momma bear, and I have no doubt she would've laid down her life trying to protect that girl.

Hayley has stuck to Jillian like glue these past few days and has been staying here. Given the trauma she'd already been through, no one has had the heart to mess with the status quo, not even the social worker with CPS, who showed up here yesterday. Jillian is now listed on all the paperwork as Hayley's foster parent.

I'm sure with time there'll be other hoops still to jump through, given the kid's massive wealth, but for now the main concern is to try and give her the space to process and heal. Which is why Jillian has not allowed Hayley to be questioned, and has shielded her as best she can from the investigation.

"She hasn't," Jillian answers. "And I know you'd like to button up your case nice and tight with whatever information she might be able to give you, but unless Hayley decides to volunteer something, you'll have to make do without."

As if she knew we were talking about her, I hear the spare bedroom door open down the hall. Next, a parade of dogs rushes into the kitchen, heading straight for the back door, followed closely by Hayley. She hesitates for a moment when she catches sight of Stephanie.

"Good movie?" Jillian asks her.

The girl spends a lot of time in her room, usually with at least some of the dogs, so Jillian had me move the TV she had in her bedroom to the spare room.

"Pretty good."

Hayley speaks in a soft voice. Everything about her is very subdued, which doesn't seem to fit the courage and spirit she's already shown, but hopefully it's just a matter of time before those return.

She moves past us to the door to let the dogs out, just as Stephanie gets to her feet.

"I should be heading out, but I'll keep in touch." Then she turns to Hayley. "If there is ever anything I can do for you, let me know. Wolff knows how to get in touch with me."

As Jillian shows the agent to the door, Hayley moves closer to me.

"Is that your real name?"

"What, Wolff? Yeah, it's my last name. My first name is Lucas, but only my mother and sometimes Jillian call me that."

"Oh." She seems to think on that for a bit before she asks, "So, what should I call you?"

I smile at her serious expression.

"You can call me whatever you like."

"I like Lucas."

I nod. "Then Lucas it is."

Jillian

"Does Lucas live with you?"

From the mouths of babes...

Hayley is poking a stick at some elk tracks we found on our dog walk along the creek.

"Not officially, but I guess it must look that way," I respond.

In fact, Lucas has stuck close to my place since Monday. Leaving for a couple of hours here and there, but always coming back. With my arm still immobilized, he's been doing most of the cooking, grocery shopping, and has even put in a load or two of laundry. Every night I fall asleep with his strong body curved around me, something I'm grateful for when I startle awake from another nightmare.

"Where does he live then?"

"He lives in a cabin at a ranch just down the road."

"A ranch with horses?"

Her voice is as excited as the expression on her face.

"Yup. Lucas has his own horse; his name is Judge. He's really big, but very gentle." I grin when I see her mouth drop open. "I take it you like horses?"

I love that she's taken to calling Lucas by his given name. As much as I think Wolff suits him, I like Lucas better, it feels more personal, even intimate.

"I love them. I always wanted one, but Dad says first I have to be old enough to look after it on my..." Her voice drifts off as she realizes what she just said.

A fat tear starts rolling down her cheek and I feel my own eyes well up. I curse my sling as I clumsily pull her into a one-armed embrace, but her two arms more than make up for it as they band around my waist.

I manage to hold my own tears at bay as I wait out hers, while the dogs crowd us, sniffing and prodding with their noses, wanting in on the action.

"You know..." I start when the dogs finally manage to pry us apart. "I'm sure Lucas would be happy to show you around the ranch."

"Really? Would you come?"

"Sure. We can talk to him tonight when he gets back."

Lucas left early this morning to deliver a horse to a rodeo training facility in Polson with Jackson. He mentioned he'd probably be gone most of the day.

The prospect puts a little smile on Hayley's face, even if it doesn't chase the shadows from her eyes. I doubt anything would be able to accomplish that.

"Would you like some hot chocolate to warm up?" I offer when we're almost back to the house. "Maybe build a fire too?"

It's been bitter cold these last few days. So cold my eyelashes have frost on them.

"With marshmallows?"

"I don't know if I have any, but we'll check the pantry."

Once inside, Hayley takes on the task of removing the booties I make the dogs wear when it's this cold, while I dive into the pantry to search for supplies.

"No marshmallows," I announce when I resurface. "But...I do believe I have heavy cream I can whip to go on top of the hot chocolate."

I find the container in the fridge and pull out a bowl and my hand mixer.

"Actually, maybe you can whip the cream while I do the chocolate?"

A few minutes later I'm at the stove, stirring cold milk into the chocolate syrup I made with real cocoa, sugar, and a splash of water, when Hayley suddenly turns off the mixer and looks up at me.

"Grandma would order me hot chocolate at the après-ski at the hotel in Whistler."

I immediately shut off the burner underneath the pan and turn to face her.

"I'm so sorry. We can make something else," I offer.

I can see her swallow hard as she shakes her head. "No, that's okay. It hurts but it's a good memory, right?"

The hopeful way she looks at me tears at my heart.

"You bet. You hold on to those good memories, because as sad as they make you now, at some point they'll become like a warm blanket to hug you when you need it."

She appears to think on that for a moment before nodding and switching the mixer back on.

Then I turn back to the stove and relight the burner, letting my mind drift back to the last time I made hot chocolate for Macy, and let the warm memory wrap around me.

Twenty-Eight

"Keep your hands low, and if you want, you can grab on to the saddle horn."

I bite off a smile when I see the intense concentration on Hayley's face.

Carmi—Sully and Pippa's thirteen-year-old—was kind enough to let Hayley use her horse, Tinker Bell. She's a pretty Haflinger, a smaller breed with beautiful fawn hide and flax-colored mane and tail, and Hayley was head over heels the moment she laid eyes on her.

It turns out the girl isn't a total newbie, she mentioned she's ridden ponies before but never without someone leading alongside. Tinker Bell is a bit bigger than a pony, and I'm not about to run alongside. Not when Hayley insisted she could do it on her own. It's the best way to learn.

I don't need to look behind me to know Jillian is

watching from the porch and probably wringing her hands again. Even though she can ride herself, she's not quite as comfortable around horses as she is around dogs, but to her credit, she hasn't interfered and seems to trust I know what I'm doing.

Still, she was out here watching from the porch the first time Hayley got on Tinker Bell a couple of days ago, and I have a feeling it'll be a while before Jillian feels comfortable enough to take her eyes off the girl. She is still in full protection mode.

"Can we go for a trail ride?" Hayley asks, a bright blush staining her cheeks and her eyes sparkling.

I chuckle at her enthusiasm.

"Maybe when the snow melts," I suggest. "The trails can be a bit treacherous in the winter."

That also gives her a chance to get some more practice in. I'd like to see her a bit more at home on horseback before taking her out of the safety of the corral. The chances of the horse getting spooked in here are slim, and even if she is tossed or falls, I'll be right here to pick up the pieces, so to speak.

"Can I go faster?" the little daredevil asks.

"Up to you. Remember what I told you? Lean forward in the saddle a little, press your knees into her sides, and click your tongue," I remind her. "And if you want her to slow down, gently tighten up on the reins and say *whoa*."

From the corner of my eye, I see Jackson walking up, and I move to join him at the fence, making sure I keep Hayley in my sights.

"She seems to be getting the hang of it," he observes.

I grunt in agreement, before adding, "She certainly doesn't seem to have any fear."

I watch as she manages to urge Tinker Bell into a gentle canter, still bouncing around the saddle too much.

"Remember to relax your butt in the seat," I call out to her.

With enough practice, all of these things will become second nature, and she won't even have to think about them.

"Are you by chance going to be around tonight?" Jackson asks.

A fair question, since I've slept in my own bed only once or twice in the past couple of weeks.

"I can be. What do you need?"

"Bought a new bed I need to pick up in town tonight. It's a heavy son of a bitch so I can't do it by myself."

"New bed? Got big plans I don't know about?" I tease him.

"Yeah, right," he scoffs. "No, I got one of those adjustable beds. It's supposed to be better for my back."

Over the past months, Jackson has slowly started opening up. Before he would blow off any questions about his physical condition, even though at times it was clear he was struggling. Then when we were making a delivery in Polson last week, and I caught him wince lowering the gate on the trailer, he mentioned his back was bothering him. Apparently, it's not uncommon for leg amputees to develop back problems.

It's the first time Jackson's ever admitted to any pain to my knowledge.

"Yeah, no problem. I'll help."

"You sure?"

"Of course. What time?"

"Six thirty okay?"

I mention it to Jillian when she joins the kid and me in the stable after Hayley's ride.

"Why don't we go grab some takeout in town—something easy—and bring it home? We'll have an early dinner."

"Did you see me?" Hayley pipes up before Jillian has a chance to answer me.

"I saw. You did really well," Jillian compliments her, a big smile on her face.

"Lucas says we can go for a trail ride," the little minx adds.

"Once all the snow is melted, yes," I amend her statement, before adding, "Don't forget to put the saddle back in the tack room and grab the grooming bucket."

Her face drops a little, but I ignore it. I'm not sure what her life was like before—whether she was spoiled or not—but I happen to believe it's important for her to learn any privilege comes with responsibility. So along with the privilege of riding a horse—or owning any pet for that matter—comes with the responsibility of looking after it.

"You know what's interesting?" Jillian says, as we watch Hayley struggle to carry the heavy saddle to the tack room. "When she first brought up wanting a horse, she said her father told her she had to be old enough to look after it first. You're teaching her the same thing."

She slips her arm through mine and gives it a squeeze.

"You're good with her. Easy and natural." She sighs deeply before admitting, "I'm finding it hard not to wrap her up and pack her away safely."

I slip a hand behind her neck and turn her toward me, resting my forehead against hers.

"Understandable. Of course you are protective of her, but as much as it costs you, I don't think you're coddling her at all.

You're still giving her the freedom to discover and explore on her own, no matter how hard it is. I don't pretend to be an expert on the subject, but to me that's what good parenting is."

"Thanks," she mumbles when I drop a kiss on her lips.

When Hayley returns with the grooming bucket, I let go of Jillian and grab one of the brushes. The kid isn't quite tall enough to brush the horse's back, so I give her a hand. I step into the stall with her, while Jillian watches from the other side of the door.

"By the way, we'll be fine if you want to spend more time at the ranch," she suggests, not sounding quite as casual as I think she'd hoped to.

I catch her eye over Tinker Bell's back.

"Do you want me to spend more time at the ranch?"

She shrugs. "That's not the point."

"Oh, but it is," I lob back, noticing Hayley is paying very close attention to our conversation.

Maybe this isn't a conversation she needs to be part of.

I toss my brush in the bucket and open the stall door.

"We'll be right back," I tell Hayley as I grab Jillian's hand and pull her to the tack room.

"It was just a suggestion," she mutters.

I close the door and back Jillian into the wall, ducking my head so we're eye to eye.

"What's going through your head?"

"Nothing. It was just an innocent—"

"Bullshit."

Her eyes flash with anger. She doesn't like getting called out, but that's too bad.

"Fine," she snaps. "I don't want you to feel obligated. I realize me taking in Hayley may have changed things. It's not exactly what you signed up for."

I'm getting pretty annoyed myself so my response is clipped.

"So you thought you'd give me an out? Do I look like I want out?"

She shrugs.

"What do *you* want?" I ask in a softer tone. "Because I like where we are. I like being at your house, with your pack, *and* with Hayley. Can't you see I'm falling for that girl as hard as you are? And God knows I've probably been in love with you longer than I care to admit."

Her mouth is slack and when moments go by without her saying anything, I repeat my earlier question.

"What is it you want, Jilly?"

~

Jillian

"I like Hawaiian pizza."

Lucas glances at Hayley in his rearview mirror.

"Pineapple belongs in a fruit salad, not on a pizza," he states firmly.

"Have you ever tried it?" the girl fires back.

"Don't need to. Pineapple is a fruit, and fruit is a dessert."

"Sometimes fruit can be breakfast, or a snack," Hayley continues to argue.

The bubble I've had in my chest since Lucas's declaration back in the barn feels like it's about to burst. Listening to the two most important people in my life bantering back and forth is a balm on my soul.

Part of me is afraid to be too happy, since this current

arrangement may only be temporary, but another part of me is reminding me to lap it up while I can. This is the life I didn't think I could have, and even if it's taken from me at some point, it's not going to hold me back from living it.

Of course, I never got the chance to answer Lucas's question, because Hayley had come looking for us, cutting that conversation short, but I still owe him a response.

The banter continues until we walk out of the pizza place with two large pizzas; one Hawaiian and one meat lovers.

At home, I first let the dogs out and get their dinner prepped, and by the time I sit down at the kitchen table, I see half of each of the pizzas is already gone.

"You ate five slices?" I direct at Hayley, who is wearing a grin on her face.

"Nope."

I turn to Lucas, who is looking a bit sheepish.

"She challenged me."

"And?" I prompt him, biting my tongue to keep from laughing.

"It wasn't too horrible," he sputters.

"Yeah," Hayley pipes up, mocking him. "Not horrible enough to keep him from grabbing another slice."

Lucas shrugs. "I had to make sure."

When our laughter dies down, I catch his eye.

"You asked me what I want?" I motion with my good arm to encompass everything and everyone. "This. This is what I want. Everyone and everything I love together under one roof. This is what makes me happy."

Lucas reaches across the table and grabs my free hand, bringing it to his mouth. Then he presses a kiss to the inside of my wrist.

"I'll pack the rest of my stuff tonight and haul everything over in the morning. Make me some room in the dresser."

Our eyes stay locked across the table, saying everything that needs to be said.

"So now Lucas *officially* lives here?" Hayley asks, referencing a conversation we had last week.

"Looks that way," he answers for me.

I wake up to a hard body curling around me from behind.

"I thought you were staying at the cabin tonight?" I mumble when I feel the familiar touch of his lips on my shoulder.

"I tried. Couldn't sleep."

He slips a hand under my nightshirt and plays with my breast, while his mouth kisses a path up my neck.

"Mmmm," I hum at the dual stimulation.

We've snuggled, but haven't progressed beyond that since we've had Hayley here, and I ended up with my arm in a sling. I'm more than ready.

"What about your things?"

My voice hitches halfway through my sentence when his hand slides down my panties, and his fingertips dip between my legs.

"I'll pick them up tomorrow."

Not only can I feel the rumble of his voice against my back, but when he presses his hips closer, I can feel the hard length of his cock pressed against my ass. My hips tilt back instinctively, seeking that connection.

"Eager much?" he teases, but I can hear the need in his voice. "Let me make sure you're ready."

He slides first one digit, then two, inside me. The walls

of my pussy tighten on his fingers. He hisses between his teeth before he retrieves his hand.

"Please, don't make me wait," I plead.

Then he takes my top leg and lifts it high, spreading me open before he slides inside, filling my body.

The next moment he fills my heart, when his words whisper against the shell of my ear.

"I love you, Jilly."

Twenty-Nine

JILLIAN

God, I'm so relieved to be done with that sling after wearing it for almost three weeks.

I'll still be seeing the physical therapist on a regular basis, but at least I won't be fumbling around with one hand anymore. I had a great night sleep, and even walking with the dogs along the creek is so much easier. It's amazing how unbalanced you feel when you're limited to one arm.

Lucas sees me coming and opens the back door, catching the dogs as they come in so he can quickly wipe their feet.

"You know what a good addition would be? Building a mudroom onto the laundry room with a designated back entrance. Room for boots and coats, dog leashes and whatever else," he suggests.

"Yeah, right..." I start but promptly snap my mouth shut, because that's really not a bad idea.

Right now, it's mostly just snow and ice we're tracking

into the house, but come spring it'll become mud, and that's going to leave a much bigger mess.

"I'm actually not averse to that idea, but I'm thinking it won't be easy or cheap," I point out, shrugging out of my coat.

"I can look into it if you like, but first we need you to try something."

He jerks his head to where Hayley is standing by the kitchen island, holding a plate of muffins.

"Where did those come from?"

"We baked them." My girl is wearing a big smile.

I point at her. "You did?"

"Me and Lucas. They're banana muffins."

"How is that possible? I was barely gone an hour."

"We were quick," she says proudly.

"Well, can I have one?"

She nods, offering me the plate, and I grab one. Then she informs me, "We packed some up for Lucas's mom as well."

"That's a great idea."

We are heading to Kalispell to have lunch with Trudy Wolff. Lucas has been to see her, and has updated her on all that happened, but she really wanted to meet Hayley and see me. Since I haven't done a session with the dogs at Wellspring in about a month, we're bringing Peanut and Nugget as well.

"Do you want another coffee with that?" Lucas asks, just as I take a massive bite of my muffin.

All I can do is nod while I chew. The muffin is delicious, and I'm about to tell Hayley that when the dogs start barking just moments before the doorbell rings.

"Quiet, guys," I call to the dogs as I weave my way through the bodies to get to the front door.

I open it to find an entire contingent on my porch. Sheriff Ewing, along with the CPS social worker whose name has escaped me, a gray-haired woman with a round face and a friendly smile, and a man in a suit and an overcoat oozing money. I've never seen those two before.

The sheriff speaks first.

"I would've called first but was asked not to."

It sounds ominous, and that delicious bite of muffin is turning sour in my stomach. In the background, I hear Lucas telling Hayley to take the dogs in the bedroom before he joins me at the door. I'm grateful when I feel his steady hand settle on my hip in support.

"I'm afraid that was my doing," the social worker pipes up. "As a matter of policy, we don't always announce our visits. It allows us to get a more... accurate representation of the home situation."

What the hell is her name? Something B...Becker? Babcock?

"And is it also policy to show up with the sheriff in tow?" Lucas questions sharply.

"Ms. Buckman didn't ask the sheriff to attend. That was me," the man in the suit announces with some authority.

Elizabeth Buckman, that was her name.

All of this feels like a weird standoff and it's making me very uneasy.

"And who are you?" Lucas demands to know.

"My name is Oliver Levitz with Chambers, Levitz, Cromwell, and Associates," he recites.

Lawyers. My stomach is officially in knots.

"Forgive us for barging in on you," the lady with the friendly smile apologizes. "I'm sure we all want what's best for Hayley. Could we come in?"

It's too soon. On some level I've known this would be a

temporary solution, but I haven't allowed myself to think too far ahead.

"My name is Heather Iverson," the woman continues when we reluctantly step aside to let the group inside. "I am...*was* the Vallard family's housekeeper."

"As per the Vallard's last will and testament, Ms. Iverson and I were jointly named guardian for young Ms. Vallard," the lawyer explains.

My heart sinks.

"We would like to speak with Hayley," the social worker announces.

Lucas squeezes my hip before letting go. "I'll go get her."

"Actually," she stops him. "Ms. Iverson and I would like to speak to her in private."

I get the sense this entire invasion was carefully orchestrated, and quite possibly intended to keep us off-balance. Still, my protective instincts rear up and, although I probably don't have a leg to stand on, I try to at least regain some control for Hayley's sake.

"Only if she is okay with that," I insist, challenging each one of them with a look.

Junior Ewing winces, the lawyer shrugs, and the social worker presses her mouth in a stubborn line, but it's Heather Iverson who answers.

"Of course."

I find Hayley cuddled up on our bed, surrounded by the pack. Her eyes are big and scared.

"There are some people here to see you."

"Are they taking me?"

I can't bring myself to lie to her, so I evade the question.

"For now, they want to make sure you're okay."

She untangles herself from the pile of dogs and climbs off the bed, grabbing my hand as we walk down the hallway.

The housekeeper is the first to react, her eyes filling with tears when she catches sight of Hayley.

"Oh, my dear girl," she softly coos, wrapping Hayley in a hug. "It does my heart good to see you."

"I don't want to go home."

Even though the words are whispered, the message is loud and clear to everyone in the room. A look I can't identify bounces back and forth between Levitz and Heather Iverson.

"But, sweetheart, what about your school? Your friends? Your things? Don't you miss them?" the woman prompts gently.

My heart breaks when I catch the internal struggle reflected on Hayley's face and step a little closer to her. She seems to sense my proximity and leans her body back against me, and I fold my arms around her.

"I do, but I miss my family more."

"I know you do, but are you sure you wouldn't rather be at home where you can remember them?"

She shakes her head and declares in a heartbreakingly solemn voice, "They're not at home anymore. They're up here, in the mountains, and I want to stay."

The older woman smiles sadly. "Of course."

An awkward silence settles over the room I am afraid to break, but Lucas doesn't hesitate to take charge.

He nudges Hayley. "Hey, kid. How about you and me take those dogs outside for a bit before they claw their way through the bedroom door? We'll leave the grown-ups to figure things out, okay?"

I give her a little squeeze and drop a kiss to the side of her head before letting her go.

"Don't let Nugget run too hard, okay?"

No one says a word until the pack, along with Lucas and Hayley, disappear outside.

"It's for the best," Oliver Levitz says. His statement is clearly meant for the housekeeper.

"Can someone clue me in on what is going on?"

"Of course," he returns. "Since Ms. Iverson and I are jointly named as Hayley's guardians, we have to agree on any decisions made for her care, her well-being, and her future. That turns out to be more difficult than it sounds."

"I thought it might be best for her to try and keep as much of her life the same as it had been," the housekeeper admits. "I only want to give her the best, most normal childhood possible."

"Whereas, I was concerned Hayley's return home would trigger ongoing harassment by the press, who lap up human misery indiscriminately. She would not only make great fodder for a story, but also a vulnerable target for every kind of criminal," Levitz clarifies before turning to the older woman. "Being hounded by press and surrounded by bodyguards would not constitute a normal childhood."

Surprisingly enough, I have to side with the expensive-looking lawyer on this.

"So...what happens now?"

Wolff

"Wow."

It's all I can think of to say.

I glance to the window where I can see Mom playing some card game called Go Fish with Hayley in her room.

Jillian and I slipped out under the guise of letting the dogs do their business, since we really haven't had a chance to talk one-on-one since that gong show at the house this morning.

By the time those people left, we had to hustle to get to Kalispell in time for our lunch date with Mom. Of course I didn't want to ask anything in front of Hayley, but I've been dying to know what was discussed.

"Yeah, I know," Jillian commiserates. "I'm almost afraid to believe it."

Only moments ago, she finished telling me about the proposed plan outlined by that lawyer, Oliver Levitz. His suggestion was to have Hayley stay in Jillian's care, but anonymously.

She would be given a different surname and new paperwork under that new name—much like in a witness protection program—so Jillian could enroll her in school and is able to get her healthcare. At twenty-one, Hayley would have the choice to revert to her birth name or carry on under her assumed name.

As for her inheritance, Vallard Holdings' board of directors is already looking for a new CEO, and Chambers, Levitz, Cromwell, and Associates will hold the remainder of the estate in trust until Hayley has reached a certain age. The trust would pay out a generous monthly stipend to Jillian to cover any expenses for as long as Hayley lives with her.

Jillian's been asked to think about it.

"It seems like a no-brainer to me," I volunteer.

"I know. That's what freaks me out. It's almost too perfect, I feel like there should be some struggle to make it more real. Nothing comes this easy."

I can't help myself; I have to laugh at that.

"Easy? Nothing about this has come easy. Need I

remind you of everything you went through to get to this point?"

I tug her close and look down into those beautiful green eyes. "This is karma the way it's supposed to work. Good things *should* happen to good people, and you're one of the best people I know."

She does a face plant against my chest. Her "God, I love you," is muffled by my down-filled parka, but I feel it down to my bones.

Over her head I catch sight of Mom and Hayley, their worried faces looking out at us through the window. I give them a reassuring thumbs-up behind Jillian's back.

"Come on, let's go back in before Mom teaches the kid how to cheat."

She tilts back her head to look up at me.

"Your mom cheats?"

I bark out a laugh.

"At cards? Like a fucking shark."

Tucking her under my arm, I start walking us back to the entrance.

"She seems too sweet."

"Oh yeah? My mother has the questionable honor of being the only resident at Wellspring Senior Living who is permanently banned from the monthly euchre tournaments."

Jillian's peal of laughter as we walk in has Marcela at reception lift her head. She cracks a smirk and raises an eyebrow when she notices my arm around Jillian's shoulders. I shoot her a wink in passing.

Peanut immediately lumbers over to my mother when we enter her apartment and lays her head on Mom's lap.

"Brrr, you guys are bringing the cold in with you," she

complains, but the sparkle in her eye tells me she's anything but unhappy.

I don't think she'd ever admit it to me, but I would bet Mom always held a spark of hope alive I would one day end up with a family.

"Look at this cool trick Mrs. Wolff showed me," Hayley says excitedly.

"My mother was Mrs. Wolff, why don't you call me Mimi?" Mom gently suggests, confirming my suspicions.

Hayley nods distractedly, she's too busy showing us how to palm a card and slip it back into the deck.

"Mom?"

My mother bulges her eyes in a failed attempt to look innocent, which has Jillian burst out laughing again.

I throw up my hands.

"See? I told you."

Thirty

"Ready for your summer break?"

Technically summer won't be here for another three or so weeks, but next week there are only three days of school left. According to Sully's daughter, Carmi, nothing really happens the last week of school.

"Sooo ready," Carmi dramatically declares from the back seat.

Hayley giggles in the passenger seat beside me.

I offered to collect the girls from school today because Jillian had something to do at the ranch. Since the girls' schools are virtually side by side, Pippa or Sully drops them off in the morning, and Jillian or I pick them up in the afternoon.

Despite the age difference between them, they seem to get along really well. Sadly, it's Hayley's traumatic experiences that are the reason she may be more mature than most kids her age. But Carmi is a great kid who didn't hesitate to take Hayley under her wing. Since starting school a few months ago, Hayley has been making a few friends of her own.

She is now officially Hayley Shaw, complete with all the paperwork needed. She named herself after Shaw Mountain, the site of the plane crash. I guess for her it was a way to stay connected to her parents. The symbolism almost goes deeper than that though; it's also where her old life ended, and her new life began, when Jillian and I found her on that mountain.

A new life for all three of us, actually, and it's been good. Not without hiccups or bumps, but nothing we haven't been able to deal with or work through together.

It's a different experience for me, I've not lived in a family situation since leaving home twenty-five years ago when I took off for college, but I've taken to it like a fish to water. I love coming home from work and being greeted by a rambunctious pack of dogs, and Hayley's soft smile from the kitchen island where she likes to do her homework.

I love feeling Jillian's hand on my back as she moves around me in the kitchen when we cook dinner together. I love waking up with her gorgeous red hair tickling my face and her tight butt pressing up against my morning wood.

Heck, I even love school pickup duty, listening to the girls' chatter and witnessing a new Hayley slowly emerging from the broken little girl we carried down Shaw Mountain.

I fucking love my girls and the life we are building.

"See you Monday!" Carmi calls out when she hops out of the truck in front of her house.

I tip my hat at Sully, who is already waiting for his daughter with the front door open, before I back out of the driveway and pull onto the road.

"What are we doing here?" Hayley asks moments later when I turn off the road toward High Meadow.

"We're meeting Jillian here."

"Oh..."

I sneak a glance at her, wondering if she has any clue. Jilly and I have done everything to keep it a secret, but Hayley is a smart cookie and extremely observant, it's possible she's picked something up.

When I park next to Jillian's SUV, Hayley is out of the truck like a shot. She's already spotted the people sitting on the bottom step of the porch, surrounded by a handful of wiggling little bodies.

"Puppies!"

Jillian is smiling when Hayley runs up to her and plops on her ass in the dirt in front of the steps. Immediately two of the puppies turn their attention on the newcomer and, to Hayley's delight, crawl on her lap.

"What do we have here?" I ask when I walk up. "Hey, Janey," I greet the vet sitting next to Jillian.

"I found these guys in a box left outside the clinic this morning," Janey explains. "I checked them out. They look healthy. I'm guessing some kind of shepherd mix; I'd say about eight weeks old. Anyway," she continues, waving her hand, "it made me think of something Jillian and I chatted about a few months back."

"You mean training specialized support dogs?"

Jillian has talked from time to time about her dream of training rescue dogs customized to people's individual support needs, particularly those of children.

Janey nods, and when I glance over at Jillian, she sports an apologetic smile.

"Do we get to keep them?" Hayley pipes up, her face hopeful.

Well, shit.

"I hate to be a wet blanket," I start, "but we live in a house currently under construction with the mudroom addition, and are already overrun with dogs. Where do you propose we keep them? And who's getting up in the middle of the night when one after the other needs to go for a pee?"

"I'll do it!" the kid offers enthusiastically. "And they can sleep in my room."

Damn, I don't want to be the bad guy, but right now, having four little puppies underfoot would be a serious pain in the ass. Thankfully, Jillian comes to the rescue.

"Lucas is right, Hayley. It would be a bit much in the house. Maybe if we had a bigger kennel with electricity for heat and light, we'd be able to house more dogs, but..."

Her voice trails off but her eyes lock on mine, and I read her like a book.

"I suppose I could ask the contractor to have a look and see what can be done, after he's finished the mudroom," I suggest, earning me a wide smile.

"You're so whipped," JD comments when he and Jackson join us.

"What does that mean?" Hayley wants to know.

"Yeah, JD...what *does* that mean?" Janey echoes, her eyebrows raised as she pins him with a glare.

Jackson barks out a rare laugh. "Burn, brother," he scoffs as he sits down on the step beside Janey and picks up one of the pups.

"Anyway, getting back to more important matters," the vet says with a final scathing look for JD before turning to Jillian. "I'd offer to keep these cuties for you until you have shelter sorted out for them, but I'm afraid I don't have the space or the manpower at the moment. If you can't take them, I'll have to find them another home."

"I'll take them."

Everyone stares at Jackson with their mouths open. Except Jillian, she's smiling wide.

"You?" JD blurts out.

Jackson simply shrugs. "Yeah, why not? I'll look after the rug rats until Jillian's got room for them, but I want to keep this one."

He holds the almost all black pup up to his face, where the little thing tries to bite his nose.

"Perfect," Jillian states, standing up and brushing the seat of her jeans. Then she holds out her hand to Hayley. "Come on, you. Wipe that frown off your face, you'll just have to be patient. But in the meantime..." She pulls Hayley to her feet. "There's something Lucas and I want to show you."

She hooks her arm through the kid's and tilts her head to the barn in a silent invitation to me.

It had taken me almost two months to find what I set out looking for, but it took Jillian and I only an hour or so to make the decision, once I found it. Or should I say; *her*.

She is a little stockier than Tinker Bell, and her coat is more of a chestnut, but her mane and tail are the same golden flax color. She's also well-trained, comfortable around other horses, and easy to handle. I made sure of that.

"Her name is Rosie," Jillian says in a soft voice when we get to her stall.

Hayley freezes when she looks over the door, and both her hands come up to cover her mouth.

"She's six years old and is as gentle as can be," I add, curling my arm around Jilly's shoulders and pulling her to my side, as we watch Hayley trying to take it all in.

"For me?" she finally manages, turning her head.

I have to swallow when I watch the fat tears running

down her face, because for once, I know these are happy tears.

"All yours, sweetie," Jillian says in a choked voice.

~

Jillian

"Marry me."

I blink open my eyes and have to squint to see Lucas's face hovering over me.

"Sorry?" I mumble, thinking for sure I must've heard him wrong.

But he confirms there's nothing wrong with my hearing when he repeats, "Marry me."

He moves back, grabs my hand, and pulls me up into a sitting position. I shake my head, trying to clear the cobwebs, because if this is what it appears to be, I don't want to miss a damn thing.

Although—on second thought—I might've preferred a proposal at a time I don't have a bird's nest in my hair, gunk in the corners of my eyes, or drool marks around my mouth. Not to mention the bad breath I know I have, thanks to the super garlicky pesto gnocchi we had last night.

The ungracious, "Now?" escapes me before I can rein it in. Luckily it only widens the grin on Lucas's face.

"Absolutely," he returns with conviction as he holds up a box with a gorgeous ring. "This ring has been burning a hole in my pocket, waiting for the right moment for weeks. I would've asked you months ago, because I know for a fact what I feel for you is a once in a lifetime deal. A rare gift I wasn't expecting but am so fucking grateful for. But this isn't about just you and me, this is about Hayley as well, and the timing hasn't been right for her." He takes my hand and presses a kiss to my knuckles. "Then yesterday we were able to put happy tears in that little girl's eyes for the first time since she lost everything. She looked at us like we hung the moon when all we've done is love her. Something I know we'll do for a lifetime if she'll let us. So, this morning when I woke up, I realized this was the moment."

Holding on to my hand he gets off the bed and slides down on one knee.

"So, I'm asking you again; Jilly, love of my life, will you marry me?"

∾

I can't stop staring at my ring.

Hayley zoomed in on it the moment she sat down at the kitchen island for breakfast this morning. To say she was happy would be an understatement. She was beaming and hugged us both hard before announcing she'd always wanted to be a flower girl. I had to laugh, because Lucas looked a little pale at that—I don't think he'd gone so far as to think about an actual wedding yet—but over breakfast it became clear Hayley was quite the little wedding planner.

So, it was a bit of a surprise when she asked Lucas how far of a ride it would be to take the horses up Shaw Mountain. When he asked her why, she said she wanted to visit the site of the plane crash. My first instinct had been to tell her no, but Lucas quietly asked her why she would want to go there. When she explained why, I instantly changed my mind.

"I want to show Mom and Dad I'm okay. I mean, I think

maybe they know already, but I want to make sure, and up there it would feel like I'm closer."

Lucas made a few calls after that, mainly making sure the actual crash site was completely cleaned up of debris, which Junior Ewing assured him it was. After, he called Jackson and asked him to put the drone up in the air to make sure the trail to the site would be passable.

Then we got dressed, went to the ranch to pick up the horses, and drove to the trailhead.

Lucas brought Pudding for me to ride. She's a sweetheart and is quite happy closing the ranks while Lucas leads the way on Judge, and we have Hayley safely tucked in between on Rosie. She's excited to be on her first trail ride. I'm just happy the weather is nice, and it's not raining like it has been most of last week, or we'd be trudging through mud.

Somehow Ama got wind of our plans, and was nice enough to pack us a picnic lunch, which is tucked in Lucas's saddlebags. When we get up there, maybe we can find a nice rock and have a picnic. Some might think that morbid, but Hayley seemed to like the idea, which is all that matters.

"Do you recognize that?" Lucas asks, bringing Judge to a halt as he points up to a rocky ledge where the opening to the small cave I know is there is just visible.

It takes a moment for Hayley to respond, first with a nod.

"I was so scared," she starts, and it's all I can do not to jump off my horse and haul her into my arms. "The last night at the hotel, I overheard my dad, my mom, and my grandma arguing. Mom wanted to stay in Canada, but Dad said we weren't safe anymore in Whistler. I heard him say my uncle wouldn't hesitate to kill us all to get his way, which Grandma got upset about. Dad caught me listening in the hallway. He was upset and made me promise not to trust anyone, and that if anything ever happened to him or Mom, that I would run as fast and as far as I could." She takes a shaky breath. "That's why, when I heard that FBI agent say my uncle would be picking me up in the morning, I ran as well."

"You did the right thing," Lucas says in a warm, steady voice.

I'm glad he did, because I don't think I could find words right now.

"I can't remember much from the crash," Hayley admits, as she points at the ledge. "Or how I got up there."

Then she turns to me and shatters my resolve to keep my shit tight.

"But I sure am glad it was you who found me."

"So are we, sweetheart," Lucas answers, because all I can do is nod at her through my tears.

This hasn't been an easy road for Hayley. She'd never really opened up about the reason she ended up hiding in a cave after the crash before now. After hearing what her father's virtual last words were to her, I understand. It was all about trust, and it moves me to the core she clearly trusts us enough now to share.

"I am so proud of you," I choke out. "And so thankful we found each other."

The midday sun is surprisingly warm when we sit down on a large flat rock overlooking Elephant Peak in the distance. Already new growth is sprouting from trees that were felled when the plane went down. By next spring I'm sure you'd hardly be able to tell what happened here, but the three of us will definitely never forget.

"I think I can feel them here," Hayley says when she finishes off her burrito and leans up against me. "Is that weird?"

I lift my arm around her shoulders and press a kiss on her head.

"No. I don't think it's weird at all. I think it's wonderful you can still feel their love for you up here."

Lucas scoots a little closer on her other side.

"We can come up here whenever you want," he promises, reaching his arm around both of us so Hayley is wedged in the middle. "And in the meantime, I hope you know how much *we* love you."

"*Duh*, I know *that*," she states with an eye roll.

I grin at her cheeky response, but bust out laughing when I glance over her head and catch Lucas looking a little shell-shocked.

Better get used to the attitude, buddy. There will be a lot more where that came from.

There is nothing as pretty as a spring sunset in these mountains.

Golds and purples streak the sky and reflect off the peaks; almost too much abundance for the eye to take in.

The first few months after taking over Doc Evans' clinic last year, any time I'd get called out around sunset, I would stop to take pictures. I must have hundreds of them eating up memory in my phone, but none of them come even close to reflecting the depth of colors nature provides.

Tonight, however, I can't afford to slow down.

I just got home and was looking forward to the leftover lasagna in my fridge, after driving all around the county to administering spring vaccinations, when I got an urgent call from Lucy at Hart Horse Rescue. One of their horses is in distress with what appears to be colic.

It's not an uncommon ailment, but it's painful for the animal, and can be dangerous if it involves a twist in the bowel. That's why proper diagnosis is key. If the horse is simply impacted, the treatment is pain control, mild exercise, and hydration, but if we're dealing with an intestinal torsion, surgery will be needed. Of course, that would require transporting the horse to the nearest equine hospital, which would be Ponderosa in Kalispell, since I don't have the facility or the equipment.

When I turn onto the property, I can see the lights are already on at the barn. I don't bother stopping at the house first and drive straight through, parking my truck right by the barn doors. I have everything I need, including my portable ultrasound, in the back. My truck has a cap on the bed, so I can keep my stuff dry and secure back there.

Bo, Lucy's husband, is already opening the barn door for me.

"Need me to grab anything?" he asks.

I hold up my field bag. "For now, this is all I need."

I follow him to a stall that is bathed in light from a flood lamp clamped to a post. Inside Lucy is trying to coax a dark bay mare to get up on all fours. She's currently sitting on her hind like a dog would and looks to be in obvious distress, her eyes wild and nipping at her own side.

"Okay, let's get her to her feet first," I order, dropping my bag in a corner before turning to Bo. "We'll need a long strap or a rope."

While he goes in search, I find my stethoscope and try to get a heart rate, which isn't an easy feat with the horse crazy with pain and sitting in this position.

"How long has she been like this?"

Lucy blows a long strand of blonde hair out of her eyes.

"She didn't eat today, and she looked restless this after-noon, so I came back to check on her after dinner and she was in obvious pain, which is when I called you. I tried to get her to drink, walked her around a bit in the meantime, and was just about to try some water again when she plopped down like this."

I do a quick check for dehydration by pressing on her gums to see how long it takes for the small capillaries to refill.

"She's definitely dehydrated," I confirm, just as Bo walks into the stall with a long cargo strap. "That's perfect. Let's double it up and slide it under her hips."

It takes a bit of doing, but we manage.

"Lucy, if you grab both sides of her halter and pull at the same time. On three. One, two..."

On three, I put all of my one-hundred-and-ninety-two

pounds into the effort. This is one of those rare times where I'm grateful to be of a more hefty variety. I'm not short at five foot eight, and the pounds are distributed well on my body, but I'm well aware there are quite a few too many of them.

Luckily because of the work I do, I am fit and strong, and I eat pretty healthy most of the time. Still, whenever I'm weighed at my doctor's office, I am sternly reminded that at my age it wouldn't take much to slip from simply over-weight into obese territory.

God, how I dread that stupid BMI scale. How can you use one single standard for the endless variety of human beings there are? It's numbers, and they don't take into account genetics, metabolic speed, health issues, mobility, and I could list an endless number of more individual circumstances that should to be taken into account when looking at what constitutes a healthy weight for a particular individual.

And that's not even the worst part; any health complaints you might have are so readily linked to that number on the scale. We're supposed to believe that losing weight is the be-all end-all of every conceivable ailment.

I call bullshit. I've never been a small girl, I grew up on a ranch, was put to work from the time I was seven- or eight-years-old, and am generally fit as a fiddle. I've always been comfortable in my skin, and I'm not about to let some arbitrary number on a scale invented by some random Belgian mathematician, for Pete's sake. The man wasn't even a physician.

"Good girl, Starla. Good girl." Lucy soothes the horse when we have her standing on trembling legs.

Now that she's standing, it's easier for me to listen to her gut sounds. There appears to be some increased activity.

"I'm going to do a quick rectal exam, and after that I'll probably use a nasogastric tube to see if there is a buildup of fluids in her stomach. Are you're okay with me giving a sedative now? Spare her any more discomfort?"

I prefer getting consent before administering any medications, especially sedatives or anesthetics, because they always come with risks.

"Whatever you need to do, Doc."

Once the sedation starts taking effect, I quickly don a disposable long-sleeve glove with shoulder protection, and set to the fun task of rooting around the poor animal's gut.

"I can feel an impaction," I report, retrieving my arm and disposing of the glove.

Luckily, there is not fluid build up in her stomach, but I leave the tube in to hydrate her. With the help of the portable ultrasound, I confirm there isn't anything else going on aside from the impacted stool she has trouble moving.

The fluids will help, as will the pain medication I give her, and after waiting to see the first signs of improvement, I leave Starla in Lucy's good care. Nature will have to take its course.

Bo walks me to my truck.

"Thanks for coming out, Doc."

"No problem. Call me if there's any change for the worse. I'll check in tomorrow to see how she is."

I smile and wave as I pull away from the barn, but as soon as I'm out of sight, I grimace with hunger pains. My stomach feels like it's eating itself.

Rather than driving all the way home to get to my leftover lasagna, I pull into the first place I come across that I know has food; Foxy's Bar. It's less than two miles from the rescue. I've grabbed something here once before, so I know it promises greasy bar food.

Just what the doctor ordered.

It's not crazy busy, just a couple of bikers sitting at the bar, a few locals playing pool, and only two tables occupied with families.

"Find yourself a spot," I'm told by a waitress toting a tray full of drinks to one of the tables.

I grab a table near the back. I'm not up for socializing and plan to dine and dash; I'm exhausted.

"What can I get you?" the waitress asks when she finds me.

"What is fast? Food-wise," quickly clarify.

"Five minutes for a pulled pork sandwich and fries."

"Sold," I tell her with a grin. "And half a pint of whatever pale ale or lager you have on draft."

"Coming right up," she promises, before walking straight through what I assume is the door to the kitchen.

As I watch her disappear to the back, I can feel a rush of cool air when someone opens the front door. When I turn around, I'm unexpectedly met by a familiar pair of dark-brown eyes that are already locked on me.

JD

"Are you heading out, son?"

I turn around to find Thomas sitting on the porch.

Thomas is my boss Jonas's father and old as dirt. I swear he spends most of his days out here on the porch just so he doesn't miss a damn thing that goes on at the High Meadow ranch. He's in his nineties and may be frail, but his mind is still sharp as a tack.

My ma runs the ranch house here at High Meadow, and she and Thomas have a special bond. They bicker like siblings, but everyone can see they adore each other. For Ma—who grew up in the foster system—Thomas is more of a father figure.

The old man sits on the porch and doles out his wisdom to anyone passing by—whether you want it or not—and is about as subtle as a two-by-four between the eyes. My mother doesn't mince words either, so in that respect they're peas in a pod.

"Yeah, it's been a long day."

We rode out early this morning to take a herd to pasture lands close to the ranch's boundary lines, where they'll graze for the summer months. Unfortunately, when we got there, we found a lot of the fencing damaged and ended up spending the rest of the day fixing those.

By the time we got back it was almost dark. Dan went straight home, but Jackson and I grabbed some dinner here.

"I heard," Thomas shares. "What do you reckon messed up those fences?"

"Not sure. Looked like a bunch of elk or something plowed through, but some of the lumber was already rotting, so it needed repairs anyway."

"Herd secure?"

"Yup. They're all set for the summer."

The storm door creaks when Alex, Jonas's wife and Jackson's mother, pokes her head outside.

"Are you gonna come in tonight, Pops, or are you planning to sleep on the porch?"

He huffs and flips back the throw blanket that was covering his spindly legs.

"Hold yer horses," he grumbles, hoisting himself to his feet.

I move to his side and grab him firmly by his elbow, when he wobbles a little as he begins to shuffle to the door.

"Weren't you on your way home?" he snaps ungraciously, even as he puts most of his weight on me.

I grin and catch the amused twinkle in Alex's eyes as she patiently waits with the door propped open.

"I'm leaving right now," I tell him as I hand him off to Alex who leads him inside. "See ya in the morning."

The old man doesn't turn around but lifts his free hand and waves as he shuffles down the hallway. I close the front door and head over to my truck.

I imagine it's not fun getting so old, your body won't move the way you want it to anymore, and you need help with the most basic things. Still, I'd rather have a sound mind in a decrepit body, than the other way around. My grandpa on my father's side had vascular dementia, and he became a person we didn't recognize anymore. I know the prospect scares my Pa, even though the disease itself isn't necessarily hereditary, the risk factors to developing it can be.

Up until last year, when Jackson—Alex's son and my friend—tried to finish the job himself after nearly losing his life at enemy hands in a military operation overseas, I hardly ever gave thought to my own mortality. But that shook me up. Since then, I've tried to exercise a little more awareness, a little more consideration, and definitely more appreciation in my day-to-day life.

Like this old 1974 Ford F-100 I fixed up over the winter. It had been sitting in my parents' barn since my grandpa died over a decade ago. It was the first and the last vehicle he ever bought new, and he kept that truck in mint condition for as long as he could. He left me that truck in his will, and I never once looked at it.

Pa put it in the barn and kept it there all those years, maybe hoping I'd want it one day. He never said anything—Pa doesn't talk much anyway—but he joined me in that barn and worked with me to get the truck road-worthy.

She's old, there's a tear in the bench seat on the driver's side I still want to fix, and it could use some rust treatment and a new paint job, but her engine is in prime shape, and I've come to love every imperfection.

I turn right to get to my place—a trailer parked on a patch of land bordering Libby Creek—and pass Foxy's Bar. I used to stop in there all the time, but I haven't been there in months. It does decent business on the weekends and during the summer months when the RV park is full, but it's fairly quiet tonight. Not many vehicles in the parking lot.

Wait, is that Doc Richards' truck?

My foot is already slamming on the brake before my mind processes the information.

Janey Richards. I don't think the woman likes me much, which is a shame, because she sure as hell has my eye. Just last week she lashed out at me when she was at the ranch dropping off a litter of puppies. I still don't fucking know what I said wrong, but the snap of fire in her eyes sure got my blood going.

I pull my truck in beside hers and without giving it a second thought, head inside.

That may have been a mistake.

My eyes zoom in on Janey the moment I walk through the door, and I see the surprise in hers when she recognizes me. I start walking toward her table, when I hear a squeal and see a flash of movement from the corner of my eye.

I turn in time to see Britt running in my direction. I barely have a chance to react when she launches herself at me, wrapping her arms around my neck and her legs around my hips. My hands automatically go to her ass to keep her from falling.

"Hey, handsome! I missed you."

Then her mouth is on mine, and I realize I should've stopped outside and thought this through.

Up next are Janey and JD in HIGH DENSITY.
Get your copy here.

Also by Freya Barker

HMT 2G:

HIGH FREQUENCY

HIGH INTENSITY

HIGH DENSITY (2025)

HIGH VELOCITY (2025)

High Mountain Trackers:

HIGH MEADOW

HIGH STAKES

HIGH GROUND

HIGH IMPACT

Arrow's Edge MC Series:

EDGE OF REASON

EDGE OF DARKNESS

EDGE OF TOMORROW

EDGE OF FEAR

EDGE OF REALITY

EDGE OF TRUST

EDGE OF NOWHERE

GEM Series:

OPAL

PEARL

ONYX

SHUTTER SPEED

FREEZE FRAME

IDEAL IMAGE

Portland, ME, Series:

FROM DUST

CRUEL WATER

THROUGH FIRE

STILL AIR

LuLLaY (a Christmas novella)

Cedar Tree Series:

SLIM TO NONE

HUNDRED TO ONE

AGAINST ME

CLEAN LINES

UPPER HAND

LIKE ARROWS

HEAD START

Standalones:

WHEN HOPE ENDS

VICTIM OF CIRCUMSTANCE

BONUS KISSES

SECONDS

SNOWBOUND

About the Author

USA Today bestselling author Freya Barker loves writing about ordinary people with extraordinary stories. With 60+ titles to her name, Freya inspires with her stories about 'real' people, perhaps less than perfect, each struggling to find their own slice of happy.

Freya has her hands full with a retired husband, a needy pup, and a growing gaggle of grandbabies, but she continues to spin story after story with an endless supply of bruised and dented characters, vying for attention!

Recipient of the ReadFREE.ly 2019 Best Book We've Read All Year Award for "Covering Ollie, the 2015 RomCon "Reader's Choice" Award for Best First Book, "Slim To None", Finalist for the 2017 Kindle Book Award with "From Dust", and Finalist for the 2020 Kindle Book Award with "When Hope Ends", Freya spins story after story with an endless supply of bruised and dented characters, vying for attention!

www.freyabarker.com